The Admirable Physician

The Gareth and Gwen Medieval Mysteries

The Bard's Daughter (prequel)
The Good Knight
The Uninvited Guest
The Fourth Horseman
The Fallen Princess
The Unlikely Spy
The Lost Brother
The Renegade Merchant
The Unexpected Ally
The Worthy Soldier
The Favored Son
The Viking Prince
The Irish Bride
The Prince's Man
The Faithless Fool
The Honorable Traitor
The Admirable Physician

The Welsh Guard Mysteries
Crouchback
Chevalier
Paladin
Herald

A Gareth and Gwen Medieval Mystery

THE ADMIRABLE PHYSICIAN

by

SARAH WOODBURY

To Deb
A truly admirable physician

Cast of Characters

Owain Gwynedd – King of Gwynedd
Hywel – Prince of Gwynedd
Gwen – Prince Hywel's spy, Gareth's wife
Gareth – Prince Hywel's steward, Gwen's husband
Llelo – Gareth and Gwen's son, investigator
Dai – Gareth and Gwen's son, Dragon member

Meilyr – Bard, Gwen's father
Saran – Healer, Gwen's stepmother
Gwalchmai – Bard, Gwen's brother
Tangwen – Gareth and Gwen's daughter
Taran – Gareth and Gwen's son

Cadwaladr – King Owain's brother
Cadfan – Cadwaladr's son
Cadell – King of Deheubarth
Rhys – Prince of Deheubarth
Richard de Clare – Earl of Pembroke
Richard de Clare – Earl of Hertford (deceased 1136)

Reginald – Commander of Ysbyty Cynfyn
Geoffrey – Warden of Ysbyty Cynfyn
Iago – Saran's brother
Everard – head physician at Ysbyty Cynfyn
Bardolf – Infirmarer/physician
Gabriel – physician
Thomas – physician
Efa – healer
Joan – Lady of Llys Arthur
Arthur – Joan's husband (deceased)
Lucan – Joan's brother

So maybe we ought to do a recap …

The Admirable Physician is the sixteenth *Gareth & Gwen Medieval Mystery*. By now, the series has covered seven years and includes a large cast, the specific details of which might not come instantly to mind. So here's a quick refresher!

A true historical event opens *The Good Knight*, the first book in the series: in 1143, Cadwaladr, King Owain Gwynedd's brother, hired a band of Danish mercenaries from Dublin to ambush and murder Anarawd, the King of Deheubarth, who was traveling to his wedding to Owain's daughter.

Yes, this really happened.

Once his treachery is uncovered, Cadwaladr flees to Dublin, where he hires more Danes to invade Gwynedd. The Danes just want to get paid, however, and they are ultimately bought off with gold and cattle. Owain allows Cadwaladr back into his court, but strips him of his lands in Ceredigion, giving them instead to his son, Hywel.

For the next several books, Cadwaladr continues to plot and plan, but without openly breaking with his brother. Then, after the death of Owain's heir, Rhun, the chronicles report a great "commotion" against Cadwaladr, who flees to England. He is known to have been at different times in the company of both Prince Henry, the son of Empress Maud, and her rival for the English throne, King Stephen.

Cadwaladr is eventually returned to Owain's favor, such that by the time *The Admirable Physician* opens, he has once again been given castles in Ceredigion.

The backdrop for the whole series is what is known to history as *The Anarchy*, a time when King Stephen and Empress Maud fought each other for the throne of England. Wales, meanwhile, is divided into multiple small kingdoms. In the south, we have Deheubarth, ruled in 1150 by King Cadell, Anarawd's younger brother. At times, Deheubarth has allied with other Welsh kingdoms against the Normans. This most notably occurred in 1136, after the Normans executed Gwenllian, King Owain's sister, who had been married to Cadell's father and was the mother of Cadell's two, much younger, half-brothers, Maredudd and Rhys.

Ceredigion itself has at times been a province of Deheubarth, but was annexed by Gwynedd after the 1136 war. The kings of Deheubarth have also allied occasionally with the Norman invaders. One of these is Richard de Clare, the Earl of Pembroke. Only twenty years old in 1150, he will be known to history one day as *Strongbow*.

In the east is the Kingdom of Powys, ruled by Madog ap Maredudd. He also faces constant pressure from the Normans and has chosen to ally with them more often than he fights them. One such ally is Earl Ranulf of Chester, with whom Madog conspired to attack Gwynedd. This tale was related in the previous book in the series, *The Honorable Traitor*.

Last, but hardly least, we have the Kingdom of Gwynedd itself. In 1150, it is ruled by King Owain Gwynedd. Although born a second son, his elder brother died in 1132, and Owain came to power in 1137 after the death of his father. He has spent his reign attempting to consolidate his control over the lands he inherited while also constantly pushing to expand them. It is he, of all the rulers of Wales, who has gained the most from war amongst the Normans. And thus, by 1150, it is he who has the most to lose ...

1

Ceredigion

Ysbyty Cynfyn

April 1150

Gwen

"**W**as the dead woman very fat?" Dai whispered the irreverent query to Gwen as he waited for Commander Reginald to summon the pallbearers forward. It was Dai's job to carry the right rear corner of the coffin, and Gwen had found a place at his right shoulder. Because there had been so many deaths at the hospital over the last few weeks, no attempt had been made to bury this woman at sunset. Instead, she was being laid to rest before the noon meal.

"Not that I would have said." Gwen edged slightly closer to Dai. She was trying not to disturb anyone with their conversation, particularly the dead woman's son. Desmond was a monk amongst the Hospitallers, the Order of the Knights of the Hospital of Saint

John of Jerusalem, who had latched onto Gwen for support in his grief. "Helen was quite thin. In fact, from what I understand, she had been ill even before this current sickness brought her to Ysbyty Cynfyn."

"Well, I have to say that this coffin is very heavy. I've been standing here wondering if they aren't burying her with rocks sewn into the hem of her shroud!"

"Hush now." At another time, Gwen would have tousled his hair, though as a grown man of sixteen, he would have barely tolerated it. "There's the commander. It's time to go."

Hospitallers were both monks and soldiers, and lived in a commandery rather than a monastery. They had two mandates: to heal and succor pilgrims and the sick; and to defend the Holy Land.

The church for this particular commandery was located within an ancient graveyard, which was one of the first things Gwen had noted when they'd arrived a week ago. The churchyard wall was built around three ancient standing stones, and two more guarded the entrance farther down the hill. According to the legend relayed to her by the Welsh laymen who worked at the commandery, pagan peoples had worshipped their gods here within a far more impressive stone circle, of which these stones had once been part, before Wales had become Christian.

In due course, the local people had built a church within that same circle, burying their dead alongside their ancestors as they had always done. It was only recently that the Hospitallers had taken over this holy site. A Norman lord, Richard de Clare, the Earl of Hertford, had welcomed the Hospitallers into Ceredigion before the 1136 war.

Even after Richard's death and the takeover of Ceredigion by Gwynedd, the monks had chosen to stay so that they might continue to provide the local people with a center for healing. As none of the endowed monks were Welsh nor spoke the language, they must have felt at times as if they were the last civilized outpost in a benighted wilderness.

It had been more than a decade and a half since their founding, but all the buildings, except for the ancient church, were still built in wood. And for all that the Hospitallers were a military order, the churchyard was the only part of the monastery encircled by a stone wall. Of course, the church, the sloping graveyard, and the wall, along with its standing stones, had already been here for centuries by the time Earl Clare had given the monks this land.

As the pallbearers processed towards the gravesite, Commander Reginald, who was leading the service, raised his hands in supplication. Gwen hadn't meant to attend a funeral today. In fact, she quite avoided attending any funerals at all if she could help it. It wasn't exactly unusual to dislike funerals. Nobody *liked* them, or at least she hoped not. If the dead person was old, they could be lovely social gatherings, where the participants celebrated the end of a life well-lived. Although this particular dead person had been old, the mood today remained somber, in large part due to the extreme grief of Helen's son, who had started gripping Gwen's arm so tightly it might leave a bruise. Desmond was in his forties, but achieving that age had not given him the ability to control his grief.

"Do you need to sit down?" she asked him.

"I will see my mother in her grave first."

The crowd parted to allow Gwen to support the weeping Desmond in his progress towards Commander Reginald, so Desmond could witness the opening of the coffin and the settling of his mother in her grave. There had been so many tears since his mother had died yesterday afternoon that she feared he would damage his own health.

Commander Reginald now made the sign of the cross and intoned the words, "May God have mercy on her soul." He spoke in French, since Reginald, along with all his brothers, whether knight, chaplain, or physician, were Normans.

Beside Gwen, Desmond gave another little sob. Although he quickly swallowed it down, the sound prompted Physician Thomas, who was a monk-physician at the commandery, to say, "She is with God, brother, in a better place than we are. Let her be."

Gwen agreed with Thomas, though she did not, in that moment, tell Desmond so. In the time she'd been at the commandery, she hadn't been impressed with Thomas's bedside manner. And yet, his words seemed to have the desired effect, in that Desmond threw back his head, shaking off, at least momentarily, his cloak of unconquerable grief.

The pallbearers began moving again, carrying the coffin the last few yards to the grave itself. At that point, the skies, which had been threatening rain all day, opened in a sudden deluge. Gwen became instantly soaked, as did everyone around her. At least the rain served to mask her companion's tears.

With the sudden rain, the fresh dirt around the grave turned to mud. One of the pallbearers, who had been holding a front corner of the coffin and had just been taking a step to close the last distance to the open grave, put his foot down on a mound of fresh earth— which proceeded to slip out from under him. He half-slid, half-fell into the newly dug grave.

With his corner of the coffin no longer supported, the other pallbearers had no hope of keeping it on their shoulders, and it hit the ground with a thud, overturned completely, and then rolled down the slope, leaving the coffin lid and the shrouded body of Desmond's mother on the ground.

Then Helen's body rolled too, exposing a second corpse, un-shrouded and face down, on the underside of the coffin lid.

The disaster was so unexpected, it took everyone a moment to realize what they had just witnessed.

Then one of the monks exclaimed, "That's Physician Everard! Physician Everard is dead!"

Under his breath, Dai commented, for Gwen's ears alone, "I guess it wasn't rocks making the coffin so heavy, after all."

2

Day One

Dai

"Mam was beside me, so she saw the whole thing unfold too," Dai said to his father when he found him in the guesthouse common room, teaching Tangwen her letters—though it could hardly be called *teaching* anymore.

Although Dai had come to reading late, he had still never known a child of five to learn to read. Tangwen was brilliant. That was all there was to it. It made him glad that she, as a girl, could never be seen as a rival to Dai.

As father and son left the guesthouse together, Dai continued, "I'm not sure Commander Reginald really wants you there, though."

Gareth's pace slowed. "Why would you think that?"

"As soon as Everard's body fell out of the coffin, Mam told the commander, *Dai should run for my husband*. Commander Reginald hesitated to agree. We all saw it."

The two shared a commiserating look. Commander Reginald was born a Norman, and it might be obvious to him that no Welshman could possibly do as good a job as one of his own kind. The closest Norman with skills similar to Gareth's would be an investigator belonging to Richard de Clare, the current Earl of Pembroke. In order for such a man to reach Ysbyty Cynfyn, however, he would have to cross miles of Welsh-controlled territory, if Earl Richard would even consent to send him at all.

And while Reginald's issue with Gareth himself might be that he was Welsh, he also wouldn't be the first leader of men to worry about an investigator in his domain. Murder investigations tended to unearth other secrets. Once Gareth started asking questions, it was anyone's guess what else would be revealed, unrelated to the initial death.

The monastery was laid out across an expansive property north of the River Cynfyn, named in honor of a King of Powys who'd ruled over a century ago. Many of the buildings were located on lower ground, so a portion of the river could be diverted to provide water for the infirmary, the laundry, cooking facilities, and the latrines. Others, like the church and graveyard, had been built on rising ground, as protection from flooding and for the views of the surrounding valley.

Gareth and Dai had set off from the guesthouse at a breakneck pace, in part because of the urgency of the summons but also because of the rain pouring down upon them.

The fact that Dai was at Ysbyty Cynfyn to witness the appearance of an unexpected body had come about through a series of events that had strung themselves together as if by chance. As Dai had stared down at Everard's corpse, before his mother had sent him to his father, he had been struck with the thought that chance wasn't something he believed in anymore.

First, not long after Gwynedd's victory in Holywell (over the forces of Madog of Powys and Ranulf of Chester), Prince Hywel, Dai's lord and employer, had received word that Cadell, the King of Deheubarth, had begun raiding northwards from his holdings in south Wales into Ceredigion. Initially, Cadell had focused on what had once been Norman strongholds, such as the castles of Cardigan, Kidwelly, and Carmarthen, the last of which he'd taken earlier this year.

Since then, Cadell had forded the River Teifi at Emlyn. Even now, he was expanding his holdings into territory Hywel ostensibly controlled, clearly planning to push farther north by the end of the summer. Prince Hywel had subsequently gathered an army of men of Gwynedd and marched south. Dai had been proud to be among them, even though they had also been joined by Hywel's uncle, Cadwaladr. Once King Owain had restored his treacherous brother to his favor, he had given him back a handful of castles south of Aberystwyth too.

Then, as if all that weren't bad enough, Saran, Dai's grandmother, had received urgent news of her own from her brother, Iago, who was a lay worker here at Ysbyty Cynfyn. He was a decade older than she, and they hadn't been close. But Saran couldn't ignore his plea to come south and bring "your son-in-law who knows about murder" with her. Iago hadn't told the traveler who brought the message anything more than that and hadn't given them anything more to go on beyond a single, dried, pink flower.

They hadn't known what he feared before they arrived.

And they still didn't.

The appearance of Everard's body was going a long way towards making Dai think Iago really had been on to something.

Dai wasn't a competent healer by any stretch of the imagination, but even he had known that the flower Iago had sent had come from a foxglove plant, common throughout Wales and blooming early this year because of the warm spring. Iago had sent the flower wrapped in a cloth because touching any part of the plant could cause a notable rash. The only place foxglove grew in the immediate vicinity of Ysbyty Cynfyn, as in Holywell whence they'd come, was in the monastery herb garden. The foxglove plant was used to treat a variety of ailments, including diseases of the heart, abscesses, and boils.

Dai hadn't known that until he had asked his grandmother.

Foxglove was also a particularly powerful poison, capable of killing even when administered in tiny doses. Maybe, then, the least surprising thing about what Iago had done in asking them to come south to investigate murder was to include the flower.

Even with a looming investigation at the commandery, Dai's mother had intended to journey as part of Prince Hywel's entourage only to Gwynedd's palace on the banks of the River Dysynni in southernmost Gwynedd. She had two small children to care for and was pregnant with her third. But when they'd arrived at the palace, they'd been warned not to enter due to a sickness that had spread throughout the area.

Because Dai's grandparents had been determined to press on, so had his mother. Besides, the hospital of Ysbyty Cynfyn seemed like a reasonable place to wait out the rest of her pregnancy. Unfortunately, shortly thereafter, the same disease they'd encountered in Gwynedd found not only a dozen soldiers from Hywel's army, but members of Dai's own family as well.

Neither Dai nor Gwen had been affected for more than a day or two. Dai's father, Gareth, had not been so fortunate, having been laid so low Prince Hywel had left him behind at the hospital rather than allow him to continue the journey south with him.

It was testament to how much Gareth had recovered that Gwen had unhesitatingly summoned him into a downpour.

Dai was at the commandery to carry Helen's coffin because he had been left behind too.

As the youngest member of the Dragons, Prince Hywel's elite squadron of soldiers, he might have resented this fact, if not for the greater task he'd been given. It wouldn't do Gwynedd any good for Prince Hywel to march south to protect his territory, only to be surprised by a force that Cadell had snuck around to the north by other paths. Gareth and Dai had thus been charged with securing the rearguard—once Gareth was well enough to ride, that is.

Up until yesterday, the sickness had also given them a few days of concern for Dai's older brother, Llelo; his grandfather, Meilyr; and little Taran. Taran had recovered fastest, praise be to God, and Saran had sat vigil beside the other two night after night, reporting that very morning that their fevers had finally broken. They would not be following the well-worn path marked out by Desmond's mother.

Or by Iago.

They'd speculated during their journey that Saran's brother had meant to imply that the murderer was poisoning his victims with foxglove, and they would be able to identify him by his rash.

But by the time they'd arrived at Ysbyty Cynfyn, whatever rash Iago had seen on any of his fellows had faded or was hidden, and Iago himself was dead, felled by the same illness that had killed dozens of others over the last fortnight. They'd asked questions—of course they had—and been met with surprised innocence from all quarters that Iago could have died of anything but this dreadful plague.

Thus, as Dai arrived back at the gravesite at his father's side and stood amidst the bedraggled group of mourners waiting for them, he couldn't help feeling a twinge of relief, immediately suppressed for the sacrilege it was. He shouldn't be happy another man was dead. Even so, out of the corner of his eye, he could just make out Iago's grave, one of many newly dug dotting the churchyard, each a reminder of all that they had so far failed to discover.

They couldn't rule out that Iago had been murdered for what he knew or suspected. But at this late date, with him in the ground, they had no threads to pull and no leads to pursue. Iago had been illiterate and thus had taken to his grave any evidence that had prompted him to send that poisonous bloom all the way to Holywell in the first place.

Now, however, at long last, they had a real lead.

3

Day One

Gareth

In deference to the rain, which continued to fall in buckets, Gwen had waited for them under one of the great oak trees that dotted the graveyard. The roots of this oak were large enough to deform the stone wall that protected it. They were still getting wet, however, since it was raining hard enough to overcome the coverage of the leaves.

"I couldn't stop Commander Reginald from burying Helen, whose funeral this was," Gwen said, "but he did see the sense in moving Everard under the shelter of the lychgate."

A lychgate was a roofed entrance to a churchyard. Helen's coffin had rested in Ysbyty Cynfyn's lychgate at the start of the burial service.

"This is the same Everard, the hospital's chief physician, who tended to me at times?" Gareth asked.

"I'm afraid so," Gwen said.

"I saw him yesterday morning. He seemed well and in good spirits." Gareth looked past Gwen to where the commander was talking intently with his second-in-command, Warden Geoffrey, along with Physician Thomas, one of the three remaining physicians at the commandery. The conversation did not seem to be going well, given the way Thomas was gesticulating.

"I should probably speak with the commander first, to get his permission to investigate as well as his immediate impressions. Then I'll look at the body." Gareth glanced at his son. "Why don't you keep to my side, Dai. You were present at the event; you can tell me afterwards if Commander Reginald's perspective coincides with yours."

Gwen recognized the importance of one of them staying with the dead body, and she headed off to the shelter of the lychgate. Brother Desmond trailed after her, as if, now that his mother was buried, he wasn't sure of his purpose or where he should go. But since he'd been following Gwen around like a lost duckling up until now, it was natural for him to keep doing it. Gareth, meanwhile, circled the filled-in grave to arrive at the commander's side.

Commander Reginald and his warden, Geoffrey, couldn't have been more different in appearance. Reginald was shorter than Gwen and weighed less (especially now that she was pregnant again). He was almost wispy, although he had a severe gaze that Gareth knew from observation could put the fear of God into any of his underlings. Geoffrey, by contrast, was tall and thickset—not fat, but barrel-chested. They had only their gray hair in common, though in Geoffrey's case, Gareth was guessing it was premature, in that he was a good two decades younger than his superior, forty rather than sixty.

The other man with them, Physician Thomas, was built more along the lines of Reginald. He was in his early thirties, however, and far more hale and hearty, even if he was as wet as the rest of them, standing in the rain. As Gareth and Dai arrived in front of them, Thomas ceased his outward agitation, stepping away and clasping his hands behind his back. His head went down too, which could have looked respectful but appeared to Gareth to be more in the manner of a man who had been told to be quiet before he'd expressed himself fully.

Conflict was the lifeblood of any murder investigation, and Gareth wasn't going to waste an opportunity to inquire about it. "I see Thomas is quite agitated. What's the issue?"

The young physician let out a barking laugh. "What's the issue? Everard is dead! It's a catastrophe for us! How are we to proceed now?"

Commander Reginald made a calming motion in Thomas's direction. "Everything is as God wills it."

Thomas immediately pulled in a sharp breath through his nose. "You are right, of course, commander. I am not myself."

"Would you see to the patients in the infirmary, Thomas?" Warden Geoffrey said. "It would be best if they heard of Everard's death from someone they trust."

"Of course. My apologies for my outburst." He nodded to Gareth and departed at a fast walk.

Warden Geoffrey sighed to see him go. "A good man, but like the rest of us, suddenly at a loss."

Commander Reginald waved a hand to indicate Gareth and Dai should walk with him and Warden Geoffrey to find better shelter under the overhanging roof of the charnel house. A burial ground this old would have centuries of dead people buried in it. In order for there to be enough room within what was a relatively small encircling stone wall, the sacristan needed to be able to remove the bones of the longer dead to make way for those who'd died more recently.

Thus, nearly every church had a charnel house as a way to keep the bones within holy ground but not within individual graves. The lower portion of the building that housed the bones was sunk into the earth, while the upper level contained a chapel. Entry into the crypt was through a trap door near the altar.

Commander Reginald started talking before Gareth even opened his mouth. As Thomas had done, he spoke in French. "In all my years, I have never encountered an incident like this. At first I thought there must have been a mistake, and somehow another of our recently deceased residents had been laid over the top of poor Helen in the darkness of the church. But then I looked upon the man's face to find that the brother who named him first was correct. It was our Everard! He was our foremost physician. Unfortunately, Thomas is right. I don't know what we are going to do without him."

Reginald had become nearly as agitated as Thomas, so Gareth made a calming motion with his hand. As someone who'd spent time in Ysbyty Cynfyn's infirmary, he was not dismissive of the magnitude of their loss. The remaining three physicians, Bardolf, Thomas, and Gabriel, were far less experienced. It wasn't any wonder Thomas was distraught, since both he and Gabriel, being in their early thirties, were still apprenticing.

For such a remote location, it was astounding the commandery had four physicians to begin with. But Everard had been the only one trained abroad and, as the chief physician at the hospital, it had been his job to train the others.

"Did nobody report him missing today?" Gareth left unasked his real question: *Once you noticed he was missing, why did you not come to me immediately?*

Reginald shook his head. "Well, we wouldn't have, would we? Yesterday I gave him special dispensation, as I have done once or twice a week for the last two years, to administer to the Widow Joan, who lives in a manor some two miles to the northeast of our hospital. Her late husband, Arthur, joined our order on his deathbed and donated his lands to the Hospitallers, with the caveat that Lady Joan would continue to live in the manor and reap the bulk of the benefits of the estate until her own death."

Gareth made a sudden connection. "Is this the same estate that includes the lead and copper mine?"

"Indeed." Reginald rocked back and forth on the balls of his feet. "The wealth is held in trust for her during her lifetime, minus our expenses, of course, and will revert to the commandery upon her death. Arthur had no heirs of his body, you see, so the entire estate will come to us when she passes."

This was new ground to Gareth. It was no surprise he didn't know about the arrangement, since he'd risen from his sickbed only yesterday morning. In fact, it was Everard himself who'd pronounced

Gareth well enough to do so. That was the last time Gareth had seen the physician, who had not at the time mentioned an imminent departure to visit the widow, Joan. Not that he'd had any obligation to tell Gareth about his plans. Gareth had been nothing more than a patient to him, one he'd treated with respect, the same as every other person who'd fallen under his care.

"Am I correct in thinking that the loan of Physician Everard was part of that endowment?" Gareth asked.

"It was not so stated at the time, since Everard had not yet come to us and Lady Joan was younger and in good health. That said, it has been a small inconvenience that most likely won't last much longer, as Lady Joan has become quite unwell." It was Geoffrey who answered this question. Even with their short acquaintance, Gareth took him for someone who gave short shrift to unnecessary thoughts or words. He reminded Gareth of Abbot Rhys in that regard. "These visits involve a journey there and back and, sometimes, if the lady is particularly out of sorts, he stays the night, as I assumed he did last night when he wasn't here for the holy offices this morning. And then, given the inclement weather, I was unsurprised he had not yet returned, even by now."

Reginald put an affectionate hand on Geoffrey's arm. "Geoffrey is in charge of monitoring the whereabouts of every man here. To that end, he takes the roll every evening after Compline, to make sure each man is where he's supposed to be. Mostly, our brethren would be in their cells, with some in the infirmary, of course. Last night, Everard was the only one unaccounted for. As Warden Geoffrey just said, neither of us gave his absence a second thought. And now he's dead under such terrible circumstances!"

"Does that roll include the lay workers and other servants?"

Ysbyty Cynfyn had a dormitory onsite for those who did much of the physical labor that kept the commandery running. Saran's brother had been among them.

For a moment both men looked disconcerted, and then Reginald said, "It does not."

"If someone rose in the night, would you know it?"

Again, they both looked uncertain, telling him the answer was *no* before Reginald agreed that they wouldn't.

Gareth could not be sorry Commander Reginald was such a talkative fellow, and there didn't seem to be any deceit in either man, nor reluctance either. Maybe for that reason, it was easy for him to ask, "If one of you, or another man you have in mind, can inquire about Everard's death, I will give way. I wouldn't want to interfere in the running of your hospital nor step on anyone's toes—"

"Another man? Who might that be, Lord Gareth? We are not accustomed to such events here, for all that we see death every day." If anything, Reginald seemed affronted that Gareth had implied, however unintentionally, that he himself knew anything at all about murder or the misdeeds of men. His horror was such that Gareth was almost wishing the commander *had* insisted he had an investigator of his own to whom Gareth could have given way.

Truly, Geoffrey appeared capable, but his expression was also that of surprise. "I am sure, were Prince Hywel here, he would insist on you discovering all you can about how our dear Everard ended up in Helen's coffin!"

Gareth bent his head. "I appreciate your confidence in me—"

Reginald cut him off, impatient now with Gareth's modesty. "Again, not at all. Not to mention the fact that it is your prince who rules us here and ensured that we knew from the moment he took possession of Ceredigion that nothing would change in the dispensation of our house or the expectations towards us. As you know, we succor all who cross our path, of whom there are many, especially as we lie on the road to Mynachlog Fawr and St. David's. We even have a few Welshmen serving with us. Your relation, Iago, God rest his soul, was among them."

"My wife's stepmother's brother, yes." Even with the intricate understanding of family genealogy that was in every Welshman's blood, Gareth wasn't quite sure of his and Iago's kinship relation. He'd met Iago only once, on the way home from Wiston Castle years ago, and had liked the fellow. Gareth had been happy to extend his sense of family to include one more and, even at the time, having a family member working amongst the Hospitallers hadn't seemed like a bad thing.

Gareth was only sorry that Iago was dead, and even more that he'd died before Gareth himself could arrive and discover why he'd been sent for in the first place. Their inability to make headway on the matter felt like a huge failure, one of the few in all his years of investigating. It didn't sit well with him, made all the worse by the fact that Iago had been family.

Neither of these men, nor anyone else at the commandery, had questioned the possibly fortuitous arrival of Iago's own sister so closely after his death. They had traveled with ill men. It had been only sensible to bring them to the hospital.

Dai spoke for the first time. "I think I can say without fear of contradiction that our lord Hywel has always appreciated the competence and compassion of the brethren of Ysbyty Cynfyn." The boy-who-was-no-longer-a-boy was definitely learning diplomacy. The statement he'd made was more artful than anything Gareth would have thought to say.

Commander Reginald bent his head in thanks. "How long do you think it will take to root out these marauders? Will you need Prince Hywel to send men to complete the task? As knights, we are ready to defend our commandery, but our walls, such as we have them, are made of wood and were not designed to withstand any concerted assault."

"Marauders?" Gareth's heart fluttered that there was more here he didn't know.

"Yes, of course." Reginald frowned. "Strangers must have entered the church, looking for something to steal, and come upon Everard, who tried to stop them. He died for his efforts. What else could this be about?"

They'd inadvertently reached a delicate moment, one Gareth wasn't entirely sure he had the skill to navigate. "My apologies, Commander. It is not clear to me that we are looking for marauders. Was anything stolen from the church?"

Reginald scratched his cheek. "I do not believe so." It was natural for him to prefer Gareth look beyond the commandery walls for the culprit and limit the disruption an investigation would bring to the residents of the commandery itself.

"No." For a moment, Geoffrey looked almost disappointed. "Nothing has been stolen to my knowledge."

Theft definitely would have sent Gareth in a different direction from the one he was presently considering.

"You have been in the church several times today already," Gareth said. "Did you see any blood on the floor or any sign of a struggle?"

"No." Commander Reginald's expression hardened. He had wanted Everard to have died by a stranger's hand. "Does that mean Everard didn't fight back? Or just that the murderer cleaned up after himself?"

"I can see in your eyes you think the latter, Lord Gareth," Geoffrey said heavily. "Do you genuinely think one of us could murder one of our own?"

Gareth wouldn't necessarily have used the word *murder* yet, though it was hard to see why Everard would have put himself in that coffin. Gareth also didn't think it wise to tell the commander that most victims knew their murderer. For now, he just said, "It seems to me that marauders would not have bothered to hide Everard's body, nor have been concerned about eliminating any trace of their passing. I cannot say for sure as yet, but it would be wrong not to direct my inquiries in many directions, both within and without the commandery."

"Can you explain exactly what that means to us?" Geoffrey was the one to ask the question, but Gareth could feel Reginald's rising concern.

"It means I must inquire into Everard's life. If someone murdered him and hid the body, I would think you would want me to discover who that was and why."

"Of course!" Reginald's anxiety had reached new heights. "Of course, we do."

"You believe this wasn't a random murder but that someone targeted him for death?" Geoffrey settled back on his heels as understanding penetrated.

"At this moment, I don't believe anything at all, but what you say is possible."

"Possible ... or probable?" Again, Geoffrey was speaking plainly.

"We'll see." Gareth, on the other hand, was working very hard to remain vague. "I can't say more before I have even examined the body or found the place where he died."

Reginald didn't appear to have understood the full extent of what Gareth was saying as quickly as Geoffrey, but now he nodded and further relieved Gareth's concerns about investigating by showing himself to be more a man of the world than he'd initially implied. "My instinct to blame an outsider will be shared by others among us. We want it to be a stranger."

"It's a natural desire." Gareth put out a hand. "I am not saying that Everard was killed by one of your brothers, especially since everyone appears to have been accounted for that night. Everard had more freedom of movement than many monks, so the murderer might still have come from beyond the commandery's walls. The death could even have been accidental. We must not prejudge more than needful."

"I will endeavor to reflect on the virtue of patience." Reginald blew out a breath. "If you will excuse us, we must settle our people. This loss has been so very distressing." He casually put out a hand to catch several drops of water coming off the roof of the charnel house. "Is there anything more that you need from us to get started?"

"I do need permission to examine the body for cause of death, as well as your consent to ask questions of everyone and anyone who might be able to shed light on how Everard came to be in that coffin. It will not be just me asking questions either, but members of my family as well." Here, he gestured towards Dai. Gareth decided not to complicate matters by mentioning that Gwen and Llelo would be asking questions too. And maybe Saran.

Even without that additional thought, Reginald really did hesitate this time, and for a moment Gareth thought he was going to deny such a comprehensive request. His glance at Geoffrey looked worried.

Geoffrey, however, merely nodded, at which point Reginald squared his thin shoulders. "Of course. As necessary."

"It behooves me to look at the body first, before any more time has passed." Gareth was bending over backwards to be polite. It cost him nothing, and might make all the difference as time went on. "In the meantime, if you could confirm that nothing has been stolen, we could at least remove that possibility from our list of motives."

"I will put myself at your disposal, though—" Now Reginald's face took on an expression of genuine curiosity, "—I do have a question for you before you go, if I may: why put Everard's body in Helen's coffin? Surely whoever did this would have known he would be found sooner rather than later. We would not have actually buried that poor woman *in* the coffin. We reuse it, as tradition and economy dictate."

"You and I know that," Gareth said. "Not all might."

"It does indicate the murderer might not be local or a member of the commandery," Geoffrey said musingly.

"Are coffins not reused in England?" Dai asked, not entirely innocently. They'd been to England, and Dai knew the answer as well as Gareth before Reginald gave it.

"It depends on the wealth of the deceased."

Geoffrey waggled his head. "Alternatively, perhaps the murderer *wanted* Everard to be found."

Gareth wasn't sure that made an enormous amount of sense, but he didn't want to say so directly, and instead modified the thought. "Perhaps he felt the need to hide Everard's body for a short while, until he could get safely away."

"Father, it could be simpler and more desperate than that." Dai looked at Reginald rather than Gareth, indicating the *father* in question was the commander. "He could have been afraid of exposure and made an impulsive decision, one that he could be regretting now. As we've discovered a time or two over the years, it isn't all that easy, even in a graveyard, to conceal a corpse."

4

Day One

Gwen

“Everard was more than just a monk and a physician,” Desmond declared once he and Gwen were alone with Everard’s body. “He was a good man. I can’t believe anyone would want him dead.”

This kind of statement was often said by people who meant the exact opposite, speaking stubbornly and with defiance, as if daring their listener to disagree. In this instance, however, Desmond sounded like he meant it. And truly, Gwen had no evidence at the moment to contradict him. Some murder victims were the architects of their own demise. It remained to be seen whether Everard had been one of them.

“Did Everard speak to you of what brought him to Ysbyty Cynfyn?” she said.

“He never talked to me personally about it, but I have heard from others that he came late to the Hospitallers, having always had an interest in physicking, and having attended school on the Continent. I'm sure you won't be surprised to hear that he was the younger son of a nobleman, with whom he had a contentious relationship. His brother, who was the heir to his father's estates, endowed him here." Desmond paused. "Come to think on it, that's probably why he endowed Everard so far away—to get rid of him."

And then he swallowed hard, having realized what he'd said.

Someone had *got rid of him.*

Gwen would have preferred to stand vigil over the body alone, precisely because she wouldn't have been only standing vigil. Given that she was here, she would have started the examination of Everard's body. But Desmond had trailed after her, and she hadn't the heart to tell him to go away. Unexpectedly too, it seemed that the combined shock of the discovery of Everard's body and the placement of his mother's in the ground had calmed him—as if the worst thing he could imagine had happened, and he was amazed to find himself not only still alive, but happy about it.

Even so, she was glad one of the monks who'd helped carry the body to the lychgate had run for a blanket with which to cover Everard's face. It was definitely better not to have to stare down at it. It was one thing to be burying Desmond's mother, who had been old and unwell. It was quite another to be confronted with the unexpected death of their chief physician, someone, according to Desmond, whom everyone had loved and admired.

Everard's story was common enough among the Normans. Unlike in Wales, where a father's wealth and lands were usually split amongst all sons upon his death, younger sons in England or France were surplus to requirements, provided the older brother lived long enough to father an heir himself. Thus, a man such as Everard had to make his own way in the world. Entry into the Church was common.

That wasn't to say the Welsh didn't have their own problems with inheritance. King Owain himself was a second son, inheriting the throne from his father after the death of his elder brother, Cadwallon. To Gwen's mind, the fact that Prince Cadwaladr was a third son fully explained (without justifying) his discontent and treason. Sometimes lands were divided equally among all royal brothers, but even in those instances, one brother usually remained preeminent. Only one head could wear the crown of Gwynedd. That Cadwaladr once again possessed castles in Ceredigion was due entirely to Owain's largesse, something Cadwaladr never allowed himself to cease resenting.

Gwen's own personal resentment against the prince was well earned. On top of all the other atrocities he'd committed over the years, Cadwaladr had abducted her seven years ago. That wasn't something a woman ever forgot.

"Can you tell me anything else about Everard?"

Desmond waved a hand. "Not more than I've already said."

That meant, now that they were alone with the body, she couldn't entirely avoid the issue at hand, which was that Everard had been placed inside Desmond's mother's coffin. As gently as she could, she asked if he himself had sat vigil over Helen in the church last night. As she should have expected, the answer was a regrettable *no.*

"I did, of course, stay with her for some time after Compline. It was peaceful in the church, with just my mother and me, since everyone else had retired for the night. But then Everard himself came to tell me that I would make myself unwell if I spent the night in the cold church, and that he would ensure the watch was kept."

Gwen couldn't help herself; she gaped at him, stunned at this easy admission and wondering if he realized the significance of what he'd just said. She could have asked *why* he hadn't led with that instead of leaving it for a *by the way*. If he hadn't realized already that he might have been the last person to see Everard alive, other than the one who killed him, he soon would. That is, if Desmond himself wasn't Everard's killer.

On the whole, that seemed unlikely, but she and Gareth had encountered stranger circumstances in their seven years of investigating together. "Was Everard well when you saw him?"

"Very well. He was never one of those dour souls, if you know what I mean, who spread gloom wherever they go. Quite the opposite! While my mother was ill, I found his cheeriness occasionally intolerable. A regret, now." For a moment tears welled in Desmond's eyes, for Everard this time instead of for Helen.

Before they could fall and Desmond could descend once more into his grief, Gwen hurried to ask, "Once he sent you away, where did you go?"

"I had a cup of ale in the warming room to settle myself and then went to bed." He made a motion that might have been by way of apology for the luxury. "Each of us has a private room."

Many monasteries housed their members in dormitories, with only the abbot allotted private quarters. The Hospitallers possessed wealth and vast support from noble benefactors, many found far beyond Wales. The men who joined their commanderies often had lived a life out in the world and had greater standing in that secular world than those in similar remote monasteries of other religious orders. And, unlike traditional Welsh houses, such as St. Kentigern's (of which their good friend Rhys was the abbot), each monastery was not expected to be self-supporting. As with the Templars, donations rolled in from far and wide. The Hospitaller's mission to protect and succor pilgrims, not necessarily only those on the road to Jerusalem, was of importance to every Christian.

Gwen could be envious of the monks' privacy, even if monastery life was clearly not for her. They would have to search Everard's quarters as soon as the commander gave permission.

"Did you meet anyone on the way either to the warming room or to your bed?"

Desmond blinked at her. "Are you wondering if *I* had anything to do with Everard's death?" In an instant, grief turned to outrage. "Are you looking for someone to corroborate my tale?"

Gwen waved both hands in front of her. "That was not my intent. I was simply wondering if you might have met Everard's killer as you were leaving the church. Taking it as a given that Everard was well when you left, someone came in after you, murdered him, and put him in your mother's coffin."

"My apologies for raising my voice. I am clearly not myself." Desmond swept a hand across his brow. "The last holy office of the evening had finished, you see, which was why I had been alone in the church to meet Everard in the first place. The next office wouldn't occur until nearly dawn."

"Did you inquire as to whom Everard had found to take your place at your mother's side?"

Desmond continued to look rueful. "I did not. I confess, I felt guilty that I had not done the service myself. Once Everard assured me that he would find someone to keep watch, I chose not to think about it again."

Gwen pitied the man in his grief. "You do not need to feel guilty; you trusted Everard because he was trustworthy. You loved your mother and could not have done more for her."

"I could have kept the vigil. Just imagine if I'd gone back to check on him! I might have saved his life."

"Or the killer would have murdered you too rather than be found out," Gwen said matter-of-factly.

"I suppose." Desmond seemed to accept that idea with more equanimity than most anything else since his mother had died. Maybe that was because his mother *had* died. "I feel responsible now. Will you let me know what you discover?"

"With the permission of your commander."

"He will give it." Desmond was surer than Gwen.

She didn't argue. "I must caution you that these are the earliest moments of the investigation. We know very little and have only questions. Answers should come in time. They always do, some rather piecemeal and others in a great revelation. Meanwhile, Gareth and I will keep putting one foot in front of the other, moving us forward towards the truth as best we can."

"As we all must do." Desmond bent his head to her and, at long last, departed.

Gwen let out a sigh of relief. She thought she'd managed that conversation well, since Desmond mostly hadn't realized it was an interrogation at all. What she hadn't told him was the very real possibility that the answers she and Gareth found might not be ones he, or anyone else at the commandery, wanted.

It was strange to think about the series of events that had brought her to this moment. They'd come here because Iago had asked for them, only to find him dead and they themselves in need of the services provided by the very hospital they had intended to investigate. They still didn't know why Iago had summoned them but, all of a sudden, she was sure they were exactly where they were supposed to be.

Iago had been right. There was definitely something amiss at Ysbyty Cynfyn.

5

Day One

Gareth

"I see you've started without us." Gareth stepped into the lychgate, Dai at his side.

Gwen had been bent over Everard's body, and now she gave something of a dry laugh and turned her head to look at her husband. "The rain isn't falling here, and we aren't bothering anybody. It seemed like a good idea." She eyed him. "I didn't know how long you were going to be able to keep upright, anyway."

Gareth endeavored not to snort derisively and instead said, "I'm fine, *cariad*. Truly."

He was of a mind by now that all of the recent fussing over him had been making him sicker than he'd experienced from his actual illness. He refused to believe he'd been *that* sick, for all that up until yesterday his body had felt so weak he could have been double his actual age of thirty-five. He'd suffered a fever, sore throat, and a stuffed head. It wasn't as if he'd vomited or had diarrhea, which could fell more men on the march than actual battle. His fever had broken by morning yesterday, after which he'd eaten a hearty break-fast, had a bath, and refused to spend another day in bed.

So while he couldn't say he was happy to learn there was a body to examine, he wasn't entirely sorry either. The sooner everyone looked to him once again for his usual skills, rather than viewing him as an invalid, the better. Not to say that Gwen's stepmother, Saran, hadn't spoken to him sternly about his wellbeing before he'd left his bed. He had given everyone a real scare, he knew.

Yesterday when Gareth had last seen Everard, he had been wearing his robes with the characteristic Hospitaller white cross, ra-ther than armor or the traveling attire in which he had died. From what Gareth had seen over the past week, in many respects, this commandery functioned similarly to every other house of the Bene-dictine Order from whence the inspiration for the Hospitallers had come. Perhaps that was because they had little to do in the way of martial activity and far more in terms of succoring travelers, pil-grims, and the local people—although that was mostly a guess on Gareth's part.

He put up one hand. "I have no objection. Honestly, you were smart to start, in case Commander Reginald refused me permission."

"But he gave it?"

"Very much so."

She eyed him. "Were you almost hoping he wouldn't?"

"Not for my sake." He gave a little snort. "I can't be sorry that you sent for me. I had just been thinking it was time I started behav-ing like myself."

"And what could be more like yourself than looking into a murder?" Gwen wasn't being entirely ironic, and relayed what she'd learned from Desmond. Gareth and Dai then shared what Commander Reginald and Warden Geoffrey had said.

Gareth concluded, "So we know our window of time."

"So far," Gwen said. "Maybe someone saw Everard after Compline or before Matins."

"That will be among the first things we ask," Gareth said.

Gwen had left Everard's head shrouded, even after Desmond had taken himself off, likely to the warming room for a resuscitating ale. Gareth now folded down the blanket covering his face. While his inspection of the body would undoubtedly mimic what Gwen had already done, he needed to see for himself. She didn't begrudge him the repetition, and he felt already with this investigation that the more heads they could put to the problems the better. Besides, there was the added element of her pregnancy. He would spare her as much of the gruesomeness of murder as he could.

Everard had been of medium height—taller than Gwen but shorter than Gareth—and burly, with something of a belly that many men acquired in middle age.

Although he'd revealed Everard's face, Gareth actually began his inspection at the man's feet, attempting to move the limbs, only to discover they were very rigid. The body was also cold, both items together indicating Everard had been dead at least half a day but not for more than two days, since by then he would no longer be stiff. This assessment coincided with what they knew from Everard's movements, since Desmond had seen Everard alive yesterday evening, more than half a day ago.

Everard also hadn't been in the church—or at least not *alive* in the church—in the early hours of the morning for today's first holy office. That narrowed the window to six hours at most in which someone could have killed him and put him in Helen's coffin.

"Everard's boots are of high quality and relatively new," Gwen said. "It was one of the first things I noticed about him."

"Abbot Rhys wears high quality boots when he travels," Dai said. "Hospitallers are knights as well as monks, not to mention a martial order. Good boots might be standard issue for them."

"Regardless," Gareth said, "they would have kept his feet warm and dry, which on a day like today would have been important."

"Sadly, he wasn't alive today," Gwen said.

"No, but if he had just returned from seeing to the widow Joan, that would explain his gear," Gareth said.

In addition to his boots, Everard wore woolen hose, a shirt, a long tunic, belted at the waist, and an enveloping cloak. The cloak was the only indication he was more than the usual traveler, in that it was emblazoned with the white cross of the Hospitaller order.

Meanwhile Gwen had moved up the corpse and made their first real discovery. "Look what's in his purse!"

Into Gareth's hand, she dumped two farthings, worth a quarter of a pence each, basically a silver penny cut into quarters; a half-pence; and one silver penny.

Dai was right there looking over Gareth's shoulder. "That's more coinage than I'd expect to see in a monk's possession."

"One might wonder where he got it and why he had it with him," Gareth said.

"And then there's this." Gingerly, Gwen unwrapped a square of cloth to reveal a pink foxglove flower, limp but not dried, indicating it had been plucked and then secreted in the purse within the last day or two. It was all but identical to the one Iago had sent north with his summons.

"Normally, when a man keeps a flower, it is to remind him of a woman," Gareth said.

"He was a monk!" Dai was outraged at the thought.

Gareth laughed. "I didn't say it was a *good* reminder."

"Monks have feelings too, even if they can't act on them." Gwen smiled at her son. "But in this case, nothing about him having a foxglove flower would be normal."

Dai subsided without taking offense. "I think it's a different shade of pink from those in the herb garden here."

"You may be right," Gareth said. "Iago's matched; this one may not. We'll have to compare in better light."

A week ago, after settling Gareth in a bed in the infirmary, Saran had gone immediately to the commandery's herb garden in order to see if any foxglove were blooming there. Although poisonous, the presence of the plant hadn't been a surprise, since foxglove was one of many powerful remedies in a physician's arsenal. The first thing an apprentice healer learned was the way, in many cases, the same herb could both heal and kill. Foxglove slowed the beat of the heart, which was what made it such a powerful medicine. But even small quantities could also produce dizziness and confusion, convulsions, excessive urination, nausea and vomiting—and, of course, death.

"Is something all of a sudden making sense?" Gwen asked. "As in, did Everard also suspect patients were being poisoned at Ysbyty Cynfyn?"

"And that got both of them killed?" Gareth said. "I would say it's more than a starting point."

"Alternatively, maybe Everard himself was the poisoner?" Dai's face brightened at the thought.

"It would be convenient to know a murderer is dead himself," Gwen said, "except we would have closed one investigation only to open another."

Gareth let out a *humph*, less in response to what Gwen had said than to what he'd just found. "He has a lump at the back of the head."

With a wave of his hand, he got Dai to help him to roll the body onto its side. It was so stiff, it was like turning over a board.

Then the three of them put their heads together to frown over the lump. Gareth touched it gingerly with his fingers, feeling around the spot. Everard's blood had pooled in the lowest part of his body, which meant his entire underside was swollen. The implication was that he'd been left on his back shortly after death. This looked to be the case, since he had been put in Desmond's mother's coffin facing upwards.

Then, as they returned the body to its former, face-up position, Dai pointed at the side of Everard's head. "He has blood in his hair too."

The body had fallen to the ground in the rain, and Everard had dark hair besides, so at first it was difficult to distinguish where his hair was wet from rainwater and where from blood. Dai's fingertips had come away red, however, and there remained a small, dried trickle emanating from Everard's ear canal.

After a brief inspection, Gareth removed his sketching pencil, the same one given to him a few years ago in Ireland at another monastery, and gingerly slid it into the ear.

"That's too far," Dai whispered. He had been involved in enough investigations by now to know murder when he saw it, as if there had been any doubt.

"Miles too far," Gareth agreed. "Now we know how he died, and it wasn't from poison—foxglove or otherwise."

6

Day One

Dai

Dai had his feet up on his brother's bed, feeling a tiny bit of satisfaction that it was Llelo who was bedridden this time, not him. While he would not have wished on anyone the illness that had laid Llelo low, he and his brother did seem to be alternating stints as invalids. He suspected that Llelo would have preferred a war wound to an illness. There was no glory in that.

The more heroic slice to the jaw that Dai had received in January had healed into a defined scar, which was starting to turn white. It would be a part of his face that never tanned with exposure to the sun, something they might not see much of this month anyway. Within a day of their stay at Ysbyty Cynfyn, the two younger physicians, Thomas and Gabriel, had taken Dai aside to study the stitching on his face. When he'd told them he'd been mended by a Welsh monk in Holywell, there'd been some nods and thoughtful looks, and a comment that they might do well to study Brother Adam's technique.

Llelo had been listening intently while Dai had related what they'd so far discovered about Everard's death. If Dai did say so himself, he had done a good job conveying the drama of the moment, worthy of one of Gwalchmai's ballads. He missed his uncle, but Gwalchmai had stayed behind in the court of King Owain, so Meilyr (Gwalchmai's father and Dai's grandfather) could travel to Ceredigion. Everyone throughout Gwynedd's royal court understood by now that Gwalchmai was a more-than-worthy successor to Meilyr, even if officially Meilyr retained the title of court bard. Gwalchmai would be nineteen years old this year, long since a man, and fully capable of surviving on his own for a few weeks or months. Likely, he was relishing the opportunity.

"Given the method of murder," Llelo said, "the implication is that Everard had to have been killed by someone with knowledge of the human body. We have many here at Ysbyty Cynfyn who fit that description."

"So it seems."

"Was nobody standing vigil over Desmond's mother all that time?"

"Did I not say? It does not appear so. Her name was Helen, by the way."

Then Desmond himself bustled in, silencing them both, especially once Desmond shot them a grin and came over. "Hello, my friends." He put the back of his hand to Llelo's forehead. "You seem much better to me." Now that his mother was buried, he was projecting much more of what one might expect from a man of his age, namely assured competence.

"I am definitely much better," Llelo said.

Dai was staring up at Desmond. "You seem much better as well."

"I am." Desmond made something of a dismissive wave. "Your mother is a blessing."

Dai could only agree, but that didn't explain the man's bright eyes and better color. Desmond had been leaning on Gwen at Helen's gravesite to the point that they'd all been concerned about his very survival. With this vibrant greeting, it was as if the morning spent weeping had never happened. Dai supposed that was the way of grief, as he should know. One couldn't spend all one's time in tears, especially when there were jobs to be done. "Are you sure you should be on duty today?"

"It is better to work." Desmond waved a hand again. "I ate and drank and am much restored."

A surfeit of ale might explain his improved color and mood. Some people became morose when they drank, especially if they were already gloomy. Dai couldn't be sorry that the hours since he'd last seen Desmond had produced the opposite effect.

Desmond patted Llelo's leg. "You may get up today."

He wasn't a physician, but with Everard dead, the others were overworked, and Llelo was willing to take him at his word. "At last!"

Desmond shook a finger at him. "Be back here at the first sign of tiredness; we can't have you relapsing."

Llelo nodded vigorously, and Dai said, "I won't let him tire himself out."

Desmond then frowned into the cup on the table beside Llelo's bed. "You didn't drink your elixir last night."

"I didn't think I needed it."

"It was prepared for you especially. It might have been Physician Everard's last act before he was killed. He hated to see any man in pain."

Llelo eased back slightly into his pillow before answering. "I fell asleep without it, and then didn't want to take it in the middle of the night."

Dai was looking from one to the other. "What elixir are we talking about?"

"It is a treatment, given nightly, for those in pain or who are unwell." Desmond dropped his voice into a lower register. "In truth, although it isn't yet night, I allowed myself a few drops just now and am feeling so much better."

"A few days ago, I overheard Nain asking Everard about the recipe, but Everard said he wasn't ready to share it widely." Llelo spoke in Welsh, his words not for Desmond's ears.

Dai frowned. "Why would that be?"

"He was being careful about dispensing it, concerned it might have other effects than the ones he already knew about."

"What did Nain say about that?" Although they were related to Saran only through a tangle of marriage and adoption, Dai and Llelo had come to refer to her more familiarly. Nain was Welsh for *grandmother*.

"She applauded Everard's caution, but I could see that she still really wanted to know what was in it."

Up until a few months ago when Dai had been wounded, his interest in herbs and healing had been minimal. In Holywell, because of his pain, the healers had given him a remedy called *dwale,* the main ingredient of which, as far as he could tell, was vinegar. It had been just about the worst thing he'd ever tasted. The concoction had numbed the pain in his face, however, at least for a while. He couldn't argue that it had worked.

Dai looked up again at Desmond and switched back to French. "Do you mean to say that you take this elixir daily?"

"I do." He bent down for Llelo's cup. "I will take this back to the remedy room so that it might be used for someone else." He walked away with steady steps, careful not to spill a drop.

Dai turned back to his brother. "For a moment just now, Desmond looked disconcerted, even afraid. Why would that be? What does the elixir do?"

"It put me to sleep, which I appreciated a few days ago."

"But you didn't take it last night. Why? What you told Desmond wasn't the truth." Of late, Dai had been noting patterns in people's behaviors when their words didn't entirely reflect their feelings. Sometimes people looked afraid when they lied; sometimes it was a matter of a smile not reaching the eyes or a curling or pursing of the lips; and sometimes, as in Llelo's case, a person leaned a bit away when answering a question with a lie, as if trying to distance himself from the answer he was giving.

"No, it wasn't." Although they were back to Welsh, Llelo's eyes were on Desmond's retreating back, and he didn't finish his answer until the other man had completely disappeared into the remedy storeroom. "Nain wouldn't let me."

"She wouldn't *let* you?"

"I know! How often does she put her foot down?"

"Not often." Not in Dai's experience.

Llelo nodded. "It was actually not Everard who left it on my bedside table but Physician Gabriel. He wanted me to drink it then and there, but she told him to leave it with her. And then, after he left, she wouldn't let me have it."

Dai knew Physician Gabriel. He was the youngest of the physicians, tall and thin, with a high voice and a twitchy manner, which might explain his interest in the stitches on Dai's face. A man had to have a steady hand to sew so finely. "You sound as if you weren't happy about that."

Llelo wrinkled his nose. "I wasn't at the time, but she was right that I was feeling better and didn't need it. To tell you the truth, I had started having a problem with my—" he gave an embarrassed cough, "—innards. Nain thought it might be a result of the elixir, though she couldn't be sure because she didn't know what was in it. She said she didn't want to come across as ungrateful for everything the monks have done for our family and the men of Gwynedd. It occurs to me that one way we can repay them is to find out who murdered Everard."

"I don't think finding out has anything to do with repaying them," Dai said dryly. "We will catch Everard's killer, whether they want us to or not." Then he paused. "Now that I think about it, though, did you hear what Desmond just said? He thought Everard was in the infirmary at one point last night before he died. Desmond wasn't actually the last person to see Everard alive."

"Well, obviously not. That person would be the murderer." Llelo hitched himself higher on the bed. Even though he had been given permission to get up today, he hadn't made a move to leave as yet. "And Everard *was* in the infirmary last night. I saw him myself."

Dai stared at his brother. "You don't say!"

"I guess I got my sense of time confused. After Nain left me, after I didn't drink the elixir, Everard came into the infirmary with his arm around another monk and assisted him to a bed. I had been asleep, but their arrival woke me." He made a face. "The monk was put in the far corner with a screen around him. I could hear him vomiting excessively, and Everard and the other monks soothing him. Eventually, they managed to get the vomiting under control, and he fell asleep. Eventually, I did too."

"Do you remember when that was? Had the bell tolled for Compline?"

"I had thought not when we were talking earlier, which was why I didn't mention it, but I honestly don't remember. Someone else might." Llelo tipped his head. "I seem to recall one of the monks carrying a cup to the ill monk similar to the one that had been made for me."

Dai really wanted to know what was in the elixir now. "Perhaps Nain will find the recipe in the herb hut." Dai looked his brother up and down. "I'm sorry I wasn't here more often this week to keep you company—and to keep an eye on things."

"Because of Iago, we knew from the start that there was more going on in the commandery than met the eye. I'm just glad to finally be finding out what that might be."

7

Day One

Gwen

Since they had a bit more clarity now as to the hour of Everard's murder, the next step was to speak to anyone who might have seen him during the course of the evening, once he returned from Llys Arthur.

Gwen's first stop, then, was the gatehouse, where a watch was kept between Matins and Compline. "Brother Mark, I was hoping I could speak to you about the events of last night."

"I would be happy to help." The monk looked over from where he was standing at the fence that surrounded the commandery, his chin on his arms where they rested on the top rail. The main commandery buildings were located to the south of the church and were surrounded by a fence low enough that Mark, being some six feet tall, was able to put his forearms on the top rail and look over it. If Gwen were lucky (and if she weren't pregnant), she just might be able to jump high enough to see what he saw.

Otherwise, the entrance to the church and the commandery were connected by a walkway that the monks traversed eight times a day in order to worship in the church. That situation was different from many monasteries, where the dormitory was either directly connected to the church, or was accessed through a covered cloister. These monks went out in all weather, day and night. Gwen had been here a week and hadn't heard any complaints.

Mark's current expression was one of curiosity, coupled with a degree of innocence. She had spoken with him before, and knew him to be fairly low in the Hospitaller pecking order. In civil society, he would be what some would call a squire, rather than a knight. That was appropriate, given his age, which she pegged as five or six years younger than she was.

"Did you see Everard arrive last night?"

"Oh yes. He came trotting down the road from the north, like usual, though he seemed more energetic than he often did after a trip to see Lady Joan."

"I have heard that he went to see her once or twice a week."

"In the past, that was true. He has taken to going more often of late." Mark's expression turned sad. "I sense she is doing poorly."

"Did you note anything different about him last night, other than his energy?"

"No. Just the usual. He greeted me, dismounted in the yard, and went about his business." These details came out almost whimsically, and she could sense him recalling the day in his mind's eye. "I will miss him."

"I am so sorry for your loss." Gwen said this sincerely, even as she organized her thoughts towards what she needed to ask next. "He died in his traveling clothes. Would that have been usual for him to wear for these visits?"

"Yes. There was nothing about his appearance that stood out to me."

"Did anybody else enter the commandery after Everard?"

"No. Not afterwards. It was a very quiet night."

"Were you outside for much of it, like you are now?"

"Well, it was a cold night, as you might recall, unseasonably so, and it had been raining on and off all day. It started again immediately after Everard's arrival. I spent most of my hours on duty at my brazier."

"Alone?"

"Commander Reginald came to speak to me at one point." He tapped his finger to his lower lip. "That would have been just after Vespers."

"Was that before Everard returned?

"Just before."

"Is it usual for the commander to visit you?"

"He stops by every now and again to see how I'm getting on. And then one of the laymen, John, sat with me a while." Before Gwen could ask if *that* was usual, he smiled and said, "We have been friends for many years. Sometimes he walks over from the village in the late evening after his wife and children are asleep. We share a drink or two before he retires and I am relieved of my duties for the night."

The village was located on the other side of the road from the commandery, a matter of a stone's throw from where they stood now.

"What time would that have been?"

"He left at Compline, the same as every night."

"What if someone were to arrive after Compline?"

"They would pull the bell, and one of the boys in the stable would come running."

Gwen bit her lip. "Is there a way into the commandery that avoids the front gate?"

"Well, of course. We aren't Jerusalem here! We have a back entrance that is never guarded, and the church itself is not locked." He paused a moment, and for the first time real concern entered his face. "I attend Compline every night. So, with everyone in the church at that time, the monastery is wide open to intruders. We have laymen and servants about, but anyone could have entered the commandery at that time. Is that what happened? Did someone enter the commandery and murder Everard while I wasn't looking?"

Gareth had told Gwen that Commander Reginald had come to a similar conclusion at a similar speed. Like Gareth, she hastened to reassure Mark, finding that his sad face brought out the mother in her. "Given where the body was left, Everard was killed after Compline. As you say, the church precincts are never locked or even guarded."

Mark bent his head. "Thank you for that."

Gwen frowned. "Everard's death aside, are there not valuables in the church to protect?"

"Between holy offices, they are stored in the vestry in their own locked box, one that would take at least two men to move, if not four."

"And the rest of the commandery's wealth? Where is it kept?"

"What we have is in the commander's quarters. But our riches are rarely in coin or silver cups. It is in our people, men like Everard, where our true wealth resides." He gave her a rueful look. "In a very real sense, whoever murdered Everard has taken from us our most valuable possession."

8

Day One

Llelo

Although Llelo was fully aware that his father had asked him to join his endeavor to look around Everard's cell as a sop to his sensibilities as his apprentice, he was nevertheless grateful for it. Initially, his simple conversation with Desmond and Dai had exhausted him, but he'd eaten a meal in the dining hall with Dai afterwards and felt better enough to declare that if he spent one more moment in his bed while the sun was above the horizon, he was going to start screaming.

His father had said exactly the same thing the day before and been set free. At that time, though Llelo had wanted to resume his normal duties, he'd felt too ill to rise. But a day later, he could practically see his sword arm atrophying hour by hour and truly felt that if his fever hadn't broken in the night, he might have wasted away entirely. If he didn't start working again soon, he'd be no good to anyone, least of all to his father.

"Are you looking for something in particular?" Llelo asked as they entered the long, low building that housed the monks' individual cells.

"You know how this goes, Llelo." Gareth stopped in front of a wooden door that to Llelo's eyes was no different from any of the others in the corridor. "If you see anything that is out of place or you think is unusual for a monk, tell me. The man was *murdered*. This won't be like some of our more recent investigations when we weren't even sure if murder had taken place."

"Mostly it hadn't. Even that dog died of natural causes." Llelo was referring to events that happened during the week of Prince Iorwerth's wedding. The investigation into the death of the dog had revealed secrets Llelo would almost rather not have known. It also included the return to Wales of King Owain's brother, Cadwaladr. But Gareth was right that nobody had been tried for murder.

Walking past the individual rooms, they'd seen that mostly the doors had been left open, revealing a space perhaps six feet wide and eight deep, large enough to fit a narrow bed and a trunk. That was more space than was allotted to most castle residents. Half the time, Llelo himself had to sleep on the floor of the great hall.

Privacy was a luxury even princes couldn't always afford. But despite being about as far from Jerusalem as could be imagined, the Hospitallers had certain standards they endeavored to maintain. Although Llelo had traveled beyond the borders of Wales many times, first with his birth father as a wool merchant and then with his adoptive parents, he hadn't ever before considered the possibility of taking the cross, leaving everything he knew behind him, and journeying to the Holy Land. All of a sudden, he wanted to see those faraway places. Crusaders were few and far between in his experience, and he wasn't even sure how one might go about starting, beyond heading east on his own (which didn't seem like a good idea).

And then he laughed at himself to remember that he was in a commandery run by the Hospitallers, who had their first great hospital in Jerusalem. The commander would be the one to ask.

The door to Everard's cell was closed but not locked. Without fanfare Gareth swung it wide.

The sight of a ransacked room was so commonplace by now that neither of them cursed.

As his father had just reminded him, Everard had been *murdered*. The murder itself could have been spur-of-the-moment, but the hiding of the body was not. As Gareth had explained many times, the driving force behind every murder was desire: murderers wanted something, whether love, money, or power (if the murder was done to advance the killer's own ambitions); or arose to protect a loved one (on the rare occasion the murderer was worrying about somebody else). Murderers justified killing in all sorts of ways. To Llelo's mind, if a person thought murder was the only resort left to them, that meant they were still thinking primarily about themselves. If a loved one was in trouble, there was always another way.

And really, as Llelo had come to see it, desire itself wasn't the real root of the problem. It was fear, driving men to do things they shouldn't.

That the room had been thoroughly searched was not in doubt. Llelo wasn't sure how dumping onto the floor everything that had once been put away neatly made it easier to look through it, but dumped everything had been. The lid of the single trunk in the room was open, but it appeared to have contained nothing more exciting than an extra blanket. Honestly, the murderer could have put everything back in a matter of a few moments, and nobody would even have known they'd been here.

The thought prompted Llelo to ask out loud the first question to pop into his head as he stood in the doorway: "Why would the murderer go to such trouble to hide Everard's body but not disguise the fact that he searched Everard's room?"

"While we put everything back, I want you to come up with at least one answer to that question." Gareth gestured with one hand. "Start on that side of the room. I'll take this side. Everard didn't appear to have much, so it shouldn't take long."

"You really want me to put everything away?"

"I don't see a need to alarm the next person who enters, even if he knows in advance that a search occurred. Clearly, no one in authority has looked in the room before now, or an alarm would have been raised."

"Don't you want the commander to see what's been done?"

When his father didn't answer right away, Llelo glanced at him, waiting.

Finally, Gareth gave a quick shake of his head. "I fail to see how that would serve us. I don't need to prove anything to the commander just yet. As he himself said, Prince Hywel is our lord. It is to him, and only to him, that I am obligated to report. Do you agree?"

"You are genuinely asking my opinion?"

"I am."

And because he'd been asked, Llelo reconsidered his initial impulse, which had been to seek a higher authority in order to exclaim, *See! Look what someone did!* "You don't think it serves our interests to share everything we know or discover with the commander?"

"My intent isn't necessarily to keep secrets. I'm not against sharing what we know. But I haven't yet decided whom we can trust. I would, of course, be forthcoming if asked a direct question by Commander Reginald or Warden Geoffrey, but we are here to solve a murder, and we have no idea who the murderer is."

"That murderer could even be Commander Reginald." Llelo narrowed his eyes. "And thus, I have a first answer to my question: we don't know if it was the murderer himself who ransacked Everard's room."

"Now you're thinking."

"In the church, he was trying to hide what he'd done, but whoever did this didn't care to be discreet."

"So is this two minds at work, or the same mind under different circumstances?"

Llelo endeavored not to swell with pride at working so closely with this father to the point that he was willing to speculate. "Could the murderer have had an accomplice who went to Everard's room while the murder was taking place? Or was the search a matter of opportunity by someone who knew about the murder?"

"One question it would be nice to answer is *when was the room searched?* If we knew that, we could better determine if it was by someone who lives in the commandery or an outsider."

"If it was during the day, nobody might have heard it happening. At night, at a time when everyone was in bed, would be a different story. These walls are made of wood."

"If it was during a holy office, nobody would have heard this happening either." Gareth made a broad gesture to encompass the whole room. "Is this the work of a man who hit Everard on the head and then stuck a skewer in his ear to kill him?"

"And then hid the body," Llelo added, as if anyone could forget. The conversation had swept away Llelo's tiredness to the point that he was feeling better in this moment than he had since they'd left Gwynedd.

"It is a unique means of murder, in my experience. I have never come across it before, and I hope never to do so again." By now, Gareth had crouched beside a small shelf next to the bed. It had held nothing out of the ordinary—a matter of a rosary, a few candle stubs, and a pocket book of the four gospels. Everard could read, after all, but also missed many of the holy offices and would have wanted a chance to make up for it.

Everard's purse had contained the foxglove bloom plus the coins. So far, there was no sign of any similar attachment to material things in this room.

Llelo went to a series of hooks on the wall and shook out a black robe, the standard color of Hospitaller garments. The Templars wore white robes with a red cross, while the Hospitallers wore black robes with a white cross, the same emblem Everard had been wearing on his cloak when he died.

"Is part of the reason we are putting everything back because you think the commander would like to pretend nothing is amiss?" Llelo had been thinking about this even before they'd come into the room. "That might be a reason to show him what someone has done here, in order to force him to accept the truth."

"It might do that." Gareth looked up from where he had been stripping the linens from Everard's mattress. The intruder had already half-pulled them off. "For now, I'm interested in letting things play out as they may. Whoever did this doesn't appear to have found what he was looking for, which means either there was nothing to find, or it is still here to find."

"How do you know he didn't find what he was looking for?"

Gareth made a motion with his head. "A search that gets more desperate as time goes on indicates frustration. Look at the mattress." There were three slashes in the top fabric, which had caused feathers to waft around the room. "I see anger there, since it didn't aid the search."

With the mattress exposed fully, Llelo thought it looked a little thicker than the usual, which made him reconsider his first impression about Everard's lack of attachment to material things. While on the surface Everard had affected the standard trappings of a monk, his well-constructed clothing and boots, his coins, and the fact that his mattress was full of feathers instead of wool, indicated he had a taste for quality and comfort.

Llelo would be interested to compare Everard's mattress to Commander Reginald's. Or any other monk's, for that matter. Maybe everyone had a mattress so fine. The desecration of it, if not the overall state of the room, was definitely something they would have to tell the commander about.

"I keep thinking about the last hour of Everard's life." Llelo made a gesture to encompass the room. "Could *he* have done this to his own room?"

"I don't know. I don't know enough about him to know why he would."

Llelo couldn't help feeling regretful. "I wish I had paid better attention to what was happening. I was just trying to sleep and didn't see him leave." At that point, he gave in to impulse and flopped down to lie spread-eagled on the mattress. It was as comfortable as he'd guessed, the slashes aside. He moved his arms and legs like he'd done when he'd shown Tangwen how to make a snow angel last winter. And then he frowned. "Does it seem like there's an unnatural lump near the head of the bed?"

"Like there was on Everard's own head?" Gareth felt at the top end of the mattress. The pressure from Llelo's head had made other areas bulge. "Shift." He made a shooing gesture. "Let's see what we've got."

"I don't like damaging this mattress more than it already is, but it's hard to see how a little more is going to hurt." Llelo started working at the stitching at the side of the mattress with the tip of his belt knife. "I'm curious how the intruder missed this. He was so thorough otherwise."

"But was he?" Crouching closer, Gareth held the seams apart to make it easier for Llelo to separate the threads holding the fabric together. "He didn't shift the trunk or the shelves. He didn't pull up the floorboards. He was anxious and in a hurry, but also impatient. It's like he didn't believe he would find anything but was going through the motions anyway. It would have been far better to study the room and work through it systematically."

"Maybe he'd never searched a room he wasn't supposed to be in before." When they had pulled the gap wide enough, Llelo put his hand inside the mattress, feeling around to find what had caused the bulge. "I have something—" he stopped speaking as he grasped the edges of the object and worked it through the gap.

In his hand was another leather purse, larger than the one discovered on Everard's person. Its size had allowed its contents to lay relatively flat, probably with the idea that this would make it harder to find within the mattress. After untying the purse strings that held the top closed, he pulled out several clumps of wool and—

Money.

Upending the purse, he spilled a dozen coins, farthings, half-pence, and another silver penny, which the wool had been protecting, onto the bed.

Gareth let out a low whistle to see it.

Llelo recalled what Desmond had told Gwen, namely that Everard had been a younger son, not destined to inherit. That was why he had become a physician and then joined the Hospitallers, with a generous endowment from his elder brother. "If he hadn't joined the Hospitallers, would his brother's bequest have gone to him personally?"

"Not likely," Gareth said. "He would have had to earn his way, just like every other younger son."

"Is it outside the realm of possibility that his brother gave him these coins for his own benefit, in case his time with the Hospitallers didn't work out?" Then Llelo answered his own question before his father could reply. "Yes, entirely outside. No brother, no matter how generous, would part with wealth if he didn't have to."

"It's less that these coins are of such great value," Gareth held one of them up to the light coming through the single window in the side wall, "than that Everard had them at all. I have farthings, half-pence, and pennies in my possession, but I am steward to a Prince of Gwynedd, not a physician at a Hospitaller commandery. I also haven't hidden what I do have in my mattress."

Llelo began scooping the coins back into the bag. "Are you going to take this money to the commander?"

"I don't see how I can." Gareth weighed the bag in his hand. "Seeing this, I trust every man at the monastery even less than I did before."

9

Day One

Gwen

Since they were dealing with a genuine murder, rather than just the possibility of one, Gwen thought she was allowed a little leeway in questioning the monks who lived at Ysbyty Cynfyn. Mark the gatekeeper aside, however, she knew from long experience that many monks would take offense at being questioned by a woman, much less a pregnant one. For that reason, she thought it best that she put herself to another use. While Gareth and Llelo looked around Everard's cell, a task for which Gwen, as a woman, was unsuited, she took Dai to the church itself. In all murders, it was important to begin at the beginning.

Since they were between services, the church was empty, though of course also well past the point that the scene of the murder would be undisturbed. They had already walked around the whole exterior, not that it had done them any good in terms of the investigation. With all the services, not to mention Helen's funeral, it wasn't as if they could distinguish one footprint from another. Whoever had murdered Everard could just have easily walked up the flagstone path to the main door. There was a second entry into the church through the vestry, where Gwen had already confirmed the lockbox resided. As the lock was undamaged, they had to take Commander Reginald's word that nothing was missing.

However, she wasn't really taking Mark, or the commander for that matter, at his word that the commandery had little wealth. Gareth had delved a bit into the source of the abbey's success. They had endowed lands, from which they supplied themselves with food, clothing, and other resources, in addition to a surplus they could sell. The manor of Llys Arthur would add to that in time, not only because of the crop and pasture land but because it included a mine. Reginald had mentioned that the commandery currently only received "expenses" for their part in the running of it. He'd been vague about what that actually entailed.

"Will you tell me what you're thinking?" Dai asked.

"As in, why are we wasting our time?" She and Dai had been doing as much talking as searching, which was Gwen's fault. She had her son alone and amenable to questions about his life, so she'd asked them. He was at an age where what was going on inside his heart and head could take precedence over what was happening in the world around him. She had a sense of the latter, but far less insight into the former. With a new child on the way, who would take most of her attention in the coming months, she wanted to get in as much mothering of her existing children as possible.

"I didn't say that."

"I don't know that we are going to find anything we don't already know, but we have to look. Everyone is behaving as though all is well at the commandery, barring the death of their foremost physician."

"Barring that." Dai gave a little laugh. "Who do you think did it?"

Gwen rolled her eyes at her son. "Your father isn't here, so you think you can ask me that, do you?"

He grinned, as she meant him to. "I'd probably be less inclined to speculate if the monks were doing it themselves. As far as I can tell, they are barely acknowledging Everard's death."

"This is a hospital in the midst of a plague. People die all the time."

"Exactly!" Dai turned on his heel in the middle of the nave. It looked no different than when they'd seen it this morning for Helen's funeral mass. "Iago could have brought us here because he had the same thought. A killer could get away with murder in the infirmary because there'd been so many deaths already. What's one more?"

"Everard was definitely *one more*." Gwen had found her way to the alcove where Helen's coffin had rested overnight on two sawhorses. These were left in the church at all times for that purpose.

"And yet, how afraid do any of these monks appear to you?"

"Not very," she said.

"Which is strange, isn't it? They don't seem at all anxious. Their chief physician was murdered last night! They should be distraught."

"They are monks. It's their job to be serene in their reliance on God."

Dai scoffed. "Nobody is that serene."

The church was built in stone, like the wall that surrounded it, with great slabs making up the floor. Gwen was only half-listening now, thinking that some of these slabs could have made up the original stone circle, before being repurposed here. She bent awkwardly to the floor to have a closer look. "Is this blood?"

Four dark drops discolored the stone. Dai bent to look too. Then he licked one of his fingers and rubbed at a spot. The pad of his finger came away filthy, but the stain looked a bit red too.

Dai circled the area. "Everard could have been by the coffin when he was murdered. That would make sense if he decided to keep the vigil himself."

"Or," Gwen said, speculating despite herself, "this was where the coffin was located, so when the murderer lifted Everard into it, his blood dripped to the floor. If at one time there were more drops where Everard actually died, they're gone now. The whole point of stabbing him in the ear, it seems to me, was to minimize blood loss, and thus the mess."

"So where is the object he used on Everard's head that made the lump? How did he subdue him before he killed him?" Dai started moving in greater circles around the interior of the church.

They had already examined the candlesticks on the altar. None showed dents in the base and all were clear of blood and tissue. This altar held no secret hiding place for treasure either. Gwen didn't see anything else portable in the church that the murderer could have used as a weapon.

"If he carried the object into the church with him, that implies he meant to kill Everard from the start." Dai looked towards the altar, motioning with his arm as if holding the object that felled the physician. "What if Everard had been on his knees before the altar, or before Helen's coffin, praying? That would have made the blow an easy one."

"You might be on to something." Gwen opened the main door and went onto the porch, thinking about what it must have been like yesterday evening. "It would have been dark by then."

Dai stepped beside her. "And a bit rainy." He scuffed his boots on the stones of the porch. "Water and mud must have been tracked into the church, though the porch roof would keep things drier right here."

"The porch and church are cleaned daily by servants. That's who I'll talk to next."

Gwen was about to set out into the churchyard itself, thinking they'd learned all they could, when her eye was caught by the rock used to prop open the door. She picked it up, expecting it to be heavy, which it was, and turned it over to show Dai the underside.

She almost dropped the rock at the sight of the smear of blood along the bottom, with maybe a scrape of skin and a strand or two of hair caught in a crack besides. Honestly, Gwen had picked up the stone on a whim. She hadn't really expected to find anything of note.

"Sit down, Mam. You just turned white as a sheet. Maybe you shouldn't be here. It isn't good for the baby."

Gwen obeyed her son, perching herself on the bench in the porch and bending slightly forward, her hand on her belly. She was too pregnant to put her head between her knees, but just sitting down helped quell her faintness.

Dai took the rock from her. "I should take this to Tad, but I don't want to leave you, not to mention the fact that the sight of me coming through the commandery with a rock in one hand might draw attention even from monks who don't want to know what happened."

Gwen leaned her head into her son's hip, feeling her heartbeat slow. "I think you may be right about the denial, Dai. Commander Reginald was upset enough about the death initially to send for your father, but as the hours have passed, everyone is just going about their business as usual. Where's the worry, the fear? They may bury Everard tomorrow with great ceremony, without ever mentioning again how it was that he died in the first place."

"This rock, though—" Dai shook his head as he looked at it.

"Living proof." Gwen was finding her equilibrium. "We have discussed in the past how there isn't a single *right* way to respond to murder, any more than there's one right way to grieve. But they're not grieving."

Dai brandished the rock again. "It's almost like they don't want to think about it."

"And is that because they don't want to know who murdered him? Or because they think they do know, and they just don't want to say?"

10

Day One

Saran

"I'm glad to see a friendly face." Aled, the elderly man Saran had been tending this evening, winked at her from the bed. "Welsh, I mean. There's not many of us here. Most of these Norman monks don't bother to learn a single word of Welsh, no matter how long they live among us."

"But some do?"

"That Everard was one. He didn't speak much, but he took the time to say *bore da* to a man in the morning. When I thanked him for caring for me he knew what I was saying."

Saran found herself liking Everard more and more and wishing she had known him better. She also recognized that liking the victim of murder wasn't as common as one might think. Often, the victims they encountered were unpleasant people, even if she would never say their death was their *fault*.

She had been helping out in the infirmary this whole week, from the moment Gareth had introduced her as his mother-in-law,

Iago's sister, and a healer. Bardolf had inspected Saran—seeing a plump woman in late middle-age, with wrinkles, thoughtful eyes, and dark hair streaked with gray—for hardly more than a single glance before assigning her a few initial duties. After that, it had taken him all of an hour to appreciate her manner and skill. At that point, he'd listened to her as much as he did to the younger, apprentice physicians.

Saran's other job in the infirmary had been to act as Gareth's spy amongst the infirmary staff. Everyone knew she was part of Gareth's family. What they might not realize was that she too had been involved a time or two in investigations and would report anything that concerned her to Gareth.

Despite her best efforts, however, what had prompted Iago to send for them was still unknown. With his death, the investigation had stalled before it had properly begun. Consequently, none of them had ever explained that they'd been headed here before any of them had fallen ill.

"Do you speak any French?" she asked her patient,

"I have to, don't I? No way to get along around here if I don't understand something of what comes out of their mouths. My son-in-law can say anything he wants, which helps too. If you went to court or entered any town when Earl Clare ruled here, you couldn't do your business unless it was in French."

Saran was unsurprised by this news, even as she was grateful that she herself was firmly entrenched in a Welsh court. These days in Gwynedd, since her husband was court bard to the king, she could go for weeks without hearing any language but Welsh. Not everyone was so fortunate. Various lands throughout Wales, north and south, had gone back and forth all of her life between Norman and Welsh. As a healer, she was always needed and, much like a bard, could travel to nearly any place and find a haven. But because of the encroachment of the Normans, she'd learned French too.

"Did you ever talk to my brother, Iago?" Saran had grown quite fond of Aled over the last week. He was older than her brother had been, but not by much.

"He was a blessing around here, he was! He died before I came to stay this time, but I had met him previously. He was one to translate for me."

"Did he ever express concern to you about his work here at Ysbyty Cynfyn?"

"Not to me." Aled looked rueful. "I am sorry he's gone. One of too many these last weeks."

"I'm sorry too. I suspect you knew him in his latter days better than I."

As a child, Saran had been the adventurous one and her brother the more timid. He'd always struggled to rein in her more reckless tendencies. Even then, they'd both worked with herbs and apprenticed to their grandmother. Because of Saran's spinsterhood, she had been the one to care for their aging parents until their death, while Iago had married the daughter of a peddler. The pair of them had sold trinkets and remedies across the whole of south Wales. Saran hadn't seen him for years until one day she'd heard a rumor that he'd joined the Hospitallers. It had been a delight to encounter him again three years ago and to know he was safely settled, even if she would never have pegged him for a monk. And, as a Welshman in a Norman commandery, he hadn't been one even here.

"When Everard tended to patients in the days before his death, did you note anything different about him, or worrisome, or just out of place?" By now, Saran had inspected Aled from head to toe. He hadn't come to the hospital because of the plague that had affected members of Saran's family. He suffered from a weeping rash on his lower legs and feet that had proven difficult to heal. It had to be uncomfortable, but he had never complained in Saran's hearing.

"I couldn't say." Aled's response was immediate, but as often was the case under questioning—usually done on Saran's part regarding the source of a particular ailment—a moment's thought brought a different result. "I did note he had a discussion with Healer Efa a few days ago that to my eyes became quite heated."

"I met her, though she and I spoke only briefly. Others have mentioned her name with respect. Is she from your village?"

Saran kept her voice polite while trying to contain her irritation at the mention of Efa's name. She had encountered Healer Efa early on during their time at the hospital, initially when Efa had popped in to speak to one of the physicians about a remedy that she didn't have in her own stores. Saran had no real cause to believe Efa was not an adequately skilled healer. Her hackles had been raised when she had asked Efa about Everard's elixir, and Efa claimed not to know any more than anyone else.

Her denial had been comprehensive, but her smile hadn't reached her eyes. Saran had felt dismissed, in truth, and still didn't know whether or not Efa actually knew anything about the elixir. Saran had watched the other woman more after that, noting the way she greeted the monks and their patients, and the way every single person responded with a smile. Gwen spread joy wherever she went too, but she didn't come off as false, and her smiles always reached her eyes.

"She lives in the next valley over from my cottage. I knew her father well when she wore pigtails! She grew into a beautiful woman, even if not so young anymore." Aled's tone was admiring, but not uncomfortably so, just that of a man who had reached the end of his life, happy to speak about a pretty woman. "She has been very helpful to the monks when they are overrun with pilgrims or those who are ill. She sees the women in particular, of course."

"Did you hear what Efa and Everard argued about?"

For the first time, Aled hesitated. "Did I say they argued?"

"You said they got heated. Do you take that back?"

"I suppose not." He scratched his neck, still reluctant to answer.

"Please don't worry about speaking ill of the dead." Sometimes this sentiment prevented people from telling the truth. "Everard was murdered, and nobody knows why. If Healer Efa can help shed light on his last days, it could only be helpful."

Aled gave himself a little shake. "I do realize."

He still didn't continue, and Saran had the sense to give him time to get his thoughts in order. Finally, she was rewarded for her patience.

"She must be close to forty and widowed twice now, I believe." He put out a hand. "No cause for alarm there. Both men were warriors. Her first husband was killed in the 1136 war and the second two years ago during a skirmish in the south. No," he shook his head, "They were speaking French, and I understood just a little bit that made me think Everard was questioning something about her behavior."

"Do you mean her skills as a healer?"

"No." Again, he made a motion with his head. "I don't know what he meant by it. Her behavior has always been kind and gentle."

"Was she perhaps *too* familiar?" Saran's career had been long and varied. In her time, she had encountered women who enjoyed encouraging monks to stray from their vocation. It wasn't entirely outside the realm of possibility that Efa, especially having been widowed twice, was one of them.

"I would not think so." His chin lifted to punctuate the denial.

There were also women who naturally attracted all men to them, while they had the opposite effect on other women. Efa certainly had had the opposite effect on Saran. "Did anything come of it? Did Everard speak of this to his commander, perhaps? Or Bardolf?"

"I wouldn't know. If he did, I did not hear of it. I would say that even if Everard did express his concerns it did not come to anything, since she is still welcome here. More than welcome. A Godsend, much like you!"

"You like her."

"She has been a friend, and I personally have had no cause to question her behavior. She is kind, as a healer should be, and thoughtful. She draws people to her, and the patients are calmer in her presence."

Maybe especially the male patients? Saran decided she wouldn't risk upsetting Aled by asking that question, which was rhetorical anyway. Such an inquiry she could leave to her son-in-law. It had been his bedside at which she'd been sitting when Efa had first arrived, and while Gareth hadn't been particularly drawn to the woman, he was married to Gwen. Only a fool would stray from her, and a fool was the last thing Gareth was, Saran was happy to say.

"Can I ask you one more thing, Aled, not related to Efa?" She was tiring him out, which had not been her intent. "Do you know why Everard would have kept a bloom of foxglove in his purse?"

Aled had already sunk down a bit more into the bed, but with this question, he perked up again. "I had a crop growing on the hill near my cottage once, but they poison sheep, so I dug them up and brought them here. That was in a better time for me, and the monks were happy to have them."

"Where exactly do you live?"

Aled motioned towards the west. "Across the river."

Saran now understood why Aled was staying in the hospital instead of returning home and visiting only during times he needed treatment. The river ran through the chasm for miles, and there were very few ways across it. The closest crossing to the commandery required a person to descend a precarious trail down a cliffside, cross a chasm on a narrow log bridge over the river, and then climb up again on the other side. It was not a trek for the faint of heart, and the old man was in no position to attempt it.

Aled continued: "On the opposite hill you'll find a stone circle, within which the flowers still grow. The local people tell stories of faeries dancing amongst them. Both beautiful and dangerous, they are."

Saran wasn't sure if he meant the foxglove, the stones, or the faeries. Maybe all three. "Would you know if Everard had visited there recently?"

"Oh yes," the old man said. "He would stop by when he came to see me, before he moved me here. And at other times too, whenever his duties allowed. He liked the peace of the place, he said, when he was burdened by the needs and pains of everyone around him. I certainly never begrudged him the time, and I don't think anyone else did either. Everyone, even a physician, needs to be able to put down his burdens every now and again."

11

Day Two

Llelo

After the excitement of yesterday, even Llelo had to acknowledge the reasonableness of Desmond's request for him to return to the infirmary to sleep. That said, the arrival of two more vomiting monks in the early hours of the morning had turned his own stomach, so he had spent the last hours until dawn curled up on a blanket at the end of his parents' wagon. He didn't think he'd even woken his little siblings when he'd crawled in.

Morning brought his first assignment of the day, which was to return to the infirmary to speak to Bardolf, whose role was both physician and infirmarer. From what Llelo understood, that particular job had never been Everard's. He'd been chief physician, but not the one who organized the day-to-day operations of the hospital. With Everard's death, that was just as well, since the remaining staff were hard-pressed to pick up his former tasks as it was.

"May I speak to you?" Llelo appeared in the doorway of the infirmary remedy storeroom.

Bardolf hesitated from where he sat at his desk, writing in a ledger. His eyes flicked up and down as he took in Llelo's person. "Watch how you go, lad."

"I'm entirely steady on my feet." Llelo didn't additionally point out that he wasn't really a lad anymore either.

"I'm glad to hear it, which means you're here for a reason other than needing my physicking skills. Out with it."

"My father asked that I talk to you of Everard."

Bardolf sighed and put down his pen. "I suppose I've been expecting you since yesterday. We do miss the man most sorely." He summoned Llelo into the room with a wave of his hand. "No sense in keeping you on your feet looming over me."

Llelo hadn't ever been inside the little room lined with shelf after shelf of remedies. If most of the concoctions were Everard's doing, the gaping hole his death had left in the running of the hospital couldn't be more evident. "This is amazing!"

His words were sincere and not meant as a means to soften Bardolf for questioning, but they were the right words to say nonetheless.

"Thank you. We are quite proud of what we have here. There are hospitals in France that have less-skilled physicians than we have here." Bardolf sighed. "Everard was among the best."

"If he was the best, why was he here?" Llelo was genuinely interested. "I don't mean to offend, but this land is not generally considered the center of society. A doctor of his stature could be serving great lords."

"I understand why you might ask that, but that isn't what we are about, is it? Everard didn't have a wife or dependents. He didn't care about clothes or fine food. Hospitallers exist to serve. Everard, when he joined our order, asked to be assigned to where he was most needed. Which was here, at the ends of the earth."

Llelo was itching to inquire about the evident quality of Everard's possessions. He really wanted to, and ultimately gave into impulse. "He had a feather bed."

"Oh that." Bardolf waved a hand dismissively. "He had a bad back. The commander authorized the bed."

"Is that why he had superior boots too?"

Bardolf's eyes narrowed. "He traveled much."

Llelo made a gesture that was half-dismissal, half-apology. "I truly don't mean to offend. I knew Everard for one week and in that time I went from feeling like I was dying to standing before you. I am grateful for everything you have done, not only for me but for my family."

That mollified Bardolf. "I know you meant nothing by it, and it is your job to ask questions. Everard did wear fine boots, but even those were from his former life." He lifted his own robe to show that he was wearing boots as well, though his were more scuffed. "We don't aspire to sandals here."

That was all very sensible as far as Llelo was concerned. His feet had been plenty cold over the course of his life. Although he appreciated the idea of wearing sandals because Christ had done so, Jesus and his disciples had lived in the Holy Land where it was purportedly very warm.

"How long ago did Everard come here?"

"Five years, almost to the day. He was trained in Salerno." He looked at Llelo meaningfully and in a manner Llelo took to be a bit of a test to see what he knew.

Llelo replied accordingly. "It is the best school of medicine in the world." He was only repeating what others had told him, but even he, in faraway Wales, had heard of the place before coming to Ysbyty Cynfyn. He had never before met a doctor trained there, however.

"If one wants to become a physician, it is the *only* place."

"I gather you didn't study there?"

Bardolf laughed. "Sadly, no. That was Everard." He threw out an arm, encompassing the world at large. "He taught all of us, to our capacity to learn. When he died, I lost not only a brother and a friend, but my teacher." He now indicated the ledger before him, as tall and wide as a Bible but not as thick. "He started us on the task of writing down every observation, every treatment, and every patient. Look—" he showed Llelo a few pages, each containing a mix of writing and images.

"My grandmother, Saran, keeps a ledger like this as well. I'm sure she would be interested in comparing her book to yours."

"She has already seen it." Bardolf watched him, eyebrows raised. "You are an educated man yourself. Not every knight's son would know what he was looking at and its significance. It's obvious to me that you do."

"I wasn't born to it." Llelo wasn't sure why this was important to him to explain. "My father, Gareth, not my birth father, learned to read as an adult, taught by a nun in a convent he was protecting. He and my grandfather then taught me."

"It is a skill of which few are capable." Bardolf canted his head. "Is there more you would like to know?"

Llelo had never before used his ability to read as a means to gain standing, but it was clear Bardolf was now according him a respect he hadn't shown him earlier. It wasn't that he'd slighted him, not the son of a knight, but he had treated him like a youth of untested worth. Although the Hospitallers were a martial order too, reading was of more value to Bardolf than knowledge of weapons and how to use them.

Still, Llelo saw no reason not to take advantage of the opportunity presented to him. "You worked closely with Everard. Do you know anything about the man that could explain how his body ended up in that coffin?"

They'd been talking in French, and now Bardolf gave what Llelo thought of as a characteristic Norman shrug. "I lived a life before coming here. I have been a physician for twenty years, albeit one less proficient before Everard came. And yet, I have never witnessed the like of what happened yesterday."

It wasn't really an answer, and Llelo decided he needed to get more specific. "When did you see him last?"

"Two days ago," Bardolf answered promptly, "in the morning before he left to visit the widow."

"But not that night when he brought in the vomiting monk?"

Bardolf shook his head. "I was abed. I attend to the hospital from Matins to the middle of the afternoon. Then I am relieved by another of our brethren. We take it in turns."

"Everard too?"

"Of course; we all do our part. Though it was understood that he was to visit the widow at least once a week and take on the most difficult cases. Thus, he could be popping in and out of the infirmary at all hours."

"Did any of your brethren resent his freedom?"

"You call that freedom?" Bardolf laughed. "Being on call every hour of every day isn't what you think, and true freedom is the absolute submission to the Will of God. It matters not at all that one man's life is less ordered or constrained than another."

This wasn't, in fact, a definitive answer, like *no* would have been. Llelo wasn't entirely willing to let it go. "Who will see to the widow now?"

"I don't know." Bardolf was no longer laughing. Instead of dismissing Llelo's question, he was considering it. "You ask who could possibly resent Everard? I can't imagine. And really, being deprived of his talents isn't the worst of it. When he entered a room, the world was immediately a brighter place, even in the midst of illness and pain. It is his laughter I will miss most."

Llelo himself had noted Everard's propensity to laugh, though Llelo himself hadn't ever been so ill that he needed much in the way of his particular attention. "Still, he *was* murdered."

"Yes, it seems so." Bardolf let out a heavy sigh.

"Any notion of who could have done that? The particular means of death was one we haven't seen before, and implies a knowledge of the human body that is perhaps not found amongst the general populace."

"I am sorry to have no answers for you." Bardolf fingered the papers in front of him. "At least I have his ledgers, both here and in the herb hut. It's enough for now, though I'm hoping to eventually find his journal too."

"He had another book?" The two ledgers so far mentioned seemed like more than enough for one man.

"Everard liked to write! He was always scribbling one thing or another. Unlike his ledgers, in which he catalogued herbs and remedies here and in the herb garden, he would never let anyone look at his journal, much less read it."

"If you never read it, why is it important to find? What do you think is in it?"

Bardolf had been showing signs of wanting to get back to work, but now he sat back in his chair, his eyes on Llelo's face. "You must realize that your family, by all standards, is remarkable."

Llelo had learned over the years that sometimes the people they questioned would digress as a means to deflect attention from a question. Consequently, Bardolf's statement made him instantly wary. "I suppose."

"Leave it to the young not to appreciate what they have." Bardolf scoffed under his breath. "Let me be the first to suggest that if you or your brother are called to the Church, the Hospitallers would welcome either of you with open arms."

"Th-thank you." Llelo found himself genuinely stuttering. "I don't know that I could come with an endowment."

"You are already a knight, are you not?" Bardolf gave a laugh at the startled look Llelo couldn't completely hide. "I saw your expression when I called you *lad*. You can *read*. You have healing in your blood." He put up a hand before Llelo could protest that he truly didn't, since he shared no blood with either his mother or his grandmother. "We don't need to quibble over the specifics. Suffice to say, we are here when you are ready."

Llelo noted that Bardolf had said *when* rather than *if*. He could think of no other way to respond than with a bow. "Thank you. I confess, the idea has crossed my mind already."

"Then we'll leave it there for now, shall we?" Bardolf smiled and turned back to his work, assuming Llelo would understand the interview was over.

Llelo was grateful for the accolades, but not so easily dismissed. "What is so important about Everard's journal?"

Bardolf looked back, his eyes crossing for a moment. He appeared to have genuinely thought the interview over. "Didn't I say? We can't find the recipe for his elixir. I do not have much left in here; there's none in the healer's hut in the garden, and we have many in need."

"I will ask my father to look for it specifically."

"Thank you."

Llelo was back outside before his steps faltered, concerned as much by what Bardolf hadn't said as his actual words. The elixir was obviously vital to the smooth running of the infirmary and the welfare of those within it. But could it be so important that Everard might have been murdered for the recipe?

12

Day Two

Gwen

After Gwen had discovered the rock/weapon yesterday, Gareth's willingness to let her go anywhere on her own had diminished to virtually nothing—and it wasn't as if he had wanted her to wander about by herself before that. During the time he had been sick, she had kept his sentiments in mind, curbing some of her possibly more adventurous inclinations.

But it wasn't only Gareth who found purpose and stimulation in an investigation.

Thus, while her three men were interviewing monks, Gwen took herself to speak to the servants whose work allowed the commandery to function. They knew now that Everard had returned to Ysbyty Cynfyn shortly before Compline. He had not attended the service, but gone to the infirmary instead. He'd returned to the church only after Compline had ended, and it was at that point he'd spoken to Desmond about keeping vigil over Helen's body.

Nobody appeared to have inquired as to why Everard hadn't attended any holy office the next morning because neither Warden Geoffrey nor Commander Reginald had realized he'd returned. The rest of the monks who had seen him hadn't mentioned it because they were used to Everard's absences.

Gwen timed her inquiries for when the servants and lay workers were eating their noon meal. Sometimes getting informants alone was sensible, but for a first interview, she thought to begin with all of them together.

She began, "Thank you for allowing me to join you today."

"You brought your children." Right off, Marvin, the head cook, had taken Taran on his knee to feed him fruit bread. Marvin wasn't necessarily in charge of all the workers, but they all deferred to him anyway. His skills in the kitchen were considerable, and perhaps nobody wanted their meals to suffer. He also appeared to be simply a nice man. "We can forgive most anything for that."

There were general nods around the table, which in this case didn't appear just to be about pleasing Marvin. They spoke in French, which all the workers understood, be they English or Welsh.

"You don't see many children here, I suppose." Gwen took a sip of ale and pretended she was enjoying it.

"We are not like most monasteries, which take in foundlings." This was from George, one of the stablemen.

"We get children in the infirmary at times, of course, but then they are usually very sick." A third man, Roger, spoke next. He was the one she really wanted to talk to, since he and his crew cleaned the monastery daily.

"May I ask which of you live here and which in the village?"

"Most of us are in the barracks." Marvin answered for everyone. "John, here, is married to a local woman, so he lives in the village." The young man in question raised his hand so she would know that it was he to whom Marvin was referring. "Your uncle, Iago, was a valued member among us too."

"Did you know him well?"

"He was one of us," Marvin said, to the general agreement of those around the table. "Terrible to lose him. You have our condolences."

"Thank you." There didn't seem any point in asking if he'd died under suspicious circumstances. They'd been over that ground already and gotten nowhere. Instead, she asked, "How well did you know Everard?"

Immediately after speaking, she realized her question was too general for so diverse a company. Twenty men sat around the table: cooks, launderers, cleaners, stablemen, and general workmen.

But the gravedigger, called Donald, raised his hand. "All of us knew him, and he knew all of us by name. Never one for putting his nose in the air was Physician Everard."

Heads nodded all around the table.

"I assume you know that my husband is investigating his death?" Gwen said. "We are trying to discover who killed him."

"In the church, no less!" Marvin shook his head. "I rise very early, so I was asleep at the time."

Again, heads nodded around the table.

"You were all asleep?"

"All accounted for too," Donald said. "We rise early, work long days, and need our rest. As soon as the sun goes down, my eyes are closed!"

"Did any of you see Everard that evening at all?'"

All she received were rueful looks and shaken heads.

Gwen settled more into her chair. "That morning, when he was in Helen's coffin but we didn't know it, which of you would have been in the church?" She spoke generally to everyone at the table, but kept her eye on Roger.

Obligingly, he lifted a hand. "My men and I sweep and clean after Lauds. It is our first task of the morning, to prepare the church for the day."

Lauds was the second morning holy office, in this monastery held immediately after Matins and taking place at dawn.

"Did you notice anything amiss? Anything unusual at all?"

His face screwed up in concentration. "No. I'm sorry. I didn't. I thought it was a normal day."

"The church was filthy," one of his underlings said, "with mud tracked everywhere. It took us hours to clean it."

Gwen endeavored to make her expression as gentle as possible. "Did you venture near Helen's coffin?"

Roger shook his head. "There was no need, beyond a cursory sweeping. It was all down the nave that mud had been tracked. We had a job of it."

"I got down on my hands and knees with a bucket before the altar!" This came from a second worker under Roger.

"Did you note anything but mud? No ... blood?"

Gwen had never seen twenty men recoil at the same instant before. To a man, the cleaners shook their heads vigorously, and Roger said, "No. Nothing like that."

Beside her, Marvin swallowed hard. "We have not been told how he died. Did Everard suffer horribly?"

"No." Gwen held out a reassuring hand and then swept her eyes around the table. "His death would have been quick."

Marvin let out a sigh. "He so hated to see others in pain, you see. I don't like thinking about him experiencing it himself."

13

Day Two

Gareth

“**D**oes this constitute a certain shirking of duty?” Gareth said as he and Gwen lifted Taran over a small downed tree.

“We are following a lead, and it isn’t as if either of us learned anything revelatory in the last hours. I would just as soon not see another shaken head today.”

Gareth himself had given up questioning the monks at the commandery after many hours of frustrating work. Everyone had been incredibly cooperative, but none could shed light on who might have murdered Everard. His questions had confirmed that Everard had been given a level of freedom within the monastery structure that was unprecedented in Gareth’s experience. Even Abbot Rhys, who truly could come and go as he pleased, had less control over his own schedule. Because Everard was so often absent to visit the Widow Joan, as meritorious as that assignment was, he could go practically anywhere and speak to whomever he pleased within a certain radius and nobody at the commandery would ever know.

That said, the one place they knew he had been was to the stone circle on the other side of the river, hence their current expedition. Although the bloom Iago had sent with his summons had come from the infirmary garden, the one in Everard's purse appeared to be a slightly different shade of pink.

It had occurred to Gareth several times over the course of the day that the fact that Desmond hadn't stood vigil over Helen would have been swept out with the morning's dust if the consequences of him retiring to his bed hadn't been so dire for Everard.

The thought brought Gareth up short, and he halted in the path. "Could Desmond have been the true target? It should have been Desmond in that church, not Everard."

Gwen resisted the way Taran was tugging on her hand and stopped to look at her husband. "I don't even know how to respond to that. Desmond doesn't appear to be a man afraid for his life, and he lives even more blamelessly than Everard did. Murder is rare enough without throwing mistaken identity into the mix."

"It would make the murderer a stranger, something that would please Commander Reginald." Gareth gave a shake of his head. "I had already been considering the need to investigate beyond the confines of the commandery. Tomorrow I should be well enough to do it."

"You must be well enough now, because we *are* investigating beyond the commandery." Gwen grinned at him. "Just because we are taking the opportunity to wear out our children on what is turning out to be a longer, more difficult walk than we expected doesn't change that fact. If you can survive this, you can survive that."

The steepness of the descent explained the wary look Saran had given him when he'd been enthusiastic about seeing the stone circle for himself. They had set off with what they thought would be plenty of time to return before Everard's funeral. Now they were worried they might be cutting it a bit close.

Gwen was right about the effort involved. Gareth hadn't realized when they'd started out exactly *how* good for him the walk would be. The plunging path to the river was slippery and steep, made all the worse by the recent rains. Then they reached the log bridge, which had a single rope as a handrail. They both looked at it, Gareth experiencing genuine palpitations of the heart. He had a vision of their small children falling to their deaths in the crevasse beneath their feet.

"Should we turn back?" Gwen queried, indicating she was feeling the same way.

Gareth swung Taran onto his back. "We're nearly there."

With Gwen holding Tangwen's wrist in a vice-like grip, despite the little girl's insistence that she could manage the bridge by herself, they navigated the crossing and headed uphill. By comparison, the steep ascent, even as it caused Gareth to breathe heavily, was a minor matter. He certainly hoped the stone circle to which they were heading, not to mention the presence of foxglove flowers, would make the entire endeavor worthwhile. He reminded himself as he huffed out another breath that there was nothing like stretching one's legs after a long spell in bed for making a man feel alive and appreciative of the life God had given him.

Ahead of them, Tangwen churned on her small legs at twice the speed Gareth could manage. When she reached the top, she raised her arms above her head triumphantly, as she'd seen her older brothers do, waiting for her much slower parents to arrive.

Tangwen was five and a half years old, and it had been an even bet when they began their walk whether the excursion would result in her crowing triumph or steady complaint. They had been working with her on the notion that she had the power to ruin everyone's day with her moodiness and contention. The sooner she chose the nobler course of cheer and a good attitude, like she had today, the better.

"Can you find the circle, Tangwen?" Gareth put Taran down, and even let go of his hand so he could chart his own course. "We are looking for plants with pink flowers. You know what a foxglove looks like. Give us a shout if you see one—but don't touch it."

"Nain showed them to me and said the same thing!" Tangwen sang out her reply as she ran off. "I'll keep Taran away from them!"

Taran chugged after her on his much smaller legs, though equally articulate. "I'll be careful too!"

"She'll be following in your footsteps before we know it, Gwen." Gareth spoke with more than a little trepidation. "You know she is going to want to apprentice with you in the same way Llelo has done with me. It's hard enough to keep her moving in a constructive direction now. What is she going to be like at sixteen?"

"Five is not sixteen. A year from now, she'll be such a different girl. Don't borrow the future's trouble." She shot him a glance. "That's my job."

Taran, meanwhile, had not only caught up with his sister, but was making his future life choice as clear as the day was long, singing one of Prince Hywel's songs about wooing a young lady. He could already carry a tune, and his little boy voice piped the wildly inappropriate lyrics with enthusiasm.

At times like this, Gareth wished their lord would keep to the more traditional ballads similar to those composed by Gwen's father and Gwalchmai. But Hywel charted his own path too and, as the *edling* of Gwynedd, was not bound by normal bards' rules. He was going to sing what he wanted, and maybe they just needed to be grateful for the privilege of hearing his voice—and to know that their son was already well on his way to carrying on the family bardic tradition.

They could have continued climbing in order to reach Aled's home in the hills, but fortunately their destination was closer. The stone circle was on level ground in a meadow that overlooked the river. In the end, it wasn't much to look at, honestly, the ring being a matter of eight feet in diameter at most. Their two children didn't seem to mind. They'd begun dancing around the outside of it, like their ancestors in the distant past, each holding high not a foxglove but a recently plucked dandelion.

"Tangwen's idea, naturally," Gareth said.

"At least she retained our instructions long enough to remember not to touch the foxglove flowers," Gwen said. "Maybe from now on every time I need her to hear and obey, I should just have Saran tell her. Taran does everything Tangwen says, as a matter of course, and will continue to do so until he realizes not every idea is a good one."

"You mean when she tells him a poisonous flower is all right to touch?"

"She is rebellious, but I don't fear that," Gwen said. "Her heart is too tender to laugh at someone else's misfortune."

"I sense you speak from experience. Was that you, once?"

"Gwalchmai is ten years younger than I." Gwen shook her head a bit at the memory. "I mothered him long before Saran married my father, so he'd better still do what I tell him!"

Then they themselves were at the circle, gazing over the landscape to the east with its grand view of the commandery below them. The sun had come out finally here at the end of the day and shone down on a world washed clean.

Tangwen pointed excitedly. "There's the church; there's the infirmary. There's Dai!" She started waving frantically. "Dai! Dai! Up here, Dai!"

Gareth didn't know if Dai could actually hear her high voice from so far away or if he merely sensed movement on the hill. Nevertheless, he turned, stared, and started waving too, both hands above his head. Gareth didn't have to imagine his smile, and that it was a match to Tangwen's own as she jumped up and down, delighted to have connected with her brother, never mind the fact that she'd given him a hug an hour ago, before they'd set off on their walk.

Dai was by far Tangwen's favorite person in the world. With Gwen's burgeoning pregnancy, Gareth figured that was just as well. Tangwen was about to find herself displaced yet again. As Gwen had said, she was only five, and that meant she might not be old enough to appreciate another baby and a further loss of her parents' attention. Taran, of course, was about to have his world transformed—and not (from a small boy's perspective) for the better!

While Tangwen next got caught up in a game of tag with Taran, each of them running through and around the stone circle, shouting at the top of their lungs, Gareth contemplated the array of flowers around which they were weaving. "I assume you have noted the color."

Gwen took out the bloom they'd saved from Everard's purse, still wrapped in the cloth to protect her skin. "We already know Everard came here often. This was just a confirmatory trip."

"But what are we confirming?" Gareth made a broad motion with his arm to encompass the valley before him. "That he liked the view?"

"Or the walk?"

"Having accomplished the climb, I can see the appeal to a man who spent his life in the service of others. According to Aled, Everard would visit him when he could."

"It seems to me that Everard may have spent more time out of the commandery than in it."

"Maybe he didn't like being confined."

"Any more than you do?" Gwen asked.

Gareth shrugged. "He came to the Hospitallers late in life. Perhaps some part of him regretted that choice."

Then, at exactly the same moment, they each said, "Or he was meeting someone."

"Iago?" Gwen said. "Is that why he sent the flower to us?"

"To say what? That he didn't trust Everard, or that they were in league with one another against a greater enemy?"

They gazed first towards the commandery and then turned completely around to face the hills behind them. Between the two closest mounds was a pass, through which even now a man walked with his sheepdog.

At the sight of them watching him, he hesitated, absorbing the unexpected scene of a family of four in the meadow. And then he continued on towards them, the dog bounding ahead with an enthusiasm that matched Taran's.

As the man approached, he said in Welsh, "I'm missing a lamb. Have you seen it?"

"We have not," Gareth said, "but we haven't been here long."

The man grunted his thanks, after which he asked, "Have you come from the hospital? I don't recognize you."

Gareth wasn't sure which question to answer first. He realized all of a sudden that they didn't look like their usual selves, since they had put on their least presentable clothes for the journey. Gwen held her coif in her hand and had a mossy twig in her hair, which he took a moment to pluck out. Gareth had even, very unusually, left off his sword. "I am Gareth ap Rhys, and this is my wife, Gwen, and our children, Tangwen and Taran. We have been staying at the hospital for the last week."

Gareth was always interested to see how a stranger reacted to him. This one nodded, as if there was nothing out of the ordinary in what he'd said. For once, the man hadn't heard of him. In truth, it was a bit refreshing. "They're good people down there, even if they are Norman."

It was the opening for which Gareth would have been waiting if he'd thought that far ahead. "Have you ever encountered one of the physicians from the hospital here, a man named Everard?"

"The one who was murdered?" The farmer had heard that, at least, and at Gareth's grave nod, continued, "I do know him. Did. Every now and again I'd see him walking these hills. My farm is that way." He pointed in the direction from which he'd come.

"Did you ever see him with anyone else?" Gwen asked.

"I wouldn't say so, but I don't come all the way over here very often. I'm here now because of the lamb. The last time I saw Physician Everard he came down to me. He told me he liked to walk and think. Often I would see him with a fistful of flowers."

"Like those foxgloves?" Gwen pointed towards the blooms.

"Nobody but a fool picks those." The man was more amiable than many farmers Gareth had encountered, some of whom appeared to spend so much time with creatures who couldn't talk back that they'd forgotten how to talk themselves. "Everard liked the pretty colors. Spring came early this year, which some didn't expect, given the hard winter."

Gareth endeavored to keep the amusement out of his face. "But you saw it coming?"

"I have daffodils along the south wall of my house. It's all about when they bloom, snow or no snow. They know best. Better than crocuses, which are fickle and come too early some years."

What Gareth knew about the weather and such prognostications, beyond what he needed to navigate his world, wasn't enough to fill a thimble. He didn't quibble with this bit of wisdom.

"How was Everard murdered?" the farmer asked.

It had been Gareth who'd digressed with the question about the weather, so he couldn't blame the farmer for wanting to get the conversation back on track. "That is why we are here." He gestured to Gwen who showed him the flower from Everard's purse. "He had this bloom in his purse when he died. It doesn't match the color of the foxglove at the commandery, so we came here seeking its source."

"He was poisoned?" The man blinked twice.

Gareth put out a hand. "No. He died by another's hand."

He still didn't want to give specifics, not yet, not before they'd had a chance to talk to more people. Not that this farmer was a suspect.

"I have seen Everard at the fairy circle before. He would lean against one of the rocks for long moments. I never disturbed him because I assumed he was praying." He contemplated the stones. "Maybe he was. He's with God now and can pray all day if he wishes." He shook his head regretfully, at which point Gareth thanked him and let him be on his way.

The man may not have recognized Gareth's name, but it was quite a lot of news overall for a Welsh farmer to know. Then again, Welsh people living in Norman territory learned what they could about those above them as a matter of course. And anyway, the average person thrived on gossip about other people, all the more so because of the power a man like Everard wielded just by his very existence.

After Gwen called the children to them, they began making their way back towards the path down to the river.

"We already knew Everard made this trek," she said. "Now we know he made it often, though still was not seen with anyone else."

"That doesn't mean he didn't meet with someone or visit a different house. Perhaps it was someone, and I can't help thinking it could be a woman, who could not get to the commandery, like Widow Joan."

"She must be first on your list of people to visit tomorrow."

"That I managed this trip to the fairy circle should be enough evidence even for my healers that I am well enough to leave the commandery."

As they surveyed the way ahead, Gwen made a face. Gareth could only agree that it looked steeper from the top than it had from the bottom. Perhaps that accurately described this investigation too. There was no help for it, though. Home was on the other side.

They started down the hill, Tangwen leaping ahead like a rabbit.

"At least we can rule out any possibility that Everard died up here. Nobody, no matter how strong, could carry a dead body from the fairy circle down this hill to the river and then back up again to the church." Gareth grinned at his wife as he swung Taran onto his back for the journey. "Not even me."

14

Day Two

Gwen

As Gwen watched Everard's corpse being lowered into the ground, she wondered how many times in this graveyard the same dead body had been part of two different funerals. Her first thought was that it couldn't have been often. Her second was that almost every person's bones were routinely prayed over twice: the first time within a day or two of death, and the second many years later, once there was nothing left of the flesh and the corpse was naught but bones. The church sexton then dug up the bones and interred them in the church's charnel house. Nobody liked to think about what was in there, but then, they didn't much like standing around in a graveyard either.

At least they had grown past some of the odd superstitions of their ancestors who'd built the stone circle and buried their dead here. According to Saran, in those days, people feared the dead could rise from their graves, so in many cases they had burned the bodies before burial. Gwen herself had noted charred bits of *something* within Helen's open grave, before the arrival of her coffin—not that she would ever have pointed them out, even if the funeral had gone off uneventfully. She was quite sure the Norman monks who ruled here now would not like to be reminded of the people who had lived and worshipped on this very spot generations before they came.

Gwen's musings were interrupted by the first shovelful of dirt thrown over Everard's body, and then almost immediately after that, nearly in the same breath, by the sound of carriage wheels coming down the road from the north. By the time the horses turned into the yard below the entrance to the church, most of the monks in attendance had turned to look. The gravedigger, Donald, once again settled into a relaxed position, with the tip of his shovel pointed into the dirt and his elbow resting on the end of the handle. Whoever had come was an important enough person for Donald to pause the funeral all on his own, in order to await the arrival of these newcomers.

At least it wasn't raining, and since Gwen was still quite warm from their walk up the hill from the river, she wasn't uncomfortable. They'd settled the children with her father just in time to get back to the church for the funeral mass.

"Who's this now?" Gwen asked Desmond, who was back at her side as if he could not attend a funeral without her for support. He had joined his brothers in the choir for the mass to celebrate Everard's life, but had waited for her once they'd processed out the door. This time, six monks had been chosen as the pallbearers rather than the four laymen who'd carried Helen's coffin.

"That's Lady Joan!" Desmond said. "She is the ill woman whom Everard visited the day he died. The commander sent word to her earlier today that Everard would be buried this afternoon. I'm sure he never intended that she would leave her home to attend the funeral!"

Gareth, who was standing on Gwen's other side, leaned past her to look at Desmond. "How did he send word?"

"Excuse me?"

"You just said that the commander sent word to Lady Joan that Everard was dead and would be buried this afternoon. How did he send that word?"

At first Desmond looked nonplussed at the question, but he recovered quickly. "He would have sent one of our messengers."

"He didn't think it important enough to go himself?" Gareth was pressing. "I thought Lady Joan was one of your most important patrons."

"She is!" Desmond looked shocked at the implied criticism of his commander. "I'm sure he meant to have followed in a day or two when things were more settled here. Her home is two miles away, and he would have had to be gone much of the day in order to visit her. He himself might have missed the funeral that way!"

Gareth put up a hand. "My apologies, Desmond. I did not mean to offend. Now that I am on my feet again, I am trying to understand how things are run here. My charge is to discover who murdered Everard and, in order to do that, I may need to ask uncomfortable or strange questions as a means to clarify a point."

Desmond subsided, accepting the apology. While Gareth would not have intended to raise his ire, he had made a legitimate query. Who had been sent? Did that person ride to Joan's manor?

Walk? Desmond had referred to him as a *messenger*, as if that was his primary job. To whom else might the commander send messages from time to time and, in those instances, whom did he send?

So far, everyone had talked about Everard as if he'd had an unusual freedom within commandery life. With him gone, it begged a host of questions. The first would be which healer would replace Everard in tending to Lady Joan, if he was going to be replaced at all. Would that person be given the same freedom to come and go as Everard? And then, *who else* might have been out and about at the time of Everard's death.

By now the driver of the carriage had leapt from his seat to greet Brother Mark, who once again had been guarding the entrance to the commandery. He had hurried from his gatehouse to open the carriage door. Gwen was shorter than most of the people around her, so she had to stand on her tiptoes in order to see the woman exit the carriage and make her slow way up the path to the grave site, assisted by a man who'd come with her.

From the way people had talked about Lady Joan, Gwen had assumed she was elderly. But as the woman came closer, she was revealed to be in her fifties at most and even possibly her late forties. The well-dressed man who held her arm was of similar age and wore the sword of a nobleman knight.

"I thought she wasn't married?" Gwen whispered to Desmond.

"She isn't. That's her brother, Lucan."

Commander Reginald stepped forward to greet her on her way to Everard's grave. "Lady Joan, you really should not have come here in your condition. I would have delayed telling you of Everard's death if I had known you would drive all this way!"

"I had to see for myself." She looked past the commander to the open grave. "That's really him?"

"I'm afraid so."

"Murdered?" Lucan put in. He was a tall man, well-built, and hearty—or maybe that was just in contrast to his ailing sister.

"Yes."

Lucan wrinkled his nose in distaste, as if Everard had displayed poor table manners instead of being murdered. "How?"

Commander Reginald looked shocked that Lucan would ask such an indelicate question at this time. "We have some idea."

Gareth had told both him and Warden Geoffrey how Everard had been killed. They couldn't prevent everyone from knowing Everard had been placed into Helen's coffin, but the how of it for now could be reserved. Truly, very few had asked, the farmer on the hill by the fairy circle being an exception. And they hadn't answered him fully either.

"*Why* was he murdered?" Lucan continued.

"We are looking into that too," Commander Reginald said.

"*Who* is looking into it?" This query came off a bit more combatively than Lucan's first two questions, which had seemed simple requests for information. The implication was that Lucan should have been involved in the vetting of the investigator.

The commander's eyes narrowed, just for a heartbeat, but enough for Gwen to wonder if he didn't much care for this brother of his patron—or maybe just didn't like his influence over her. Then Reginald gestured to Gareth that he should approach. "You will have heard of Gareth ap Reese, of course. He serves as steward to Prince Howell."

"My lord." Lucan bent his head in respect. It wasn't often a Norman responded to Gareth that way, and Gwen was pleased to see it.

Reginald continued: "Lord Gareth, may I introduce Lucan, brother to Lady Joan, who I believe I have mentioned. My lady, this is the man investigating Everard's death."

Gareth bowed over Joan's hand. When he came up, he said, "I must agree with the commander that Everard wouldn't have been happy if you made yourself ill on his behalf."

"I am already ill." Her tone was tart, implying she was losing patience with the men's concern. "Traveling these few miles isn't going to hasten my end. And even if it did, it would be no loss to anyone, least of all me!"

"Joan!" Lucan protested. "Don't say that."

"Why not? It's true."

Gwen was definitely warming to her.

"I bow to your wisdom, my lady." Gareth gave way to allow Joan and Lucan to approach the grave. Joan continued to lean heavily on Lucan's arm as she walked, both of them stone-faced as they looked down at the body.

As was tradition, the first shovelful of dirt, which was all Donald had managed before their arrival, had not covered Everard's face. Gravediggers always worked from the feet to the head, though as Everard was wrapped in funeral linen, nobody could see his face anyway.

Even though Commander Reginald was equivalent in height to Joan, he was half-bent over in a solicitous manner. "Would you like a moment alone with him?"

There was an instant Gwen thought Joan was going to say yes or, even worse, ask that Everard's corpse be pulled out of the grave so she could see his face to make sure it was really him. She wanted to, Gwen could see it, but she managed to restrain herself. Instead, with a handkerchief she patted at the tears that leaked from the corners of her eyes and shook her head regretfully. "I merely wished to attend his end."

The relief in the commander's face might have been comical in another context. His emotion was also mirrored in Lucan's expression. Although Lucan's demanding manner was off-putting, Gwen was willing to give him the benefit of the doubt for now because he had been respectful to Gareth and clearly cared for his sister.

As those around her approached the grave in order to toss a handful of dirt on Everard's body, Gwen stepped back, and then back again. The other monks, including Desmond, who at long last had forgotten that he needed to cling to Gwen's arm at all times, completely filled the space in front of her.

Once Gwen extricated herself entirely from the crowd, Dai fetched up beside her. "You should know the commandery's right to Joan's estate isn't quite as set in stone as Commander Reginald makes out."

"How do you know that?" Gwen spoke out of the corner of her mouth, her eyes still on the crowd around the grave.

"Brother Mark, our gatekeeper."

"Does the widow herself know that?" Gwen had talked to Brother Mark too, but he hadn't mentioned this bit of gossip. Dai had a way with people. They told him things they might not normally speak about, and enjoyed doing it.

"Mark was unclear on that point. But if Joan were to remarry, her lands would act as her dowry."

"She is no longer young enough to produce a child for any husband," Gwen said.

"Yes, but the final bestowal of the land to the Hospitallers would be delayed further until her new husband's death."

"I see." Gwen plucked at her lower lip as she thought. "A new husband might object to the current running of the estate."

"Not to mention the fact that any of his heirs from a previous marriage, or even worse, a later one, might contest the bequest. It's good land. With a mine! Nobody would want to give it up."

Gwen glanced towards Commander Reginald, who was still hovering over Joan. "No wonder the commander is so anxious to please her."

Having paid his respects, Gareth returned to Gwen's side, at which point Dai related his news again.

Gwen kept her eyes on Joan as her brother helped her take a few steps back from the grave. "Unless we are very much confused about Joan's situation, she could not have hit him on the head, skewered him, and placed him in Helen's coffin."

"You'd need a strong man for that. I'm not entirely sure *I* could manage it. But *he* could have." Dai gestured towards Lucan, now standing with his sister on the opposite side of the grave from the commander, who'd just raised his hands again to renew the benediction. He had prayed over Everard before the first shovelful of earth, but with Lady Joan here, Gwen agreed that it felt right to do so again.

Gareth's expression turned dubious. "Hard to see how murdering his sister's physician gains him anything, and her grief looks real to me."

"It might be real. But it also might be that Lady Joan sought to shape her own destiny, if the death of Everard in some way affects that." Dai's expression was bright, even if wildly inappropriate for the moment. "Just because she didn't wield the weapon herself doesn't mean she couldn't have asked her brother to do it for her."

15

Day Three

Dai

The previous evening, Dai had been happy to generate suspicion about Lucan (and Joan) out of whole cloth. At the best of times, his father hated speculating, however. Rather than continue to do so, Gareth had taken action and gone to speak to Commander Reginald again. The commander had made it clear that Lady Joan was not to be questioned at the funeral meal, but he personally arranged for Gareth and Dai to see her this morning. Thus, after breakfast, Dai found himself riding at his father's side, enjoying a rare sunny day.

Only the two of them were traveling because Llelo was still not well enough to ride, and Gwen too had a plan (as she'd said with an arch smile) to peer into some corners they'd so far neglected.

"You really are feeling well enough for this?" Dai asked his father for what might have been the third time since they'd left the commandery—on top of the roughly five times one or another of his family members had asked him something similar before he'd mounted his horse. Even Taran had wrapped his arms around Gareth's neck and said, "Be safe." Since Taran himself had no concept of such behavior, he was simply repeating his mother's words.

"I'm not in my dotage, you know. I'm not fragile."

"I didn't say you were!"

Gareth scoffed. "Regardless, being out and about can only do me good."

"I am actually really glad to see you back on your feet, Tad. I want everyone at the commandery to see that we are doing something about Everard's death."

"Even if they don't want us to?" Gareth glanced over at Dai with a wry smile.

"Like Mam said, they should be more worried," Dai said. "Someone hit Everard on the head and then skewered him. Why aren't they afraid about who did that? It's almost like they still can't believe it really happened."

"Maybe they can't. They run a hospital, so they know death. But these monks aren't warriors like their brethren in the Holy Land. They don't know violence the way we do."

"You would think, living where they do, they'd be more worldly." Dai pursed his lips. "Or they could be pretending."

"What do you mean by that?"

"Lying, then," Dai said. "It's like they're all trying too hard. They want to be perfect. Is that because they fear Prince Hywel might shut down their commandery if they admit anything is wrong?"

"I don't know, son. You may be on to something. So far, we've asked questions, but we've struggled to delve deeper into community life, to find what might be happening beneath the surface." Gareth smiled. "You're good at that."

"I am?" Dai glanced at him. "Thank you, though ... I'm still a Dragon, not an investigator, you know."

Gareth laughed. "As if I could forget!"

They traveled the rest of the distance to Lady Joan's manor, hardly more than two miles, with Dai warm from the compliment. Even walking, the journey would have taken them no more than an hour. On horseback, even with his father still not entirely well, they were managing it in half that time. Dai could see, however, why Commander Reginald, being older and frailer, had been reluctant to make the journey himself.

Finally, they rode along the ridge overlooking the beautiful valley that the Hospitallers were so anxious to own, with its good pasture, cropland, and, of course, its mine in the mountains beyond. Though primarily a source of lead, it also produced zinc, copper, and bits of silver. Food production was definitely important to the running of the monastery, and they could sell any extra, but real wealth was to be found within the earth.

"It is no wonder the Hospitallers are so solicitous," Dai said as he gazed down the valley. "If one of the monks at the monastery felt the need to murder someone, it should have been Joan, not Everard."

"I'm glad you are comfortable speaking your mind to me, my son, but please don't say that to anyone else!"

Now that he knew the extent of the estate, Dai had to give further credit to Commander Reginald for not balking at arranging this interview.

And it spoke also to what he'd said earlier to his father: the Hospitallers might have good reason to be concerned that Prince Hywel would realize the amount of wealth capable of being generated here and take the mine, if not the whole estate, for himself. Dai didn't think his lord would violate the privileges of a monastery in that fashion, since he was devout in his own way, but the monks here did not know him like Dai did. Or like his father did.

Which also meant, because he *did* know him, that Dai needed to be realistic about Hywel's proclivities. If he was pressed for money, the mine might be the first place he looked to generate income quickly.

"I wouldn't say that to anyone else." Dai made a face. "Still, money is a powerful motive for murder."

"But maybe not the most powerful."

"That would be love," Dai said, "and hate."

"Two sides of the same coin." Gareth clicked his tongue to start his horse down the track towards Joan's manor. "We'll see if anyone here knows who flipped a coin on Everard."

16

Day Three

Gareth

It was with significant curiosity that Gareth and Dai approached Joan's home, with its earthwork ramparts, moat, and palisade. Within these encircling defenses was a substantial manor house, known locally as *Llys Arthur,* meaning *Arthur's palace.* The place had not been named for the great warrior-king of Wales whose victories held back the Saxons for a generation. *Arthur* had simply been the name of Joan's husband.

Although the manor itself was built in wood, stones had been used to divert the river into a moat that enclosed the outer defenses, and portions of the wall had been reinforced in stone at their base. A wooden fence encircled the entire complex. Arthur had been a vassal of the Earl of Hertford, the former ruler of this region, and would have been seen as an interloper by the local people. Before the Hospitallers had spread their wings of protection over the estate, Arthur would have had real cause to worry about attack from Welsh forces.

Gareth and Dai crossed the drawbridge to be instantly admitted beneath the gatehouse. Like the walls, the gatehouse was built in wood with stone foundations, making it apparent that the manor had been constructed over the top of an earlier outpost. Arthur wouldn't be the first newcomer to take advantage of what was already here, as the Hospitallers themselves had done at Ysbyty Cynfyn.

Long ago, the Romans had established forts all through this area, because they too had valued and worked the nearby mine. Hywel's army had followed the old Roman road down from Gwynedd, the same one that connected the mine to larger settlements farther south. The manor itself was two stories high, built in a square, with rooms around a central courtyard. From the looks, it had been built on the remains of a Roman plan too. King Owain's castle at Aber had a beautiful interior bath room for the same reason.

Before they'd even dismounted, the front door to the manor opened, and Lucan himself, rather than a steward or housekeeper, stepped out. Of course, given the long vista the manor's location granted its residents, he'd had warning of their approach. As they'd been riding, they'd been visible from the towers the entire way.

"My sister is feeling much better today and has been expecting you." Lucan smiled broadly. "We thought you'd be here earlier."

Gareth hesitated, noting the odd juxtaposition of the smile and the censure. Lucan's manner was so welcoming otherwise, and his eyes guileless, that all of a sudden Gareth wasn't sure if he could trust his own observations.

Last night, Gareth hadn't sensed much in the way of welcome from either Lucan or Joan, but he had reminded himself that she'd just lost her physician. And friend, he suspected, given the extent of her grief. Lucan had been significantly harder for Gareth to evaluate, not having spoken to him once they'd left the graveyard. At the dinner, he'd stayed at his sister's side and provided such a buffer that Gareth hadn't tried to approach her. He'd felt lucky to have been granted even this visit, thanks to the intercession of Commander Reginald.

"Thank you. I myself have been ill this week, though of course not like your sister. My apologies for not rising sooner. I didn't know we were expected at a particular time."

He had answered a back-handed censure with a non-apology. Normally, Gareth tried not to play games like this—and in truth wasn't very good at them—but his reading of the situation indicated a game was on.

Lucan seemed to accept his words as he said them, waving a hand in dismissal. "It isn't important. We are just happy you're here." As they passed through the courtyard, he added, in a confiding tone that made Gareth feel bad about his lack of apology, "Yesterday was such a difficult day; I was very concerned that the loss of Everard would set back my sister's health significantly. When Commander Reginald requested a meeting with you, I counseled against her seeing you. She insisted on it anyway." Then he smiled, in a manner that was both casual and disarming. "The expectation of seeing you today seems to have done her good."

"I will be careful." This time Gareth felt able to be entirely sincere. "I promise if she at any time becomes unwell, I will take my leave."

Lady Joan's personal quarters were in the southeast corner of the manor. On a day like today, the sun shone brightly through both large windows of her solar, filling the room with light. Inset in a far wall was a door that led to a chamber with a bed.

Joan had been sitting beside a fire, one that wasn't roaring, exactly, but crackling well and giving off a significant amount of heat. One of the windows was open too, letting in the outside air. Gareth was glad he'd shed his cloak before entering the house, having folded it neatly and tucked it into his saddle bags. Were it June, he might have risked leaving it behind in his wagon. But April weather was as variable as the wind. As much as he'd like to say he had recovered entirely from his illness, he would be wrong to think so. It wouldn't do to catch a chill.

Yesterday, Joan had been dressed in enveloping layers. She had appeared slender, but he hadn't been able to tell if her thinness was more than that. Today, she wore an underdress and overdress, with a blanket on her lap. With only one layer of fabric on her arms, they were revealed to be painfully thin, even emaciated. She needed the warmth generated by the fire.

At the sight of Gareth and Lucan entering the room, Joan didn't stand, but she did smile and wave Gareth forward. "Lucan, you don't need to watch over me. If you could ask Agnes to bring wine to share, that would be sufficient. Then you may go about your business. I don't want to disrupt your day any more than I already have."

A spasm of displeasure crossed Lucan's face, not dissimilar to his look when Commander Reginald had admitted that Everard had been murdered.

Joan gave him a stern look. "I'm fine. No need to hover so."

"As you wish, my dear." Lucan gave way with a bit more grace, back to the more amiable host he'd been up until now. Still, it was clear he didn't like being dismissed. Gareth didn't know if that was out of concern for his sister, because he wanted to be part of their conversation, or (at the very least) he wanted to know what she was saying to Gareth and he to her.

Joan, by contrast, appeared determined to speak to Gareth alone. It had him thinking he might actually be about to hear some truths. For that reason, he looked at Dai, who'd been hovering in the doorway, hesitating between staying with Gareth and following Lucan. Gareth made a slight motion with his head, which Dai correctly took to indicate the latter was the better choice. There was more to be learned here today than just from Joan, and Gareth himself didn't expect to have the chance. If questioned as to what he was doing or why he wasn't with his father, Dai could always make the excuse that he was seeing to the horses. Dai was experienced enough with investigations that he didn't need to be instructed further.

Gareth bent over Joan's hand, as he had done at the gravesite. "Thank you for seeing me. I do not mean to impose."

Joan looked up at him, surprise in her face, and then let out an unladylike snort. "Really? If we are going to work together to solve Everard's murder, I suggest we don't begin with lies."

17

Day Three

Gwen

"Have you met Healer Efa?" Bardolf held out one hand to Gwen and the other to the newcomer, speaking all the while in measured French, slowly so he could be sure both women understood him. Gwen's French was more than adequate to the task, but perhaps Efa's was not. "She has been of invaluable assistance to our hospital for many years now. Efa, this is Gwen, wife of Sir Gareth ap Reese."

"Prince Hywel's steward?" Efa's voice was lilting. And while she was not traditionally beautiful, when she smiled at Gwen, real joy lit her face. Perhaps this was how she greeted everyone, but regardless, Gwen couldn't help smiling in return.

"Yes, that's Gareth. It's so nice to meet you. I've heard so much about you."

"Good things, I hope!"

They weren't all good things, but Gwen certainly wasn't going to tell her so. "I was hoping I could have a moment of your time."

Efa's expression turned rueful. "It is rare for me to be this busy, but this illness is widespread, and most can't travel to the hospital. Thankfully, more recently the deaths have been fewer than I feared, and most are on the mend."

"We've had a hard time here, that's for certain." Despite his words, which were no less than the truth, Bardolf looked pleased that everyone was getting along. "Efa, I think you have already encountered Saran, Gwen's mother, who is an accomplished healer herself."

Gwen didn't bother to correct Bardolf that Saran was her stepmother. It wasn't important. And certainly, after Gwen's mother had died when she was ten, Gwen had been mothered by other women, Saran among them, who had cared for her even before she'd married Gwen's father. Gwen also didn't mention that Saran had not warmed to Efa.

Even if Efa knew how Saran felt, she didn't correct Bardolf either, instead smiling even more widely. "I am always happy to speak on matters of healing."

Humming a tune now, Bardolf took himself off to attend to other business, leaving Gwen to add, "May I express my condolences at the loss of your friend."

"My friend?" The corners of Efa's mouth turned down in puzzlement.

"I'm speaking of Everard." Gwen had thought to start with the assumption they were friends rather than the opposite, despite the argument between them, which Aled had witnessed.

"Oh, of course!" Efa put a hand to her chest. "My apologies. I was afraid someone else I knew was dead!"

Few patients or doctors might appreciate Efa's expression of relief, but she and Gwen had been speaking in Welsh, the native language of both. Gwen herself chose not to judge Efa too harshly. As she had said, it had been a busy few weeks at the hospital, and people died all the time. If Everard hadn't been a friend, then his death would not be the first thing on Efa's mind.

Efa hurried to explain. "I worked with Everard here at the hospital, but I didn't know him all that well. I wouldn't want to lead you astray in thinking that we were more than acquaintances."

Gwen couldn't decide if Efa was protesting too much or was simply distancing herself from his death. Gwen would like to think the latter. While Efa had rubbed Saran the wrong way, Gwen's job was to elicit information. As far as she could tell, Efa had done nothing wrong but have a beautiful smile.

"Would you take a walk with me?" And then, before Efa could agree or decline, Gwen walked out of the infirmary, assuming Efa would follow. Good manners would dictate it and Efa did, in fact, keep pace. There was a little path along the stream that was the main supply of water to the hospital. Once outside, Gwen set out along it. The day had dawned beautifully, and was continuing in that vein, not even threatening rain. "Even if you wouldn't call the doctor a friend, you must have worked with him on multiple occasions. I was hoping you could give me some insight into him." She gestured towards the infirmary building they'd just left. "An outside perspective could be useful."

It was the truth, even if not the whole of it.

Efa made a motion with her head. "I confess we never really talked about anything but medical matters. He didn't speak Welsh, for starters, and my French could be better."

"Still, you are a healer and observant. What was your sense of him?"

"In terms of physicking the ill, he was accomplished, if not brilliant in his ability to diagnose a problem."

"And as a person?"

Efa spread her hands wide. "As I said, I didn't know him particularly well."

Getting Efa to speak candidly was tougher going than the trail they were on. So far she hadn't even admitted he had a good bedside manner. Thus, Gwen decided to try a different tack. "What about you? Where are you from originally?"

"Here. I have lived in these hills my whole life."

Gwen knew this to be true already from Aled, which was the point of asking. She couldn't evaluate how Efa lied if she didn't also know what she looked like when she spoke the truth. "How is it that you ended up working at the hospital?"

"My mother was a healer too, and I apprenticed under her, as I'd wanted to do since I was a little girl. Over time, I became more trusted by the people of the area and, after my mother died, I slid into her place. It just happened that one day the commander himself came to see me."

"We're talking about Reginald?"

"Oh no. An earlier commander. They've had three or four different ones over the years, just like they've had different physicians, Everard among them, obviously."

They were back to Everard, which was all to the good as far as Gwen was concerned, since Efa hadn't wanted to talk about him earlier. However, Gwen didn't want to appear too eager, so she didn't allow for a change of subject. "What did that commander want to see you about?"

"He had a rash that nobody could cure, and he had heard good things about me. I made him a salve, and what ailed him was gone within a fortnight."

"This would have been before Everard's time too?"

"Oh yes, years ago now." Efa smiled. "Although, I should say that when Everard heard about it, he recorded my recipe in his ledger, so they have it now. I was happy to share. This commandery was fortunate to recruit someone of Everard's standing and skill. Admittedly, he wasn't always the easiest man to get along with. He was skilled, and he knew it. That meant he had definite ideas about how things should be done and little patience for lesser men."

"Or women?"

"You mean me?" Efa laughed. "I never had a problem with Everard. To him, the patient always came first, and I could not help but appreciate him for that."

"Do you mean to imply that he cared more for his patients than for his vocation?"

"I suppose I do, at that. His vocation was to be a physician. Being a monk was second, always, if not further back, behind being a scholar and a good man."

"You would call him a good man, then?"

"Oh yes. Most of the time." She grinned. "He could be amusing too. When he was talking about a treatment or procedure he'd learned, he had a way of imitating the style and accents of his instructors that was both endearing and cutting. You couldn't help but laugh, even though you knew you probably shouldn't."

If there had been any sense that Efa and Everard had shared a romantic attachment, Gwen would have pressed her about their relationship, since the more Efa talked, the more it became clear that she and Everard knew each other quite well. But Everard had been a monk, and nothing Efa had said so far indicated a deeper relationship. Gwen wasn't yet ready to overstep with someone who wasn't a real suspect, in what was supposed to be a general conversation.

However, she could get to the heart of the matter that Saran had elicited from Aled. "We have heard that you and Everard had an argument in the days before he died. What was that about?"

She could have phrased her question more obliquely, even to say, *I was hoping you could tell me what that was about*, but she didn't want to imply to Efa that she had a choice about answering.

Efa heard the change in tone and came to a full stop in the path. "I don't know what you're talking about. Why would you even ask me that?"

Gwen stopped too and turned to face her. Despite Gwen's best efforts to keep things casual, any pretense that this wasn't an interrogation had vanished. Efa saw right through her. Maybe that was just as well. "My husband is charged with investigating Everard's death. Someone overheard you and Everard having a disagreement. I don't know if it is relevant to his death, but I won't know until I ask. My apologies for not making clear earlier what I was about."

"And here I thought we were just getting to know each other. Do you enjoy manipulating innocent people into answering your questions?"

"Was that what I was doing? I *was* getting to know you, and I don't like murder."

"Are you implying that I do?" Efa's hostility—and her refusal to answer Gwen's question—felt illuminating.

"I wasn't, actually." Gwen said mildly. "Should I be concerned about your movements on the night Everard died? Why won't you tell me what the two of you argued about?"

Efa glared at her. "Do you genuinely think I have the ability to put Everard in that coffin?"

"No, I don't."

"But someone does think it? Your husband, perhaps, or Commander Reginald, wanting to blame Everard's death on an outsider?" Efa suddenly laughed, but without amusement this time. "Why do I even bother asking when I already know the answer? Warden Geoffrey never liked me. I'm sure he's dripped plenty of poison in your ear in the time you've been here." When Gwen just smiled, Efa snorted slightly under her breath. "Who overheard us? Bardolf? Or did Everard talk to him afterwards? That would be just like him."

If Gwen had thought the earlier part of the conversation was illuminating, this was positively revelatory. She still didn't answer, though. She had no answers to give.

For her part, Efa scoffed again, and finally said, "I had nothing to do with Everard's death."

"In which case, you might as well tell me where you were between Compline and Lauds the night Everard died."

She sobered. "I was sitting with an ill man."

"At Ysbyty Cynfyn?"

"No, on the other side of the valley." She made a gesture to indicate some place to the east. "I admit to dozing at times, taking turns with the man's wife to watch over him. He rallied, and his fever broke just before dawn. He lives still." She put a hand on her heart. "It was he, actually, whom I was afraid you'd learned was dead!"

As an alibi, it was a good one, though if the wife had slept while Efa sat with the man, that could have given her time to get to the church and back, depending upon how far away the house actually was. That said, Efa was right that she was a slight woman, and it would have been quite a feat for her to lift Everard, who was a good-sized man, into the coffin, not to mention overpower him enough to stick a skewer in his ear.

"If you had nothing to do with his death, you shouldn't mind telling me what the two of you were discussing that became heated enough to be noticed." Gwen could be stubborn too, and it seemed the time for it.

Efa gazed at her in what looked like disbelief. "What does it matter?"

"When a man is dead, anything and everything can matter."

Efa sighed. "Is it your husband who is Prince Hywel's investigator, or is it you?" And then, before Gwen could reply, though she wasn't sure what she could have said, Efa continued, "Everard accused me of being too friendly with the men in my charge. I challenged him that I was no more friendly than he, that I came to know my patients and those who treated them, and if I am to heal the sick, they need to trust me. I asked him how I was supposed to do that without being *friendly*. He had no answer. Did Bardolf agree with him?"

"I can't answer that." And she couldn't, since, of course, Bardolf had nothing to do with this. At the same time, Gwen completely appreciated Efa's response to Everard's conjecture. Not only that, but rather than being rubbed the wrong way by her forceful defense, Gwen found herself admiring the woman's assuredness. She wasn't afraid of any monk. She hadn't been intimidated by Everard. She would stand up to Bardolf if she had to—and maybe Commander Reginald and Warden Geoffrey too.

She also might speak French better than she was letting on. And, maybe, her umbrage and comprehensive denial were meant to deflect Gwen from a truth. Efa would not be the first to disguise a lie with outrage.

For all these reasons, and because Gwen wanted to note her reaction, she told a truth of her own: "As far as I know, Everard's concerns about your behavior have not spread to the point of being common knowledge."

"Thank you for that." Efa's expression turned musing. "Maybe I should take the bull by the horns, so to speak, and confront Commander Reginald directly. If I am not wanted in this hospital, I have plenty of patients outside of it. I would have hoped my service to this community might speak for itself."

She spun around and began walking, or maybe even stalking, back the way they'd come. She hadn't gone more than a few paces, however, before she turned back, striding up to Gwen with an equally determined air. "I just want to say that you have impressed me. The way you asked me questions, at first without me realizing the direction we were taking, was well done. I answered as if you had authority over me, which you don't." She paused. "What would have happened if I'd refused to talk to you?"

"I would have told Gareth, and he would probably have come to see you in a more, shall we say, official capacity."

Efa laughed. "To make it clear to someone even as witless as I that I have no choice but to talk?"

"I didn't say that," Gwen said. "That's not Gareth's way."

Efa subsided. "I apologize. You are a good wife, and I should not have disparaged your husband. Our conversation has upended me a bit."

"And me as well," Gwen said, still being honest. "With your alibi, which should be easily verified, you are well out of the running as to actually committing the murder."

"Good to know." Real interest entered her eyes. "Can you tell me how Everard died? You've kept the method well under wraps."

"We have, but by this point, that's less because it must be kept secret than because it's awful." Gwen then explained how Everard had been hit on the head and skewered.

Efa sucked in a breath, understanding immediately the brutality of that death. "I have never heard of anyone dying that way. It sounds so painful, and Everard hated to see anyone in pain." But then, almost immediately her expression turned curious again. "Any one of us who work at the hospital would have known how to murder that way. I can see now why you had to talk to me and why you didn't ask any of us to examine the body before Everard was put in the ground."

All of a sudden, Gwen herself felt a little ashamed for not at least asking Saran her opinion. Maybe she and Gareth had become a bit too assured of their own abilities and too used to working among the ignorant. "In truth, there is little else we know for certain except that Everard didn't put himself in that coffin."

"And is even that certain?"

Gwen blinked. "I-I—"

Efa waved a hand, smiling now. "I'm teasing. Of course, he didn't."

But she had induced doubt. *Could he have? And why would he have?*

Efa was moving on. "Are the rest of us in any danger, do you think?"

"I hope not. My children are here with me."

Efa's eyes went to Gwen's protruding belly. "If you need anything in the coming months, please don't hesitate to ask."

If Efa had said those words earlier, before she'd answered Gwen's questions, Gwen would have suspected she was trying to divert her. She didn't now. "Four months to go."

Efa put her hand over Gwen's. "I had three children live to grow up. I'm fortunate enough to have six grandchildren too."

They smiled at each other in that silent understanding only mothers shared.

"I wish you luck." Efa looked at Gwen with pity and sincerity. "For the sake of the baby, I would suggest you keep your distance from this investigation. You just never know what the future holds." Still with a smile on her face, Efa finally did turn away.

But in so doing, she left Gwen wondering if that last comment had been merely an observation ... or a threat.

18

Day Three

Gareth

"I don't believe that you mean me harm, but you *do* mean to impose."

Because Gareth was taken aback, he fumbled his recovery and found himself apologizing again. She was right, of course; she'd caught him in a lie. Any one of his family members would have seen through him instantly as well.

Joan cut him off with a wave of her hand. "Don't apologize. I was abrupt. I have little patience these days with the niceties of manners. I know you are sorry about Everard's death and about having to disturb me. Truly you don't need to thank me. If I'm being honest, it is you who are providing me with a service, since it is much better to think about finding Everard's killer than how much I miss him or how terrible I feel myself." Suddenly, she looked to be fighting back tears. "He was so full of life! I can't believe he's gone."

"I am so sorry for your loss."

She wiped at her cheeks with her fingers. "It is astounding to me that I have outlived him. I feel like I have been dying for so long, you see. That's how I came to know Everard, of course."

"How did your relationship with Ysbyty Cynfyn come about?"

"Arthur and I came in the train of the Earl of Hertford, as I'm sure you know. Arthur himself was mortally wounded in the fighting after the earl was killed, though he didn't die immediately. He had time to be transported to Ysbyty Cynfyn, more's the pity. On his deathbed he became a Hospitaller and willed everything to them."

Her offhanded *more's the pity* had Gareth stepping warily for a moment. He didn't know if she was referring to the fact that Arthur had suffered a good deal before his death, rather than dying immediately on the battlefield, or if it was the transportation to Ysbyty Cynfyn itself that was at issue. "Was his promise a surprise to you? You were still married, after all. If he'd lived, his allegiance to the Hospitallers would have been awkward."

"To me, certainly! There is, however, accommodation for that very situation in their charter." Her mouth made a moue of disaffection. "Suffice to say, my husband didn't always consult me on business matters."

Gareth was still treading carefully, but he also wanted to make sure he could ask every necessary question. "Do you feel the bequest could have been made under duress?"

"He was dying. Of course, it was under duress. That doesn't mean he didn't intend it or that he was coerced by the commander at the time into making it."

"Were you not there when the bequest was made?"

"I wasn't. They sent for me, but it was a time of war; Earl Clare was already dead. I could not travel until the following morning, by which point Arthur was dead too." She met his eyes. "You have a suspicious mind. I like that. You might even be wondering, as I initially did, if Arthur made the bequest at all, given that he died in the middle of the night with only two men to hear him."

"The thought had crossed my mind," Gareth admitted. "For a man of Arthur's standing to leave everything he had to a religious order isn't unusual, but at the same time, it was very much in his caretakers' best interests."

"The commander was with him and sent another monk for paper and pen. Arthur put his mark on the agreement, sealed it, and died not long afterwards."

That still sounded to Gareth like his decision could have been coerced, but he also didn't think there was anything he could do about it, especially since the bequest had been witnessed by more than one person, as all such agreements had to be.

"At first, I was not happy, to say the least. In fact, I was furious, and I was going to contest the bequest. But since I had nobody to contest it with, since the Welsh had conquered the region, it gave me time to think. I came to see that Arthur willed everything to the hospital in order to protect me. He knew by then that Richard de Clare was dead and his lands would be under dispute, possibly for many years. With Arthur's death, I would have been left defenseless. I might even have lost everything. By giving his lands to the Hospitallers, but not completely until my own death, he ensured my survival. He'd done it because he loved me, and I no longer regret his choice."

She made a motion to encompass her physical form. "Especially now."

"Did you meet Everard before or after your husband's death?" Gareth already knew Everard had been at Ysbyty Cynfyn for only five years. He was asking if they'd known each other before, from childhood perhaps.

"Oh, after! I wasn't ill then, and not even forty. I could have married again. I might even have given a new husband a child. Arthur had ensured I was not seen as eligible, however, and with the change of suzerainty of Ceredigion, I had no lord to find me an appropriate husband." She made a motion with her head. "I can't say I was sorry about that."

"You have no father living, then?" They had moved on from Arthur, which Gareth thought might be just as well. He didn't want to tire her too much, and needed to leave time to discuss Everard. He was deliberately delaying that painful topic, even if she kept saying his name, to give her a chance to speak about her life. He also wanted to make her more comfortable with him as a person to talk to.

"No father; only a brother I told in no uncertain terms had no business marrying me off to further his position. He lives in Hertford on our family's lands, with a wife of his own and a dozen offspring." She laughed. "I could have gone to live with him, but I had no desire to become a nanny."

"I gather the brother we are speaking of is in addition to Lucan?"

"Lucan is a younger son, shut out like so many from the family inheritance. I must say, the Welsh practice of allowing every son to inherit does have its merits, even if it's against the edicts of the Church." They'd been speaking in French, and for a moment Gareth wondered if she'd forgotten that he himself was Welsh. The ill and dying often had trouble with memory. But then she met his eyes, and there was mischief in hers. "You don't protest?"

"Why would I? You speak the truth. I would say that nowhere in scripture does it say that only the eldest can inherit, nor that only legitimate sons have value. We will have to agree to disagree on those points if this conversation is to remain amicable."

"I just said I agreed—with you!" She snorted laughter. "I think I like you, Gareth ap Rhys." She actually managed to say his name the Welsh way.

Gareth bent his head. "I am honored. Others might prefer you didn't."

Her smile this time was pleased. "They might, but when one is as close to death as I am, one begins to care less about what others think."

"While we are speaking of the Church's will, as well as your husband's, can you tell me the identity of the witnesses to Arthur's bequest?"

"One was the commander at that time, as I said. In those days his name was Robert. He died some years ago."

"And the monk with him? Do you remember his name?"

"Of course, I do. He's our current commander, Reginald."

19

Day Three

Dai

Dai hadn't known exactly what his father was thinking when he had waved him away from Joan's receiving room. He hadn't taken offense because he too assumed Joan would do better talking to Gareth alone. Dai had really come along on this journey more as a companion (and to make sure Gareth didn't relapse) than because his presence would lead to any great insights.

But as he paced away across the courtyard of Llys Arthur, it occurred to him that his father might have brought him because he did want Dai to investigate on his own. Well, he could do that. As he'd been taught, one had to follow where the investigation led.

Right now his curiosity was leading him to follow in Lucan's footsteps, which went outside the main house structure and into the courtyard. Beyond was the ring formed by the moat, inside of which were the defensive earthworks upon which the wooden palisade had been built.

When they'd first arrived, Dai hadn't realized quite how extensive the earthworks were, but now that he had a chance to really look at them, he realized they encompassed a space as large as sixty yards east to west and forty yards north to south. The house was on one side of this protected land, along with the stables, workshops and laundry, all of which filled the northern half of the space. To the south were gardens, including a workshop to which Lucan was leading Dai (inadvertently because he hadn't yet looked back to see Dai following). The garden was particularly impressive in its order. Plants were organized by height and type, staked in neat rows or arranged on climbing trellises. This early in the year most still had a long way to go.

At one point, Gwen had tried to teach Dai about herbs, but he had been much more interested in what his father had to say to him. In retrospect, Dai had been a bit brusque in his disinterest. This last week, however, he'd asked his grandmother to show him a few things, having realized that, as a soldier, it might behoove him to know how to treat other men when a healer could not be found.

With just those brief lessons, he had grown to recognize several of the herbs. Some, such as thyme, had a hundred uses, both medicinal and for cooking. Others, like the many varieties of poppies, had fewer—and in the case of the oriental poppy, only one.

As Dai gazed at the plants, he realized he had learned more from his brief stint at Ysbyty Cynfyn than he'd thought. Lucan's garden contained both the field poppy, which was native to Wales, and the oriental poppy, from faraway lands. These latter poppies were the source of poppy juice, *dwale*, and other concoctions to reduce pain.

In order to make any of the remedies, a healer extracted the milky juice from the poppy seed heads. These poppies weren't in bloom yet, so that harvest was upcoming. Field poppy was used in a less potent medication, derived from the fresh petals to make a syrup, or dried petals in hot water to make an infusion.

Lucan had pulled open the door to the herb hut and was just about to enter when he glanced back and saw Dai stopped in the middle of his garden. His expression tightened just for a heartbeat—in concern or distaste Dai wasn't quite sure from this distance. Then, almost instantly, his face was transformed by a smile.

Dai didn't think he was imagining that the welcome didn't reach Lucan's eyes.

Lucan closed the door again and advanced back to where Dai was standing. "May I help you with something? Were you looking for me?"

Dai gestured to the plants in front of him. "Your garden is amazing."

"We have worked hard to make it so. If you were to return a month from now when everything is blooming, it would be even more impressive." Lucan gazed out over his domain, his hands on his hips and a look of genuine satisfaction on his face. "Do you know anything of plants?"

"Not as much as I would like. This week I have felt that lack more acutely. My grandmother is Saran, who is a healer herself. Have you met her?"

"I can't say I have." Lucan seemed to have overcome whatever had caused his initial negative response to Dai's presence in his garden.

"Did you do all this yourself?"

"Mostly." He shrugged. "I have helpers, of course, who do much of the heavy labor."

Dai glanced towards the garden hut in what he hoped was a casual manner. The hut was a bit larger than the one at the commandery. "Is that where the herbs are dried and worked?"

"It is."

"May I have a look?" Dai was trying to appear like a novice, which in regards to herbs he was. "I promise I won't touch anything!"

Lucan cleared his throat, his native good manners overcoming the initial reluctance which had prompted him to close the door to the hut and intercept Dai before he could follow him inside. "Of course. This way."

"Thank you! As I said, I have been taking instruction recently from my grandmother. I know I am just a beginner, but I would very much like to see what you have here." He truly wasn't forcing his enthusiasm; he genuinely wanted to see what was inside, though not because he had aspirations to become a healer. From Lucan's manner, he might not know that Dai was one of Prince Hywel's Dragons. In fact, he could be assuming Dai couldn't be much of anything yet since he was only sixteen.

But although Lucan allowed Dai to enter the hut, as soon as he crossed the threshold, he pointed to a spot three feet inside the doorway. "I'm going to have to ask you to stand there. I have many delicate processes going on that I don't want disturbed. Even a few extra heavy feet on the floorboards could disrupt them."

That wasn't something Dai had ever heard before, but he wasn't going to argue with what was looking like a singular opportunity. He planted himself where Lucan had indicated and looked around with an eager expression. "I am happy to see whatever you are willing to show me. I have been inside the herb garden at the commandery. This is even more extensive! Do you supply remedies to them?"

"Very occasionally when they have run out of a particular item." Lucan eyed Dai, who kept his expression open and, hopefully, without guile. "As you may already have figured out, Everard was integral to helping me create all this."

He spoke like he hadn't wanted to admit it and would have lied if he thought he could have gotten away with it. Dai had learned to watch other people's faces closely, so he knew how hard it was to control one's expression. Everyone tried, but most people were not accomplished liars. The key, as he was beginning to understand, was to lie to yourself so completely that in the moment you spoke, you believed what you were saying was the truth.

Most people weren't capable of such deception, even as they told little lies ten times a day and thought nothing of the ways they gave themselves away.

"He taught you how to garden?"

"And how to make remedies. I can't say everything I know came from him, but much of it did. My sister is not the only person at Llys Arthur who lost a friend when Everard died."

Lucan continued speaking with what appeared to be the truth: "The commandery has physicians who aid in healing directly, but we at here are becoming known throughout Deheubarth for supplying herbs and remedies. In the winter, after the garden has been put to bed and much of the work on the estate is in hiatus, I travel south to offer my medicines and expertise to some of the great lords there."

They'd been speaking in French, in which Dai was fluent. So while Dai could never forget that Lucan was Norman, he found himself settling more comfortably into the Norman French accent. By doing so, he might even be able to make Lucan forget that he was Welsh. Certainly the other man didn't seem concerned about telling the son of the steward of the ruler of Ceredigion that he routinely traveled into Norman-held territory. Having been steeped in intrigue since he was ten years old, Dai was suddenly considering all the ways putting on the mantle of a traveling healer was a great disguise for a spy.

Not that he had any cause so far to suspect Lucan of anything untoward.

But his smile really didn't reach his eyes very often.

"This is an incredible achievement." Dai's fingers itched to pick up any one of the vials or jars on the workshop's central table. Instead, he rested both hands on the hilt of his sword, in mimicry of Gruffydd, his commander among the Dragons, when he didn't know what else to do with his hands. "Are you worried about what will become of you and your garden when the Hospitallers take over completely?"

"You mean when my sister dies?"

Dai hadn't wanted to speak so bluntly. Now that Lucan had done so, he simply added, "Yes. I do mean that. My apologies for bringing it up at all, but your success here begs the question of what happens after."

"Afterwards, the garden will no longer be my problem."

"You don't think the Hospitallers will keep you on?"

"I don't know that I would want to stay on without my sister." Maybe Dai's French accent really had lulled Lucan into speaking truths, because that certainly sounded like one.

"You could join their order."

"The Hospitallers?" Lucan scoffed. "I don't think so. That life is not for me."

Again, the truth.

That life wasn't for Dai either—he definitely liked girls too much for that—but since Lucan had been telling the truth in this moment, he thought he might be able to get away with pressing a little bit more. "Why not? I'm just asking because it might serve them to keep you on, running the manor and estates which you know so well—and caring for the garden, for which you clearly have a gift."

He hoped he wasn't being overly effusive or too familiar. He was genuinely impressed with what he saw here. He was just sorry he didn't have his grandmother with him to recognize the remedies Lucan was cooking up. Dai didn't necessarily suspect that there was anything unsavory about them, but he knew as well as anyone else in his family that an herb that healed could also kill.

Then again, Everard hadn't been poisoned.

And what he hadn't seen in Lucan's garden, now that he thought about it, was any foxglove. His parents had already matched the color of Everard's bloom to those at the fairy circle—and Iago's to those at the commandery—but it was good to confirm that neither could have come from here.

Lucan shook his head. "Even were the commandery my calling, or could become so, it has been made clear to me that the monks are happy to go their own way." For a moment his eyes turned sad as he took in his domain. "I will miss all this." Then he shook himself. "Plants can be regrown, and I have all the seeds stored safely away. I will survive." He tapped his temple. "What's in here nobody can ever take away from me."

He went back to chopping a root. Dai watched him, knowing that he had about outworn his welcome, even only a few feet inside the door, but he was not quite ready to leave. He still wanted to suspect Lucan of murdering Everard, but he honestly couldn't come up with a way Everard's death would have served him.

Then Lucan swore and clutched at his hand. Blood seeped from between his fingers.

Instantly disobeying Lucan's command to stay put, Dai grabbed a folded cloth from a stack on a nearby table and wrapped it around the bloody wound. Lucan himself had staggered back to sit on a stool set against the wall. His face was pale, and his eyes wide and staring. If Dai hadn't witnessed the event himself, he would never have believed such a big man could tremble in such a fashion from a little cut on his finger.

Dai squeezed the cloth tighter before releasing it in order to inspect the wound. Lucan had definitely sliced his left forefinger, but he hadn't cut to the bone. It was bloody, but not disastrous. "Can I clean this for you? Do you have a salve I could put on it before I bandage it?"

"Yes." Lucan cleared his throat. "Thank you."

Dai bustled about at Lucan's direction, collecting the necessary items to tend the wound and bind it. As Dai tied off the bandage, Lucan's color began to improve. He took a deep breath, still resting the back of his head against the wall. Then, at last, he managed a wry smile. "Don't tell my sister about this, eh? It wouldn't do for anyone to know the master of the house shrieked like a girl at the sight of a little blood."

"I would never," Dai assured him.

Lucan indicated the door. "If you don't mind, I'd like to be left alone."

"Of course." Dai thanked Lucan and departed to find his father, glad Lucan hadn't asked him not to tell Gareth.

As he walked back through the garden to the house, Dai considered all that had happened. Lucan *had* shrieked like a girl. Had that been deliberate, to put Dai off his trail? Was Lucan that good a liar? If so, it had been well done. Lucan had the necessary size to have murdered Everard. As a healer, he had the knowledge too. But after that performance, Dai would be hard pressed to believe he could ever have had the will.

20

Day Three

Gareth

As Joan herself had said, by bestowing his lands on the Hospitallers, her husband had protected both them and her—from Gwynedd, as it turned out. As to the other parts of her story, Gareth couldn't decide if the fact that Reginald had been the other witness to Arthur's bequest was significant or not. By Joan's own admission, she was as satisfied as the monks with the current arrangement. By now, nobody thought any crime had been committed.

Except, perhaps, Joan's brother? With her death, it looked to Gareth like he had the most to lose. In fact, he had everything to lose.

"Has Lucan always lived with you?"

"Just since Arthur died." For a moment, through the discontented look on her face, her familial connection to Lucan was obviously that of a sibling, despite their differing size and gender. Then the look was gone, her expression turning matter-of-fact instead. "During our marriage, Arthur thought Lucan should do more to make his own way and wouldn't allow him to live here permanently. Now he manages the estate for me, with the guidance of the Hospitallers, of course. He's very busy, as I'm sure you can imagine."

Gareth longed to ask if the older brother, who'd inherited the family's lands in Hertford, had also declined to have Lucan in his home, nannying or otherwise. Such a question could wait until he could ask the man himself. Or Dai would do it for him.

For that reason, it might have been better for Dai to have stayed in the room a little longer. But, from the start, Gareth had been feeling that Joan would prefer a more confidential conversation and didn't need Gareth's sixteen-year-old son listening in. In addition, neither she nor Lucan looked to be going anywhere. If Gareth had more questions that weren't getting answered, he could always return.

Had Gareth and Joan been younger, and Joan not so ill, there might have been some question about the appropriateness of them sitting alone together. As it was, Dai had left the door open, and just as their conversation hit a lull, the maid came through it with a carafe of mulled wine. The drink was too warm for Gareth today, but he looked more favorably upon the plate of baked treats. For nearly a week, his illness had prevented him from eating normally, and all of a sudden he was ravenous.

Joan indicated that the maid should leave the tray. Then she asked Gareth to pour the wine, which he did, both for her and for himself, in order to be companionable. He also laid a cloth on Joan's lap and added one of the treats. She didn't touch it, but she did take a sip of wine. "What did you really come here to speak to me about? Surely it wasn't about my husband and the disposition of his estate."

This was the opening he'd been waiting for, and he wasn't going to waste it. "I did come to talk about those things, since I can never know what information might be useful over the course of an investigation. I would like to hear from you now about your relationship with Everard and, in particular, about his last evening with you."

"My relationship?" She raised her eyebrows at him. "He was my physician."

Gareth bent his head. "I did not mean to imply otherwise or that you were engaged in anything unconventional."

"Or inappropriate? When you say it out loud, it becomes even more absurd than thinking it." She scoffed. "I suppose I do believe you, but I also know that you are looking for intrigue where there is none. Yes, Everard was my friend; no, our relationship did not rise to anything more than that of two people who enjoyed each other's company, despite the circumstances of our meeting."

"Might it have if you were not unwell?" Gareth found himself speaking more straightforwardly than he might normally have done. Joan was on the edge of death, looking into that vast chasm of the unknown, and he knew for certain she could not have murdered Everard. At the same time, Gareth was happy they had finally reached the main point.

"And were he not a monk?" She chortled, and Gareth found himself smiling too. "I couldn't say. It was impossible, regardless, and we left it at that." She tipped her head. "It was freeing, really, in many ways just like this conversation here between the two of us. Because of my illness, we can speak easily without all the usual sparring and jostling that happens between men and women, married or not, compatible or not. As death approaches, all pretense falls away."

That was also refreshingly straightforward. And true. "How was he that last day?"

"It's funny you should ask that, or maybe not so funny, given what came after. I did notice that he was a bit out of sorts. I don't have many visitors, so the ones I do get are inspected from head to foot." She raised her eyebrows at him. "Beware."

"I would expect no less." Despite her assurances of earlier, Gareth had a sense she was flirting with him. And again, maybe that was because, at long last, she could be herself, in whatever fashion that meant. But if this was how she'd treated Everard, Gareth could imagine they'd come to be quite companionable. Friends, as she'd said, loving each other but not lovers. It was hard not to admire the woman for her resilience and refusal to bow to what obviously was a terrible disease that was taking her life moment by moment. Her intelligence was self-evident, and she was enjoying the back and forth of thoughtful conversation, which Gareth hoped he was providing her. "Did you get a sense of what was wrong?"

"I did ask him. As you must by now be aware, these days there aren't many boundaries I'm not willing to cross. Because Everard and I were comfortable with each other, I felt I could inquire as to his wellbeing. He deflected my question with a wave of his hand, implying it was nothing worth talking about, and asked me about what I'd eaten that day. I confessed it wasn't much. It is amazing how long it actually takes to die once a person gets started on it." The corners of her mouth turned down. "Did Everard take long? Did *he* suffer? *How* was he murdered? The commander wouldn't say."

Gareth hesitated to say either, genuinely not wanting *her* to suffer with the news. She waited patiently, seeming to understand that he needed a moment to consider his answer. Finally, he gave her the bald truth. "He was hit on the head with a rock and then murdered with a metal skewer shoved into his ear canal."

Her instant recoil caused Gareth to regret his candor.

He put out a hand. "I am so sorry. I shouldn't have told you like that. To answer your question, he may have had a spurt of pain, but his death came almost instantly, and he likely had no real consciousness of what was happening to him."

Joan took a more lengthy sip of wine before putting down the cup. "Thank you for telling me. I apologize for my instinctive response."

"It was a natural one to an unpleasant description."

"If only my own death could be so quick."

"May I ask what ails you?"

"At one time I refused to talk about it, but it hardly matters now." She moved a hand towards her breast. "It started with a lump that grew and grew. I think it's everywhere now. That is what Everard thought too. He was well educated, an accomplished physician, and had seen it many times before."

"You are in pain." It was an assertion, rather than a question. Gareth didn't need her to reply to know it. "I am sorry about that too."

"Strangely, the pain hasn't been bad today. Once it is, I take the juice of the poppy. When I first fell ill, Everard tried many remedies to ease my suffering. These days, poppy syrup has become the only thing that lets me sleep. I try to put off taking any until I can't stand the pain a moment longer, to the point that my whole body is shaking with it." She lifted her cup in Gareth's direction and saluted him with it. "Wine helps to keep the edges softer."

Gareth took the liberty of pouring her some more. "What did he do for you when he visited?"

"That last visit was after a *bad* night. Nothing had allowed me to sleep. In the hours before he arrived, I had been crying on and off. He took one look at me and dispensed a stronger dose." She took in a breath and let it out. "You cannot imagine the relief. Normally, I won't take it during the day, because it muddles my mind far worse than this will." She raised her cup to him. "It makes me feel like I'm stuffed with wool. Or maybe stuffed *in* wool."

"He would give you straight poppy juice, not *dwale*?" *Dwale* was used the world over as a sleeping potion and to lessen pain in men injured in battle. Perhaps Arthur himself had taken it for his wounds before he died. The healer could give a patient *dwale* before amputating a limb or sewing up a gaping wound, and even if it didn't entirely dull his senses, the next day he would remember little of what had gone on.

One of its main ingredients, however, was vinegar, which made it taste dreadfully bitter. Joan pulled a face at the thought. "No. I can't bear the taste. I'd rather live with the pain than drink that."

"Poppy alone is an even more powerful medicine—though I can see why it would be exactly what is needed in your case."

Joan nodded. "Any physician worth his salt is careful with its use, as you know. But Everard did not need to be careful with me. I am accustomed to taking it; I can't live without it; we both knew it and accepted it."

"Do you have enough to keep you going now that he is gone?"

"We grow it here," she gestured towards the open window, "and make it here. Everard showed my brother how."

This news was a little startling to Gareth. "You have that extensive an herb garden?"

"Lucan and Everard worked on it together." She waved a hand, surprised at Gareth's surprise, and then dismissing it. "You must admit it makes sense, given our distance from the hospital. We grow more than poppies, you know! In fact, my brother has become quite a proficient healer in his own right. He tends our people when they are ill. Miners, in particular, are often injured, and we provide assistance."

Even with her insistence that Lucan ran the estate for her, Gareth had still been thinking of him as a ne'er do well and lazeabout. Suddenly, he was revising his opinion. "Does he administer to you now?"

"That day, the day Everard died, my brother demanded that I take what he gave me, but I refused until Everard arrived." She sighed. "Now I have to use my own judgment, which I distrust."

"And Lucan's?"

"I do trust him."

Though she stated this clearly, Gareth still thought there was a measure of reluctance in her voice. "Was Lucan here the day Everard died?"

"Of course he was. Didn't I just say?"

"Was he here when Everard left?"

Now Joan's brow furrowed. "What an odd question. He's always here." Then she made a qualifying motion with her head. "He does frequent that inn, known as The Castle, on the high road. Come to think on it, he went that night, though he didn't stay long. I heard him come in after an hour or two. He poked in his head to ask if I needed anything."

Gareth would definitely be asking about Lucan's movements that night. As dosed with poppy as she'd been, Joan might not be a reliable witness. For now, Lucan's alibi seemed as strong as hers. "How was Everard by the time he left?"

"He was still distracted, but then finally admitted he was going to meet with someone. I'm not sure what gave me the impression exactly, but I had the sense it was a woman, and that was why he didn't want to tell me."

"He feared you'd be jealous?"

She smiled gently. "I already told you there was nothing between us. We were friends. Friends care about one another."

Hoping what he was about to do was in any way sensible, Gareth drew a paper from his coat and quickly sketched a likeness of Healer Efa in charcoal. Then he turned the paper to show Joan. "Do you know her?"

"What a wonderful drawing! Of course, I know her. Efa has come to my home many times too. She and Lucan have learned to work together." She bit her lower lip. "In truth, I am quite sure it is to see my brother that she comes here so often, not to check on me, though she has been helpful on the days Everard is not available."

Lucan's relationship with Efa was another line of inquiry to pursue, but again, not with Lucan's sister. Not yet, anyway.

"Did you get a sense that Everard was going to see Efa?"

"If that were the case, I think he would have said, given that we know each other." Her manner was dismissive, indicating as plainly as if she'd expressed the thought out loud that Efa was of no interest to her. She wasn't jealous. She wasn't concerned about her brother's attachment either. Instead, her eyes turned thoughtful as she looked at him. "Could … could I ask a favor? You work so quickly. Could you draw a picture of Everard for me?"

Gareth instantly pulled another paper from his pocket, glad he'd resupplied himself from the commandery's scriptorium. "I will do my best."

It was a matter of a few moments' work, easier than drawing Efa, whom he'd encountered less often. This time, he was drawing from all the times Everard popped in and out of the infirmary while Gareth was unwell. For now, he blocked out any vision of what he had looked like in death. For a dying woman, Gareth needed to render Everard very much alive, but maybe just out of reach, as he was now, though perhaps would not be soon, not to Joan.

In the end, he drew Everard half-turned away, with a hint of a smile on his lips and what Gareth thought of as friendly eyes.

"Thank you. That's exactly like him." Joan took the paper in both hands, staring down at it. Then she wiped a tear from her cheek before it could drop onto the paper and mar the image. "Part of me dreaded you coming here because I knew you were investigating his death. It wasn't as if I didn't know Everard had been murdered, but I wasn't sure how I would feel about talking about his loss.

"All of a sudden, you have captured the very essence of him, and whether you meant to or not, you have given him life again and me a measure of relief ... and joy. I will welcome you into my home any time you have need to return."

21

Day Three

Gareth

"That is a lot of poppies." Gareth surveyed the garden, Dai at his side, though speaking to Lucan. "You work hard."

It was exactly the right thing to say.

"I do. I am not sure very many people have appreciated that fact." Lucan was digging in the dirt of a raised bed. He had exchanged his gentlemen's gear for workman's clothes.

Gareth was truly impressed. Although both Joan and then Dai afterwards had told him about the extent of the garden, he hadn't realized what they'd meant. The man did know how to get his hands dirty, in really one of the best ways possible. Today he was readying his garden for the fullness of spring, staking out small plants, refitting trellises, and planting seeds in neat rows.

"Your sister spoke well of you."

Lucan was focused on the plants before him, and simply waggled his head. "She is the exception to most everything."

Dai had told Gareth about Lucan's forthrightness regarding his sister's upcoming death. In the main, it mirrored Joan's own, so perhaps Lucan's intent had simply been to be honest about what his life was going to be like after his sister died. Dai had also told him about Lucan's feigned welcome into his herb hut. Dai still thought he was hiding something. The set of his shoulders in this moment spoke as loudly as words that he was too busy to talk. Lucan wanted them to go away as quickly as possible.

But Gareth wasn't done asking his questions, and he'd rather get them over with now than have to come back, even with Joan's invitation. "Did you speak to Everard when he came here on the day he died?"

"I always do."

It wasn't quite a monosyllabic answer, but it was close.

"Did you talk about anything in particular?"

"Just the usual. My sister's health, the weather, the garden, my sister's health."

"And what did he think about your sister's health?"

At last Lucan consented to put down his spade and look at Gareth. His expression was one of impatience, if not exasperation, but Dai wasn't the only one who noted the upraised brows and wrinkled forehead. That was fear. Lucan was a good liar, and that was saying something among Normans, particularly noble Normans, who had a skill for lying matched by few others.

But still, Gareth had been lied to by some of the best.

"What do you think he thought? She's dying. That's what we talked about. He doesn't know how long she has. It could be a day, a week, a month."

"A year?" Gareth said.

"Unlikely. I wake up every morning terrified that it's today."

Gareth spread his hands wide in apology. "I had to ask, you understand? The man was murdered."

Lucan wiped at his brow with the back of his hand, leaving a swath of dirt on his forehead. He was wearing gloves, which was understandable since one of his fingers was bandaged. Without the glove, the wound would have become filthy with garden dirt. "I understand, but I don't know what you want from me."

"Everard came here weekly. I want to know what you knew about him and if there was anything in particular that struck you as different, odd, or concerning on the final day of his life. You appear to have been one of the last people to see him alive."

Lucan had been on his knees, but now he pushed to his feet. "There was nothing unusual about anything he did here that last day." He still held the spade, and he waved it about as he spoke.

"But ..." Dai pounced, because there had been a moment of hesitation in Lucan's manner that Gareth had seen only in retrospect.

Lucan sighed. "I suppose I could say there was something unusual about what he did afterwards." When Gareth didn't prompt him for more, he sighed again. This had been a difficult conversation, and if Lucan wanted to take his time now that he was talking, Gareth was going to let him. "In truth, I wasn't one of the last people to see him alive. Not even close."

"How do you know that?"

"Because I followed him."

"To where? And why?"

"At first, I didn't mean to. I was going to The Castle—that's the inn on the road before the turn to Ysbyty Cynfyn. I often go, seeing as how it's a matter of a mile from here. As it turned out, that was his destination too."

"This was unusual?"

"I had never seen him there before. He met a woman."

"A woman!" Gareth believed him, since Joan had thought Everard was going to meet a woman too, one she didn't know. "Who?"

Lucan shrugged. "She wasn't someone I had ever seen there before."

"Can you describe her?"

"Not young but not old either. Red hair! I stayed far away because I didn't want him to think I'd been following him. They had a close conversation by the fire and then he left. She went to her chamber in the inn. I honestly expected him to go with her. Maybe that wasn't what they were about."

"How do you know what she did? Did you follow her?"

Lucan looked sheepish, which wasn't an expression Gareth had seen on his face up until now. "I asked the proprietor about her afterwards."

"And?" Gareth truly shouldn't have had to prompt him.

"He knew who I was talking about, since she was staying in his inn. If nothing else, it is rare for a woman to travel alone. She told him she was a healer, in service to the Earl of Pembroke, which was why she met with Everard."

Dai had been studying Lucan's face. "You didn't believe her?"

"If she really was a healer, why didn't she wait for Everard at Ysbyty Cynfyn? Why arrange to meet in the inn? The commandery has a guesthouse, and as a servant of the earl, she could have stayed without charge."

"Maybe she did stop by the commandery and was told he was at your manor," Dai said.

"She didn't. Last night I spoke with the guard at the gate—"

"That would be Brother Mark?" The answers were coming, and Gareth wanted to keep them coming. For someone who had said almost nothing up until now about anything that was in any way relevant, Lucan had suddenly become a font of information. Gareth didn't know if he'd been storing it up, waiting for the right time to talk, or if he had meant never to speak of it until Dai and Gareth had started poking around his manor. People with secrets tended to think too hard about them and that was often what tripped them up. Lucan could have feared Gareth and Dai would stop by the inn on the way home to slake their thirst, speak to the inn keeper, and the news that Lucan had questioned him about Everard and the woman he met would be revealed.

Quite frankly, Gareth relied on this type of convoluted thinking from informants. And suspects. They tied themselves up in knots because, even if people told little lies all day long, big ones were much more difficult to sustain. Secrets only became harder to keep as time went on.

"Yes. Brother Mark told me he hadn't seen a woman fitting her description."

"Did the proprietor give you a name?"

"Brigid ferch Gruffydd." Lucan sneered as he spoke, indicating he was skeptical that it was her real name—but in so doing, he also revealed that he spoke a little Welsh.

"Your accent is excellent." Gareth switched instantly to Welsh himself.

"I wanted to learn." And with that sentence, the entire tenor of the conversation changed. Gareth had never before met a Norman who had bothered to learn his language. He almost didn't know how to respond. *Llongyfarchiadau?* That meant *congratulations,* but Gareth didn't want to appear to be throwing the word in Lucan's face if he didn't know it.

Instead, he pulled out the sketch of Efa he'd made to show Joan. "Is this the woman Everard met?"

Lucan laughed. "Of course not. That's Efa. She doesn't have red hair anyway." He held out a hand. "May I?"

While Lucan studied the drawing, Gareth got ready with yet another piece of paper. He was going to have to restock the moment he got back. "Please describe Brigid to me."

Lucan looked up, his eyes a bit unfocused, making Gareth think Joan had been right about his attachment to Efa. That she was Welsh might explain his desire to learn the language. "As I said, the first thing you would notice about her is her red hair and freckles." He went on to instruct Gareth to draw an upturned nose, pointed chin, and high cheekbones. As he drew, Lucan also added. "She wore a green cloak, too finely woven for a healer, in my opinion, which was one reason to think she wasn't who she said she was."

"How old?" Gareth asked.

"Older than you. Older than me too. Maybe fifty. Off-limits to Everard, regardless, or should have been ..."

Gareth looked up from his sketch. "You really were thinking she was his lover?"

"At the time. Why else would they be sneaking around instead of meeting in the open at the commandery?"

Gareth could think of a number of reasons, none of which he was going to share. He worked on the sketch until he achieved a nod of agreement from Lucan, whose mood improved as the exercise progressed. As Gareth prepared to leave, Lucan indicated the sketch of Efa, which he still held. "Do you need this back?"

Gareth shook his head. "You may keep it." And since it was a perfect opportunity to ask one more question, he didn't hesitate to do so. "Is she more than just a friend to you?"

Lucan wrinkled his nose. "I think that's a question only Efa can answer."

22

Day Three

Llelo

Llelo could have been upset or jealous that his younger broth-er had gone with their father to pursue the investigation out-side the commandery. At another time he probably would have, but since he had woken up feeling pretty terrible, the fact that his father hadn't given him a choice about going meant Llelo hadn't had to admit how unwell he still was.

In that case, his mother might have put him back in bed in-stead of sending him to interview Commander Reginald's messenger to Lady Joan. Llelo wasn't going to give up the chance to still be a part of the investigation.

The messenger turned out to be a young man named John. By appearance, he was not much older than Llelo. This was the same man that Brother Mark, the gatekeeper, had spoken about spending time with of an evening in his hut—and particularly the evening Everard had died. Llelo's mother had also noted him around the ta-ble when she'd talked to the commandery's servants.

Llelo found him walking a horse around the yard. As Llelo approached, he looked up from checking one of the horse's hocks. "What do you think of her, my lord?"

It wasn't the query itself that pulled Llelo up short but the *my lord*. As a knight, it was his right to be called that, but he didn't spend a great deal of time outside his immediate circle, so not very many people ever used the honorific. *My lord* meant Gareth. That John had used it also told Llelo that he himself was not a knight of the Hospitaller Order. He supposed he already knew that from Mark.

Llelo bent to run his hand up and down the horse's leg. "It's warm. Is that what you were wondering?"

"Yes. It feels so to me as well." John looked towards the stables. "She was fine last night when I checked on her."

Horses were expensive and worth their weight in silver. Anytime a horse was unwell, it was a cause for concern. Llelo patted this one's neck, sorry that her leg was hot but pleased to have had such an easy opening into a conversation with John. "You have a good number of horses here, beyond those we brought from Gwynedd. Do you tend to them all?"

"I suppose I do at times, though—" he made a gesture towards a man just walking through the archway into the stable complex, "—Brother James oversees us all. He's a healer too, actually, though of animals rather than of men."

"How many are you?"

"We have eight dedicated stable hands, and some days that isn't enough! Then there is Brother James, of course, and another rider like myself, Ralf, who is out."

"Out?"

"He carries a message to another monastic house."

"Where would that be?"

John's expression turned wary. "In Shrewsbury, at the Abbey of St. Peter and St. Paul. They succor lepers at a hospital, which we aid with our own remedies when they run out or when the crop of a particular herb fails."

"I know of it," he said, thinking of his parents' investigation in Shrewsbury. It was there they'd met Conall, their Irish friend now serving as ambassador to the court of King Brodar of Dublin.

John's expression cleared; he had been worried how Llelo would react to hearing that this commandery, located well within Wales, was corresponding with a Norman abbey. Llelo decided the best way to reassure him further was to get on with his questions. "Is it true you were the man to ride to Llys Arthur to tell the Widow Joan of Everard's death?"

"I was. Is that what you've come to ask me about?"

"My father wanted to know if you were often sent out of the commandery in that capacity, but I can see now that you are. You and Ralf." He paused. "When did Ralf leave?"

"Over a week ago." John's shoulders were no longer tight at these easy questions. "Our commander corresponds with all our holdings, as well as with monastic communities throughout the region. It is only sensible."

Llelo had never before thought about the logistics of communication, but he knew that Abbot Rhys, the monastic with whom he was most familiar, spoke often with other abbots, not only locally, but throughout Britain. "You aren't with the Hospitaller Order, though, are you?"

John laughed. "Do I look like a monk? I have taken no vows beyond a pledge to serve the Hospitallers to the best of my abilities."

"Is that usual for this Order?"

"Usual? I wouldn't know. Necessary? Definitely. They would not survive without lay workers. Obviously, none of the staff who cook and clean are monks. That wouldn't be seemly. These men come with endowments, of which I have none. Still, the commander saw no reason not to use me, once I came to his attention." He took in a breath, showing a bit of wariness again. "When I was younger, I was a servant in the train of Richard de Clare."

He meant Richard de Clare, the Earl of Hertford, who'd died in 1136, not the current Richard de Clare, the Earl of Pembroke, who was twenty years old. They had met this younger Richard de Clare three years earlier at Dinefwr. Richard's father had died the next year, leaving Richard to succeed to his father's estates at the age of eighteen. These days, he was supporting King Stephen, who had confirmed him as Earl of Pembroke and Lord of Striguil.

"You must be older than you look!"

"Thirty this year." He bobbed his head. "I stayed initially because I had nowhere else to go and then stayed because I wanted to. I have a Welsh wife now and three children so ... not a monk!" These last words were said in Welsh.

Llelo laughed with him and then switched to Welsh too. "May I ask where you have traveled recently?"

John handed off the horse to a lad, who walked with it towards the stable. "I visit other commanderies, outposts of our order, abbeys like Shrewsbury, and lords who have endowed or might endow lands with us. I have ridden to Aberystwyth many times since Prince Hywel took control of Ceredigion. I have even ridden all the way to the Hospitaller commandery at Standon in Hertfordshire."

That was a long way to go, near to London, a place Llelo had never been. His imagination was sparked by John's description of his work. Here was another job Llelo could do, if called to it. Though, as a knight, it would be beneath him unless he was carrying word from his king or prince. "Are these messages verbal or written?"

"They can be both, but usually written. Whatever is needed."

"Was the message to the Widow Joan in writing?"

"No, that was verbal and not one I enjoyed, let me just say. I did my duty, as always."

"So riding to the manor was nothing out of the ordinary?"

"Not to me. I am sorry for Everard's death, though. I have been known to ride for him too."

It took a moment for John's words to penetrate. "Have you? To where?"

"Most recently? To the Earl of Pembroke."

"When was this?"

"I returned ... a week ago. Less, maybe?"

Llelo managed not to swallow hard in his effort to disguise his sudden, extreme interest. "Do you know what that message was about?"

"Not that time. It was written and sealed." He frowned. "I must admit Everard's behavior was odd in that instance. I was going there already, you see. I had letters from Commander Reginald to both the earl and to the Bishop of St. David's. Everard asked me to take his message to Earl Richard too." He paused. "He also asked me not to mention his request to anyone else."

"Did you? Mention it, I mean."

John bit his lower lip. "Not until now."

"Not even to your commander?"

John waggled his head. "I didn't like the secrecy, but Everard said the earl was consulting with him about a private, medical matter."

Llelo knew enough of the world to guess what condition he was implying the earl had, as did John, obviously. "Was there a reply?"

"Yes, there was, though I felt that made the situation even more odd. After the earl handed me the letter, he gave me a pink flower to go with it."

This time, Llelo couldn't help his gasp.

"I gather that means something to you?" John said.

Llelo avoided the question. "At the time, did you ask what it meant?"

"I have learned not to," John said shortly. "It sounds like you're not going to tell me either."

Llelo waved a hand, intending to imply apology. "But you thought about it afterwards, especially after Everard's death." This wasn't a question on Llelo's part. He could tell it was true, and John didn't deny it.

"Yes, but I never learned what it was about, and I wasn't going to ask Everard, especially since I lost the original flower along the way."

Llelo's mouth dropped open in surprise, both that John had lost it, and that he would admit it. "What did you do about it?"

John scoffed. "I know a foxglove flower when I see one. Before I gave Everard the message, I replaced it with one I found along the road."

23

Day Three

Gareth

Clearly the first thing to do after leaving the manor house was to stop at the inn Lucan had mentioned. It was even on the way back to Ysbyty Cynfyn. They had the sketch now too. Provided Lucan had accurately described the woman Everard had met, they might not need it.

With Dai in tow, Gareth pushed open the door of The Castle to find the common room all but empty. The people in this land were hardworking, and few would have coinage or time to socialize in the middle of the day.

That wasn't to say nobody was present. In one corner sat a man and a woman, both dressed for traveling, which probably explained the carriage in the yard behind the inn. This was the main road across the belt of Wales. Following it east could take a traveler to Shrewsbury or Worcester, and then ultimately to London.

Giving in to an impulse Gareth didn't care to suppress, he stopped at their table. "Good afternoon. I'm Gareth ap Rhys, steward to Prince Hywel. Is everything well with you?"

He said all this in Welsh, despite the fact that the travelers didn't necessarily look Welsh to him, just to see what they'd say.

But the man replied in the same language. "Very well, my lord. We journey to see my father near Llanrhystud."

Gareth knew that castle. It was located south of Aberystwyth, above the River Wyre and close to the coast, with views of Cardigan Bay towards the west and the Ystwyth Valley and mountains to the east. It also happened to be one of Cadwaladr's reacquired holdings.

"He serves Prince Cadwaladr?"

"He holds lands just to the north of the castle."

Gareth noted that the man had hedged on the matter of his father's allegiance, but didn't press. A lesser lord had no choice about the identity of the lord above him. King Owain had given Cadwaladr the castle at Llanrhystud, and that was to whom this man's father tithed. That didn't mean he would have chosen to serve him.

Gareth held out a hand to Dai. "This is my son, Dai."

The man put a hand on his chest. "I'm Pedr ap Bleddyn. This is my wife, Mary. She has little Welsh."

Dai bowed over her hand like an accomplished court lackey and then said in elegant French, "It is a pleasure to meet you."

The woman smiled. She was probably ten years younger than her husband, a matter of five years older than Dai. "Your French is perfect!"

Gareth put a hand on Dai's shoulder and spoke in French himself. "One of his many skills, my lady." He bobbed his head. "Safe travels."

The pair thanked him, and Gareth steered Dai away.

"Spies?" Dai said in an undertone.

Gareth almost didn't know if he was joking, and answered as if he wasn't. "Our first task in staying behind at Ysbyty Cynfyn, beyond living through the sickness, was not, in fact, to investigate murder. We are Prince Hywel's rearguard, and we need to know what we're dealing with. I know too little of these lands and cannot advise the prince properly if my information is wrong or lacking."

"And then, if nothing else, it's good politics."

Gareth let out a little snort. "Did you note the lack of enthusiasm for serving Cadwaladr? That could come in useful down the road."

At that point, a man walked along the passage that led from the recesses of the inn and stopped at the sight of Gareth and Dai leaning on the bar.

"May I help you, my lords?" He spoke Welsh.

Gareth replied in the same language, introducing himself again and Dai. "I was wondering if I could talk to you about some visitors you had in here the other night."

"If I can help, I will." He moved to a spot behind the bar where he kept his cups and carafes of mead and ale.

"Two meads, please," Gareth said.

The innkeeper obliged, though he kept an eye on Dai, smiling at him out of the corner of his mouth. "We get all kinds in this inn, young lord. Few Welshmen speak French as well as you do."

"You overheard that?" Dai said.

"Sound carries to the back." He set the two meads one after another on the bar.

Gareth glanced towards the back wall, on which was hung a huge tapestry. If he pulled it aside, would he find an opening through which the innkeeper spied on his patrons? "And you are?"

"Rhodri. Rhod, usually." He ducked his head in something of a bow. "It's an honor to serve you."

"I appreciate the sentiment, though you are free to revise your view after you hear my questions." By now, Gareth was used to people having heard of him. Much of the time, it made things easier. He didn't know if Rhod knew of him as an investigator or only as Prince Hywel's steward. He wasn't sure which identity might get better answers. "This is about a red-haired woman who was here the other night speaking to Everard the Physician."

"Oh." Rhod rocked back a bit on his heels. "Brigid."

"That was fast. You don't even have to ask me to describe her further?"

"Not at all. She would have stood out even if she hadn't stayed here and spoken Welsh like one born to it."

Gareth pulled out the sketch he'd made at Lucan's direction. "Just so we're clear, this is the same person?"

Rhod's eyes widened admiringly. "I knew a man once who could draw like that, years ago. Come to think on it, his name was Rhys." He looked up. "Not your father?"

Gareth found himself gaping at the man. He was rarely rendered speechless by a conversation, but this was definitely one of those times.

Fortunately, Dai was there to step in. "My grandfather died when my father was five years old, so I never met him. Are you speaking of Rhys ap Trahaearn?"

"Indeed, I am." He looked from Gareth to Dai and back again. "Well, this is an unexpected pleasure."

Gareth so rarely talked about his father that he was surprised Dai had remembered his full name. As Dai had said, Gareth's father, along with his mother, had died of a sickness when he was five. He had been raised after that by an uncle, and he'd never known, in all these years, that his father could draw. His uncle had never mentioned it. "How did you know him?"

"He was in the service of King Gruffydd of Gwynedd, King Owain's father. Long ago, that was. Back then, I was a cook in his encampment."

Gareth found himself shaking his head, though he supposed he shouldn't be surprised at what a small world Wales turned out to be. "I am very pleased to meet you. How did you know he could draw?"

"He once drew a picture of me as I was cooking. Come to think on it, I still have it." He spun around and headed into the depths of the inn, to return a moment later with a packet. He'd carefully preserved the drawing between two other pieces of paper and now held it out with both hands for Gareth and Dai to see.

Gareth swallowed hard, moved beyond speech.

"You have the same way of drawing lines, Tad, so easy and clean. If I didn't know better, I would have said this was one of yours!"

"That's what I thought when I saw how you'd drawn Brigid." Rhod looked at Dai. "How about you, son?"

Dai put up a hand. "Drawing is not one of my talents."

"I suppose that would be unfair." Rhod raised his eyebrows at Gareth. "Would you like to keep it? It sounds as if you have very little left of your father."

Gareth passed the drawing back to Rhod. "I have enough. This has meant something to you all these years. I'm just glad to have seen it and to have talked to you."

Rhod bobbed a nod and returned the sketch to wherever he had stored it. By the time he returned, Gareth had himself under control and pushed the picture of Brigid towards the innkeeper. "You were saying?"

"She's a healer." He paused. "Or so she said."

"What do you mean by that?"

Lucan had implied the same skepticism.

"Brigid said she wanted to speak to Everard about matters of healing, but I did not see evidence of vials or herbs when her servant carried her belongings upstairs to her room."

"Servant?"

"A young man. Well set up. He slept in the loft—" Rhod broke off, uncharacteristically hesitating.

"Was there something strange about him sleeping in the loft?" Gareth asked.

"Not about that, more his manner when I showed it to him. He seemed amused." He shrugged, dismissing the servant's behavior as one of any number of oddities he might come across in the course of his day. "They were gone by the time I arose the next morning. I keep late hours, as you might imagine. It is my cook who serves the customers breakfast."

He paused again.

"There's more?" Gareth said.

"I suppose there might be at that. All might not have been well when Brigid left. My cook said she was agitated, eating alone and leaving alone, no sign of the servant. Maybe he really didn't like his quarters."

"Do you know where she went?"

"I do not, and I'm not sure if she told me I'd have believed her."

"I'm not sure I understand." Gareth peered at the man. "Your face tells me you were concerned."

"Even at the time, I wondered where my duty lay in regards to her. As an innkeeper, I try not to involve myself in my customers' business. Because she didn't return, I put it from my mind."

"But you are concerned enough to tell me now."

"You are steward to Prince Hywel, who rules here, and you asked. I might not have mentioned it even now if Everard hadn't died."

"But he did die. He was, in fact, murdered." Gareth forced himself not to loom over the man. "What about her has you mentioning it now?"

"I overheard her say to Everard that she would speak of his concerns to Earl Richard."

Gareth reared back. "Earl Richard de Clare of Pembroke?"

"Is there another?"

There had been, of course. It was Richard de Clare, Earl of Hertford, who'd died nearly fifteen years ago, in whose train Arthur and Joan had come to Ceredigion. There were too many Clares overall, in Gareth's opinion.

For now, Gareth took Rhod's point. "Why would a physician from Ysbyty Cynfyn be talking to a healer who is of such a station that she can arrange an audience with Richard de Clare?"

"I couldn't say." Rhod shook his head. "That's why I have my job, and you have yours. But I was in the army, as I said, and have owned this inn for many years. I know a spy when I see one."

24

Day Three

Llelo

Llelo had not felt discontented when his brother had ridden off with their father. But by late afternoon when they still hadn't returned and Llelo was stuck minding his young siblings, he'd been feeling quite a bit more sorry for himself. Sometimes Llelo felt Dai's natural abilities in almost every area of everything were entirely unfair—as if he were constantly pushing up at Llelo from behind. It was Llelo who was the plodder, following the path laid before him because it was all that he could see or know. Dai probably had even more gifts they hadn't yet discovered.

Whenever Llelo's thoughts traveled down this path, he tried to remind himself that it was he, Llelo, who had made a friend of Prince Henry and his half-brother Hamelin, not Dai. It was he who'd been knighted. Nobody could ever take that away from him. More times than Llelo cared to admit he'd hugged that fact to himself, taking comfort in the fundamentals of his life.

And then, just as Llelo had finished consoling himself one more time, as well as deciding it was time to return to the common room for the children's dinner, Rhys ap Gruffydd, the youngest brother of King Cadell of Deheubarth, stepped out from within a stand of trees to the northwest of the commandery.

Over the course of the afternoon, Llelo had wandered with Tangwen and Taran quite far from the back gate. They'd climbed a bit of a hill, while still remaining on the commandery side of the river. He and Rhys spied each other practically at the same moment and recognized each other instantly too.

Three years ago in Dinefwr, when Llelo and Rhys had both been fifteen, they hadn't been natural friends, not like Llelo and Hamelin, despite the fact that they were the same age and both Welsh. At the time, Llelo had been trying to find his feet as his father's apprentice. When Gwen had made an offhand comment about how Rhys was probably the smartest person she had ever met, her words had stung. Sensing it, Gwen had explained that just because a man was clever didn't mean he was wise, or that he didn't have more to learn, or was allowed to walk around with a puffed up idea of himself. It just meant that Llelo should assume everything Rhys did had been thoroughly considered in advance.

At a minimum, Llelo should not forget that Rhys had been integral to the resolution of their investigation. He was also a prince of Deheubarth and first cousin to Hywel, since Rhys's mother had been Gwenllian, King Owain's sister.

Today, the two of them were eighteen and both knights: Llelo by Prince Henry's hand, which he'd reminded himself about yet again; and Rhys, by the hand of his elder brother earlier that year, after their forces took Carmarthen Castle, which even now Cadell was refortifying to hold against the Normans. Honestly, Prince Hywel would have been completely happy for Cadell to take every castle the Normans had built. It was Cadell's insistence on opening a second front against Hywel's holdings in Ceredigion that was the problem.

Gareth had often said that if the Welsh would only stand together, they could really drive the Normans out of Wales. Abbot Rhys believed it. King Owain believed it too. The problem was that, even if each of the Welsh kings agreed with the idea in principle, they each also wanted to be the preeminent ruler, the *princeps*. And, as with the throne of Gwynedd, only one head could wear that crown.

None of them had seen Rhys since the events at Dinefwr Castle three years ago, and he had changed a great deal, probably in similar ways to Llelo. He was tall, broad-shouldered, and sported a real mustache, something Llelo had yet to be able to grow. He had also shrouded himself in one of the plainest brown robes Llelo had ever seen. It was ragged and frayed at the edges, presumably to blend in with the common folk, though Llelo could see his riding boots peeking out from beneath the hem.

"Llelo." Rhys put out his hand, and they shook forearms, man to man. "I need to speak to your father."

"He rode out of the commandery this morning and, as far as I know, has not returned. Can I help?"

"I need what I gave him three years ago." He peered into Llelo's face. "I see that you know what that was."

Llelo bent his head. Rhys was referring to a bag of gems that had come out of the investigation at Dinefwr, a bag which he'd asked Gareth to keep for him. "My father told me of it only recently, because I am his eldest son, in case something happened to him. He should be returning at any moment. Let me take you to him. Where's your horse?"

"In the woods." Rhys pulled the hood of his robe up over his head. He wasn't even wearing his sword. That he had left it behind, either entirely or with his unattended horse, was a risk few knights would ever take. Llelo peered into the darkness of the wood, looking for the animal. Rhys saw him doing it and added, "He's black as the night that's coming on. Nobody will find him."

Llelo had to take Rhys at his word, especially since he'd already ridden so many miles in the middle of a war. To have reached this point would have required a great deal of thought, at which, as Llelo's mother had said, Rhys excelled. He had the appearance of a man prepared for anything.

Llelo made a gesture to encompass Rhys's disguise. "Am I to suppose your brother does not know you have come to us?"

"This?" Rhys looked down at himself. "This is not specifically for your benefit. I've worn it for days now and was wearing it when the king sent me out as his spy. He does not know I have come to Ysbyty Cynfyn to see you, however. Neither brother does."

"I see," Llelo said, and he thought he really might.

Rhys was referring first to Cadell, the current King of Deheubarth, who was only his half-brother, a child of his father's first marriage; and then to his full brother, Maredudd, who was two years older than Rhys and a child of Gwenllian. Rhys had once had two more full brothers, both of whom had died with his mother in battle in 1136; and one other half-brother, Anarawd, who'd been ambushed by Danes at the behest of Prince Cadwaladr and assassinated. To say the family history of the royal houses of Deheubarth and Gwynedd was complicated was to woefully understate the case.

"I would prefer it to stay that way. They don't know I have any relationship at all with Gareth or with your family." Rhys shrugged. "Or with my cousin, Hywel."

"Please know that we still consider you a friend. I believe I can say without hesitation that Prince Hywel does too."

"I appreciate your candor and feel the same way. I sincerely wish circumstances were not what they are. I never wished to go to war with Gwynedd. I am a man of Gwynedd by blood as much as of Deheubarth. Cadell doesn't see it that way, obviously, and he is my liege lord."

At a gesture from Rhys, they had set off back to the commandery, Llelo having swung Taran up onto his shoulders so they could move faster. Tangwen skipped and hopped beside him to keep up. After a moment, Rhys lifted her into his arms too before she stumbled in the gathering darkness on an unseen root or stone. Llelo really had left his return a bit late. He hoped he hadn't caused Gwen to worry more than she already must be about Gareth and Dai. "Is that why you need your wealth now? Because you fear if you don't ask for it today you'll never get it back?"

"Such would never be my concern. Your father is the most honorable man I know. It is rather that I should soon have some extraordinary expenses that might inhibit our further connection."

Llelo took Rhys's meaning. "You mean to marry, and as a prince of Deheubarth, this upcoming alliance is sure to be one that is meaningful to your brother."

And likely, though Llelo didn't say this, less meaningful to Rhys himself. Llelo hoped for Rhys's sake that the girl was at least young and pretty.

To this query, which hadn't actually been a question, Rhys merely glanced at him.

"I see. Is she a daughter of King Madog of Powys?" Llelo asked this, knowing that Rhys's prospective bride had to be either the daughter of a Norman or the daughter of one of Owain's enemies. King Madog of Powys seemed a likely choice. Rhys couldn't marry one of Madog's legitimate daughters, since their mother would be Susanna, Rhys's own mother's sister. But Madog had plenty of illegitimate ones from which to choose. Iorwerth, King Owain's son, had already married one of them in a love match.

"I dare not say." Sometimes when men looked away while answering a question, it meant they were lying. Other times, they kept their gaze fixed on the questioner, daring them to disbelieve. Rhys had chosen not to answer at all rather than to lie. Llelo's respect for him increased, and he was sorry already that he would not be able to get to know him better.

"And this is the only reason you're here?"

Rhys kept walking, in no hurry to answer. Llelo sensed he was struggling with *how* to answer. As when Tangwen behaved similarly, or anyone he was interviewing during the course of an investigation, Llelo knew better than to get in the way.

Finally, Rhys sighed and met Llelo's gaze fully—or as fully as he could in the darkened path within a few yards of the back entrance to the commandery. "As we stand here, someone newly returned to your king's favor is betraying him again."

Llelo felt his stomach drop into his boots. "What you just said is too important for us not to speak plainly; if you can't, I will. You mean to say that Cadwaladr is betraying King Owain by allying with your brother?"

Rhys simply met his eyes and let the truth hang in the air between them. "If you could find your father and meet me in the church after Vespers, I would be grateful."

"He will be there."

25

Day Three

Llelo

As Llelo entered the commandery proper, he heard his father's shout of welcome to his mother, and then the clattering of horse's hooves on the slate walkway beneath the gatehouse. With Taran on one arm and holding Tangwen's hand, he hustled forward until he could see his parents, greeting each other by torchlight. Dai was already leading the horses away.

"Mam. Tad." Llelo came to a halt. "We have business to attend to." And in a low whisper in Welsh, which thankfully few members of the commandery understood, he related why he had come to find them.

Vespers would be happening right now, with the setting of the sun. That gave Rhys a half-hour to work his way around to the church, and Llelo's parents the same amount of time to settle the children with Meilyr and Saran.

The monks were just filing out of the main gate when the four of them, Dai included, approached the upper entrance to the churchyard. Gareth put a finger to his lips and they held still, waiting until the last of the monks' footfalls fell away into silence.

The wooden gate swung open on leather hinges, making no noise, and Llelo held it until everyone was through so it wouldn't bang. He knew he was privileged to be allowed to come with his mother and father. No longer was he feeling disaffected by the nature of his tasks today. If he hadn't been minding the children, Rhys might have had to enter the commandery to find him, increasing the risk that his treason—it was probably important to call it what it was—would be revealed.

The nave was empty and quiet, with just two candles left burning on the altar. Only when a king was put under interdict by the pope were the candles put out. It hadn't happened in Llelo's lifetime.

Dai took up a position at the main door of the church, guarding against intruders, while the rest did a full circuit of every nook and cranny, not that the church was large enough to have very many. Llelo ended up standing in the entrance to the vestry, so there was no chance they could be interrupted through that doorway either.

Once Rhys appeared, still in his plain clothes and cloak, Gareth held out the bag of gems. "What you asked for."

"Thank you. That day at Dinefwr feels like a long time ago."

"Much has changed," Gareth said. "It isn't as if we didn't expect it."

"I am grateful for your constancy, despite the fact that we are enemies now."

"Never that."

Rhys let out a sharp breath to hear Gareth's assurances. "Cadell underestimates Gwynedd. He always has."

"You don't have to say anything more," Gwen said gently. "Llelo told us."

"Honor demands that I do." Rhys let out a low *harumph*. "What I am about to tell you wasn't conditional on your welcome. I think I knew before I came, and maybe this is *why* I came, that you would not betray me. What I know about honor I learned from you." He bent his head, seemingly gathering his thoughts. "Cadell, more than Cadwaladr, has up until now escaped censure for what he has done. I told you, back in Dinefwr when I gave you these stones, that I would try to warn you when Deheubarth and Gwynedd ceased to be allies. I must apologize that I was not able to fulfill my promise. It is my hope that the news I bring tonight can in some small way make up for my failure. I tell you this, and I betray my brother. If he knew I was here, he might take my head."

"And yet, you came," Gareth said.

"I do as my conscience dictates."

"One day you may be king and not have that luxury."

"I will decide what is right. Nobody can do that for me."

Llelo stood a little straighter to hear his words. Although Llelo's early upbringing had been difficult, he had loving parents now. Rhys had faced challenges throughout his life many times more difficult than Llelo's. And yet, he was strong enough to say those words. He'd been put into the flames, as in the Bible, and come through as gold.

Gareth hadn't replied to Rhys's last statement, letting the younger man's words penetrate before he spoke again. "I am not nearly as perfect as you think."

"Maybe others expect perfection from you. I expect you to do what you say when you say it." Rhys managed a smile that reached his eyes. "I can see by your face that you think that's a low bar to step over. For most men, even that is out of reach."

"Including your brother?" Gareth asked—bravely, Llelo thought.

"Will it come as a surprise to you that Cadell had a hand in the death of his elder brother, Anarawd, seven years ago, a death for which Cadwaladr was blamed?" As he spoke Rhys watched Gareth's face closely, and then he took in everyone else's expressions. "I see that it doesn't."

Gwen put out a hand. "We can't say we are surprised; we suspected this, but we didn't know for certain."

Rhys focused on her. "What you might also not know is that it was meant to be an equal bargain: Cadwaladr would arrange for the death of Anarawd and, in turn, Cadell would eliminate Owain Gwynedd for Cadwaladr. There have been attempts over the years; none have succeeded, obviously."

Llelo had heard King Owain at one time suggest that Cadell was neither smart enough, nor devious enough, to have instigated a plot to murder his brother. Gareth—and Prince Hywel—had always thought otherwise.

Now Gareth looked at Gwen. "It seems we have consistently underestimated Cadell's mastery of deceit."

But Gwen was looking at Rhys. "I imagine it took a great deal for you to come here to tell us this. He is your brother. Perhaps he has even been like a father to you at times."

"I had one father, and he was so much more than Cadell."

She bent her head. "As are you, as evidenced by the fact that you are here."

"Hopefully this isn't a matter of bringing you too little too late." Rhys's eyes were back on Gareth. "It is the assassin you don't see coming who will succeed."

All of a sudden, Llelo felt a chill from the top of his head to his toes in his boots. "One is on his way now?"

Rhys didn't move, so Gareth did instead, closing the distance between them. "Cadwaladr knows of this?"

"Why do you think he journeyed south with you? He wants to be nowhere near his brother when it happens."

Gwen let out a breath. "Instead, he is here, actively undermining Hywel's rule in Ceredigion."

"That too is true." Rhys swung around to look at her. "Cadwaladr has castles of his own again. You should take it as a given that he holds these for my brother, not for my cousin."

"Do you have proof of what you're saying?" Gareth said.

"You don't believe me?" Rhys's face held some frustration.

"I believe every word you have said, but I am not the one needing to be convinced." Gareth made a gesture with both hands, conveying a measure of helplessness. "I can tell Prince Hywel what you have said, and he will believe it too, but he can take no action against Cadwaladr without someone willing to testify before King Owain. I'm guessing that can't be you."

"It cannot."

"Nor can you say when the assassin will strike?"

"No. But you must be ready when he does." Rhys gripped Gareth's upper arm. "It will come, for you, for your prince, and for your king." Then he spun on his heel, prepared to stride down the nave and out the door, as if he had disconcerted himself with his adamancy and his treason and needed to put both behind him.

However, after one stride, he turned back in order to wrap Gwen up in a hug. He held on tight, his face down on her shoulder, like he was her own son. "Please take care of your family. You are the best of us."

He released her without looking at her and, a moment later, had retreated out the door.

By the time Gareth and Llelo moved to follow, he had disappeared from view, in a manner in which he appeared to have become accomplished.

Llelo came to a halt in the doorway of the church, where Dai had been standing throughout the conversation. "What are we going to do about this?"

"*We* will do nothing." Gareth took in the faces of his two sons, both of whom had words of protest on their lips. "I already have an investigation to pursue. But you two are a different matter. Normally, I would send you to King Owain to warn him of this assassin, but for that I will borrow Llelo's messenger friend, John. He can't get me the rest of what I need."

"Which is what?" Dai was as intent as Llelo, standing straight and ready for whatever adventure Gareth had for them next.

"What I am going to ask of you could be too much for any man, but I have to ask it of you anyway. At first light, I am sending you to Cadwaladr's seat at Llanrhystud. Bring me proof of his treachery, something I can take to Hywel. Maybe, if you find it, we can finally rid ourselves of Cadwaladr forever."

26

Day Four

Dai

Dai and Llelo had just reached the crossroads to the north of Ysbyty Cynfyn and turned west when they came upon a gray horse, trailing its reins and cropping the grass beside the road. They reined in, looking around for any sign of the rider.

Tossing his own reins to Dai, Llelo dismounted and made to approach, but the horse shied away.

Dai looked on pensively. "Who would leave a horse out here on its own?"

"Nobody," Llelo said.

Horses were valuable, even more so in time of war. Llelo was right that no man, no matter his station, would abandon one like this unless forced to. Most likely, the rider had been thrown and was lying somewhere in a ditch.

"Could it be Prince Rhys's horse?" Dai's breath was suddenly catching in his throat.

For a moment, Llelo looked stricken, but then his expression cleared. "He told me his horse was as black as night, which made it invisible in the woods where he left it when he came to see us at Ysbyty Cynfyn." He put his hand to his heart, indicating it had been beating as fast as Dai's. "It isn't his."

Ysbyty Cynfyn and Llanrhystud, Cadwaladr's castle, were separated by fifteen miles as the crow flies. Had Dai and Llelo begun their journey by crossing the River Rheidol on the log bridge, those miles could have been managed in a relatively straight line. That route would be precarious, however, and the road poor. They could also have ridden south and crossed the bridge over the canyon of the River Mynach. The subsequent tracks to Llanrhystud from there were also poor and indirect.

Thus, they had ridden north first until they reached one of the few fords across the Rheidol before it plummeted into the canyon that went past Ysbyty Cynfyn. The plan was to continue west on the high road until they reached Aberystwyth, at which point they would turn south and take the coastal road to Llanrhystud. While this route meant they'd have to cross the Rheidol twice, both times would take place in much less harsh terrain. In addition, with the sea so close, they could never lose their way.

The castle at Aberystwyth had been the site of much intrigue before Dai's parents were married. Seven years ago, the current King of Dublin, Brodar, had merely been the son of a dying co-king, who'd raided Gwynedd on behalf of Prince Cadwaladr. It was on the beach below the castle that Brodar had offered to take Gareth to Dublin to rescue Gwen from Cadwaladr—and from his own brother, Godfrid.

Today, Brodar was King of Dublin, and Godfrid was not only one of Dai's parents' closest friends, but married to Cait, the sister of the Irish diplomat and spy, Conall. It felt worthy of a bard's tale that this selfsame castle would provide Gareth and Gwen's two sons a place to lay their heads for the night—provided this sudden issue with the horse didn't waylay them too long. Regardless, they couldn't just pass by without stopping.

"Hello! Is anybody there?" Llelo cupped both hands around his mouth and called towards a stand of trees to the north.

Dai, meanwhile, headed towards a house to the south of the road. It had tables and benches set in groups outside, and a man was just coming out the door with a small barrel on his shoulder. "Excuse me!" Dai made his way across the yard towards him. "Do you know whose horse that is?"

The man set the barrel down on one of the tables. "I tried to catch him earlier, but he spooked. My stable boy couldn't even do it."

Dai surveyed the house, which was much less grand than the inn at Dyffryn Castell where he and Gareth had interviewed Rhod … yesterday? It felt like so much had happened since then. "Is this your inn?"

"We aren't an inn." The man laughed. "We are merely a cool spot to quench the thirst on a long journey." He tapped his right thigh. "I can't do much these days, not with this old wound, but I brew a fine ale for the visitors and mead for the people."

That was an interesting and politically astute way to categorize his customers. Back in Gwynedd, the local Welsh viewed both Normans and English as invaders and didn't get along with either of them. Apart from the trading ports at Nefyn and Llanfaes, any stranger—even a Welshman from a different kingdom—could be viewed with suspicion as a matter of course.

Here, the local people had faced conquest time and again. While a Welsh lord was in the ascendancy at the moment, he wasn't native to Ceredigion either. Dai could understand why it wouldn't be an easy world to navigate, but was also one that could provide profit to a smart merchant who was prepared to put aside any grievances if it produced a purse full of coins.

"Do you know whose horse that is?" Dai repeated.

"No." The man picked up his barrel of drink again and stumped over to the bar. When he set down the barrel again, he added, "This is the third time I've seen her in as many days. I thought I would have been able to catch her by now, since she looks well cared for. You'd think she'd want a stable. I even put out a bag of oats for her, but she shied away before I could grab her reins."

Three days ago, they'd just learned about Everard's death. Everard's own horse was safe in its stall at Ysbyty Cynfyn. As far as Dai knew, nobody else was missing one. They'd come all of a mile and a half from the commandery, and were already facing a mystery. With the amount of traffic on the main road heading across Wales, who was to say how many others had ridden this way in that time? Well, perhaps this man.

"Have you noticed anything else unusual these last few days? Have you had any visitors who stood out to you?"

The man frowned. "Funny that you're asking. A woman rode through here a few hours before I saw the horse for the first time, asking if I'd seen her servant. He hadn't come back to that inn that's up the road aways where they'd spent the night. She waited all night for him and then went searching. Do you know the place?"

"I do." Dai's heart started beating a bit faster again. "Did she have red hair?"

"Bright as the sunset over the water. Do you know her?"

Dai chose not to answer that. "Which way did she go?"

"West."

"By herself?"

"I offered my lad to see her on her way, but she declined. She was in a hurry." He paused. "And scared."

"Did she mention that he had a horse?"

"I suppose she did. I didn't remember that until now." Then his attention was drawn to Llelo, who had not only captured the strange horse, but mounted it. He clopped across the road to the tavern.

The man cleared his throat. "Aren't you a fine horseman! Pardon my familiarity, my lords. You're knights!" He looked at Dai. "Both of you?"

"Llelo is. I'm just the son of one." He grinned, hardly needing any effort to put away that bit of longing. While Dai wanted the honor more than anything in the world, he was only sixteen, and he trusted his father's assurances that it would come.

As Llelo dismounted, Dai quickly related what he'd learned from the tavern keeper, who then asked, "Why all the questions?"

"We have been tracking the woman you mentioned. Our father is Gareth ap Rhys." Llelo spoke as if that should be enough for the tavern keeper, and it appeared to be so because he bobbed his head in a nod.

"I heard he was among those made unwell by this terrible plague."

"We are all back on our feet now." Llelo kept close to the captured horse, with a firm grip on the reins.

"May I ask why you're interested in the woman?" the tavern keeper said. "I admit she stood out. It wasn't just the hair but because she surely wasn't from around here. What is she to you? We have many travelers on these roads. Without them, I wouldn't have a business!"

"We are investigating the death of the physician, Everard."

"A fine man and a fine doctor. He gave me a salve for my leg that eases some of the pain."

"Did he give you an elixir as well?" Llelo asked the question in a tone Dai thought was casual enough not to cause alarm.

"Ack," the tavern keeper slapped his leg again, grinning, "this old thing has hurt since the day I was wounded. Mead is enough for me."

Llelo patted the horse's neck. "If you could oblige us, I would have you send this horse and a message to my father at Ysbyty Cynfyn."

"You will be paid," Dai added hastily, having seen the man calculating the cost of the request in his head. Even if he, or one of his people, rode the horse to the commandery, they would have to walk back. This would mean several hours out of his day.

Llelo was already pulling a coin from his purse and a piece of paper, pen, and ink from within his gear. This wasn't because he was capable of drawing like their father. He needed to write a letter, and he was the one to do it. Dai's handwriting remained abysmal, and he had resigned himself to the fact that it always would be.

Dai could read just fine, however, and he looked over Llelo's shoulder as he wrote out what they had discovered. Then Llelo asked the tavern keeper for a candle by which to seal the letter with wax. Dai took that moment to go through the saddlebags on the stranger's horse. The leatherwork was well done, but the bags contained nothing more exciting than a spare blanket and a portion of bread and cheese, both dry. Whoever owned the horse had traveled lightly.

The tavern keeper also found his stable boy. After offering the horse a drink of water in their trough, he was able to mount and set off back the way Dai and Llelo had come. "Don't worry. I will find your father. You can leave it to me!"

Dai and Llelo rode away in the opposite direction.

"What if we discover this Brigid woman turned north?" Dai said. "Then what do we do? Our real charge is to find out what Cadwaladr is up to."

"Mam would suggest we don't borrow trouble."

"Leave it to you to be sensible. My head is full of possibilities." Dai urged his horse into a canter. Even with half the morning gone, he couldn't regret the delay. "I'm starting to think we might be on the trail of a conspiracy to rival Cadwaladr's own."

27

Day Four

Gwen

"**M**y lady, I need you to come with me." Desmond kept his voice low enough that it didn't penetrate beyond a few feet from where Gwen was standing, observing her father playing his flute for Taran and Tangwen. All through her growing up, even when Meilyr had sunk deep into his misery, fueled by over-consumption of alcohol, he had still played. The children were clapping along to the lively tune.

She approved of what he was doing. This was a lesson as well as entertainment. Learning to clap along with music was a skill that not all children had by instinct. Tangwen had taken time to learn it, but whether because of her example or his own natural talent, Taran had kept perfect time practically from birth. Her father already had Gwalchmai, to whom his talent had passed without dilution. Meilyr wasn't the only one who'd been hoping for his skills to reach a third generation. Taran was a knight's son, but he was also the grandson of the most renowned bard in Wales of his generation. With Hywel providing an imitable example, in their world a man could be both knight and bard.

The look on Desmond's face when he spoke to her indicated his news was grave and urgent. Gwen put up one finger to her father, who nodded in the midst of playing without losing a beat. Then she backed out of the doorway.

Desmond was already two steps ahead of her. They left the guesthouse and set off across the yard. Of their family, only Llelo and Dai had rooms inside the guesthouse, but the common room was still a comfortable place for Meilyr to practice and entertain his grandchildren. Some monasteries frowned upon too much joviality within their precincts, but Ysbyty Cynfyn had welcomed his music and singing, particularly for those in the infirmary. Even during the time he hadn't been well, Meilyr had played every afternoon.

But Desmond wasn't taking her to the infirmary, nor to any of the other buildings within the commandery. Instead, he led her outside the walls and across the field to the west, the sun shining on her shoulders through a gap in the clouds. Farther on lay the chasm through which the river ran, and she could see another ray of sunshine lighting up the fairy circle on the hill.

The nearer they came to the river, the more her heart beat with a fear she couldn't suppress at what might have happened that was so grave Desmond couldn't put it into words. She was having a hard enough time of it as it was, having said goodbye to Llelo and Dai a few hours earlier. As Gareth had promised last night, he had sent them together to investigate Cadwaladr's doings. Even as she told herself her boys were capable of taking care of themselves, she was struggling with her peace of mind.

This was *Cadwaladr* they were talking about. If he suspected Dai and Llelo of deceiving him, on their way to exposing his new treachery, he might imprison them. Or kill them.

And there would be nothing anyone, much less Gwen or Gareth, could do about it.

Her anxiety overcame her respect for Desmond's reticence. "Can you at least tell me something of what this is about?"

"I'm sorry. Didn't I say? They found a body in the river."

By telling her this, he had not lessened her anxiety one iota. If he had meant the River Cynfyn, which was the stream that meandered directly past the commandery, he would have said. Thus, Desmond's use of the word *river* was very specific language in this region to mean the River Rheidol.

"A body? Whose?"

"That of a young man."

Still not helping. "Not—" So great was her fear she couldn't force her next query past her lips.

It was only at that point that Desmond seemed to realize something was amiss with her, though even then his brow furrowed in puzzlement. "It is not someone we know."

Gwen put a hand to her breast, forcing herself to breathe again. And then she gulped again because of the other young man of her acquaintance she'd seen recently, Prince Rhys. The monks wouldn't know him to look at.

By the time she arrived at the bank above the river, which rushed as loud as ever through its winding chasm, she and Desmond were just two among many who had gathered. The farmer they'd talked to the other day by the fairy circle had crossed the log bridge and was standing beside Gareth. He appeared calm to Gwen, which eased her concerns somewhat. If the body were that of Rhys, he would not be so relaxed.

She recognized most of the observers, between the monks and the locals who had visited the commandery at one time or another over the last fortnight. Rather than isolating themselves, as with some abbeys, the monks at Ysbyty Cynfyn sought to be part of the community. From what she could see, Iago's summons aside, they were doing a commendable job.

"You're sure it isn't a woman?"

Desmond looked at Gwen, startled. "I'm sure." He crossed himself. "Why would you think it was a woman?"

She didn't want to answer that question, since he didn't know about Brigid.

Then Gareth left the farmer talking to a monk and came huffing his way up the bank to where she waited. "They have the body out of the water now and are bringing it to the commandery."

"Desmond says we don't know who he is."

"At the moment that's true. Nobody recognizes him." Gareth grimaced. "Not that they might, given the body's condition."

"So he—he's been dead a while?" Gwen held her breath.

"Definitely, Gwen." Gareth put a hand on her arm, recognizing her fear and seeking to assuage it. "We don't know him."

"Many people do pass along this road," Desmond said. "It could be anyone."

"While true, his cloth is finer than that of a farmer's," Gareth said, "and he still wears his boots."

If Gareth hadn't been so sure the man had been dead a while, he could have been describing Rhys.

"So he wasn't robbed?" Gwen asked. "Hywel will need to know if he is facing banditry as well as war."

Gareth held up a small purse. Again, this was not the bag of jewels they'd both witnessed Rhys tuck inside an inner pocket of his coat. "Not that I can see."

"That means he fell in." Desmond was naïve enough to think this was the only other possible explanation. He heaved a sigh and turned back towards the commandery. "Just another poor unfortunate who lost his footing trying to cross the river. It happens all the time."

The comment prompted Gareth to put out a hand to stop him before he could leave. "Do you find bodies in the river that often?"

"Several times a year, for certain. Travelers unused to the conditions have been known to slip on the path and tumble to their deaths. Our bridge can be quite slippery."

"We have been on it." They watched Desmond go until he was out of earshot, at which point Gareth added, "I might agree with him if not for two things: the first is that the body was caught on a branch *upstream* of the bridge. I suppose it's remotely possible that he was trying to cross our bridge here and somehow flung his body upriver."

"But unlikely."

"Very unlikely, if not impossible. That means he fell into the water at some spot to the north. Now, he could have been walking on the edge of the chasm and lost his footing, but why would a wealthy man be here at all?"

"We are quite far from the main road," Gwen agreed.

"Right here, we are," Gareth said, "but farther north the main road to Aberystwyth crosses the river at a reasonable ford. Again, he could have fallen in accidentally, but we have seen that crossing, and it is nothing like as treacherous as this one. That then begs the question, *when* did he fall in? Wouldn't we have heard of a missing man?"

"Not only that," Gwen said, "if he was a traveler in this region, where is his horse? His possessions?"

"And then there's this." Gareth untied the strings of the man's purse and opened it wide so she could peer inside. "It's a foxglove flower, in case you were wondering."

She had to gasp. "Another one?"

"The water has leached some of the color, but it is still a bit pink." Gareth pulled the strings tight on the purse again. "He's connected to Everard."

"I suppose he could have walked to the stone circle, as we did, and liked the flowers there so much he kept one."

Gareth laughed. "You mean he plucked it, not knowing he'd have a rash on his hands afterwards, and then just happened to die on the way back? You don't believe that."

"You're thinking he was murdered? That's the last thing the commander is going to want to hear. Did you ever tell him about the other flowers?"

"I did not." Gareth clutched the purse in his hand. "And if I can help it I'm not going to tell him about this one either."

28

Day Four

Gareth

They had plenty of people working together to figure out how to carry the body up the east bank of the river and across the field to the commandery, so Gareth saw no reason to put his back out helping. Besides, he would learn more by talking with the people who'd come to spectate. Already, and contrary to Desmond's supposition, two different people within Gareth's hearing had postulated that the man had taken his own life. It seemed reasonable, then, to address the matter head on when he and Gwen overtook Physician Thomas and Warden Geoffrey on their walk back to the commandery.

Gareth cleared his throat as they approached. "You're not thinking he did himself in, are you?"

"I would never presume to say so," Warden Geoffrey said. "And yet, he was a well-built young man. It is hard to see him slipping into the river by mistake."

"Anyone can slip," Thomas said mildly.

"That is true, Thomas. And, in cases like these, we have always erred on the side of caution. Only God can ever know what is in another man's heart." Geoffrey crossed himself piously.

For Gareth's part, he was already impatient with the conversation. On the whole, he respected Geoffrey, and he agreed that anyone who was under suspicion of suicide deserved the benefit of the doubt. Unless the young man had left a note, Gareth wasn't going to believe this was anything but an accident—or murder, which so far nobody had said out loud.

He wasn't going to suggest it either, not without incontrovertible proof.

Gareth's agitation had lengthened his strides, to the point that he was some yards ahead of everyone else when he reached the commandery's back gate. As he pulled it open, he heard his name shouted near the front yard: "I must speak to Lord Gareth! Is he here?"

Gareth hustled towards the main gatehouse, fearing what new trouble they might be facing. At least the dead body would be required to come this way to reach the laying-out room near the laundry. Gwen would ensure that nobody touched it before Gareth could.

As he arrived beside Brother Mark, a boy of perhaps twelve was waving a letter and speaking in Welsh, little of which Mark understood. "I need to speak to Lord Gareth immediately!"

"I am Lord Gareth."

The boy turned to him like a parched traveler in the desert where Gareth was a water carrier. "My lord!" He bowed deeply. "I have a letter for you from your noble sons."

Gareth would have laughed at the way the boy had clearly been practicing speaking like a courtier all the way here from wherever Dai and Llelo had found him, but he didn't want to diminish his enthusiasm for his task.

"They sent me with this letter and this horse." He held out the reins, which Gareth took, along with the letter. "Are they well?"

"Your sons?" The boy ducked his head. "I left before they did, but they were hale last I saw. They said they would be continuing west."

Gwen had arrived at Gareth's side by now, and she allowed herself a tremulous sigh. This had been a rough morning for her heart, as it had been for Gareth's, though he had known sooner than she that the dead man couldn't be either Prince Rhys or one of their sons.

Gareth made a motion with his hand to indicate the boy should continue. He hadn't broken the letter's wax seal yet.

"We first saw this horse trailing its reins near the bridge on the main road, just above the River Rheidol."

"Who do you mean by *we*?"

"My master and me. I work at the tavern located on the western bank. One of your sons caught the horse, and my master, the tavern keeper, sent me here with their letter."

Gareth surveyed the horse, which was saddled still. "Anything in the bags?"

"Nothing beyond a blanket and food. Your sons looked."

"Provisions for a traveler." Gwen was able to see as well as Gareth that the horse was well-shod and cared for, other than lightly sweating from the ride down the road to the commandery.

Having opened the letter, Gareth recognized Llelo's hand immediately. Gareth himself had come to writing late in life and that fact had been encouraging to Llelo, making him think that he was capable of learning the skill. Dai still didn't have the patience for it, and in his mind's eye Gareth could see his sons distributing their labor according to each one's proclivities.

Gwen edged closer in order to read over his shoulder. After skimming the letter once and then reading it more slowly a second time, Gareth handed it to her. By now, Physician Thomas and Warden Geoffrey had reached the yard too. Gareth contemplated not sharing what Llelo had written with them, but despite his thought to keep the bloom a secret, it was clear he needed to share *something*.

Over the years, Gareth had discovered that relating the details of an investigation to a third party was something of an art. He needed to impart enough information in sufficient detail to sate curiosity but, in so doing, distract from the parts of the narrative Gareth had no intention of sharing. In this case, it was more important to keep secret the visit by Rhys and his accusations against Cadwaladr than the details of Everard's death. Gareth had already implied that Dai and Llelo had left on a quest for information about Everard's travels during his last days. He hadn't lied exactly; he just hadn't corrected their misperception.

"My sons believe the horse belonged to the servant of the same woman Everard met in the inn the night he died. If they are right about the horse, then this body might be the servant's. Even after several days in the water, he bears a resemblance to the young man the innkeeper described."

"Is someone dead?" The boy asked.

"I'm afraid so." Gareth looked down at him. The boy had spoken to Gareth in Welsh, but it seemed he had enough French to understand something of what Gareth had related to the monks. "Can you speak to me of this woman? Did you see her yourself?"

"Yes, although I didn't talk to her. Even so, I can attest to what my master told your sons. She definitely had red hair! When she asked after her servant, my master offered me to accompany her down the road, but she declined. And then she rode away west towards Aberystwyth."

Gwen tsked. "She'll be long gone by now."

"Most likely." Privately, Gareth commended his sons to God's care, knowing that if they were meant to find her they would. They were on her trail now, perhaps as much as they were on Cadwaladr's. If they were forced to choose which mission had priority, he had to trust that they would make the right choice. He hadn't told anyone at the commandery about Brigid's connection to the Earl of Pembroke, but Dai had been present for that discussion. It would be at the front of his mind, and he would know what to do.

"Thank you for coming so quickly." Gareth put a hand on the boy's shoulder, before turning to Warden Geoffrey and switching to French. "Might we find him something to eat before we send him back to his master? He has a walk ahead of him."

"Of course." Geoffrey held out a hand in a gesture of welcome.

But the boy's eyes were riveted on the shrouded body just coming into the yard, heading for the laying-out room. Not all monasteries had robust facilities for dealing with the dead, but this was a hospital, designed and built to succor the ill and the dying. It had the largest laying-out room Gareth had ever seen, with room for five bodies on tables.

He surely hoped this investigation would never reach a point where he needed all the spaces. He also wondered how differently this week might have gone if Desmond's mother, Helen, had still been in the laying-out room that night instead of in the church.

29

Day Four

Gwen

Another day. Another body.

Although, really, Everard's death was days ago now, so that was really just two bodies in four days. It had taken only a brief inspection to determine that the young man had been murdered. Gwen's despair, then, was more about the tragic path of destruction this murderer had left in his wake. He had killed Everard, which was bad enough, but to have murdered this young man felt worse.

Commander Reginald stood beside the body, shaking his head. "You're *sure?*"

"It's the same method." Gareth took his pencil and slid it all the way into the ear, curdling Gwen's stomach as he did so.

Commander Reginald's nose wrinkled in distaste. "Do you know with what instrument?"

"Not yet."

"Could it be as simple as a pencil?" he asked. "Like yours?"

Gwen caught her breath, uncertain if she was misunderstanding his implication. Had Reginald just accused *Gareth* of murder?

Gareth answered in an utterly calm tone. "I wouldn't have said mine was sharp enough to kill. Whatever was used must have been longer and more dagger-like."

Reginald wasn't ready to concede the point. "The body is in poor shape, unsurprising given the rocks within the chasm. Is there any chance this is a result of damage after death?"

"Given that Everard died by the same means, the answer has to be no. Besides, do you want to risk your life and the lives of everyone here on the possibility?"

Gareth's tone was an indication that he was losing patience with Reginald's hesitation. While she could understand the commander's reluctance to face a second murder, his behavior highlighted their ongoing sense that the monks at the commandery had taken Everard's murder in stride. They would just as soon have continued as if it had never happened at all. As Gwen had said, first to Dai and then to Gareth, *Where's the worry and fear?* Truthfully, there was plenty of worry and fear here, but about the *wrong* things. Reginald wasn't afraid of being murdered. He was afraid of having his world upended.

Reginald smoothed the front of his robe. "Do you really think we are in danger?"

Gareth spread his hands wide. "Two men are dead. With their connection to this woman, Brigid, their deaths cannot be a coincidence."

"I admit that."

Reginald appeared to still be having trouble getting his head around what Gareth was telling him, so Gwen stepped in to try a different tack. "What most people—and certainly most murderers—don't realize is that an experienced investigator can tell the difference between an injury that was sustained before death and one that happened afterwards. Before death, a man bleeds. After death, the heart stops beating, which means his blood stops flowing. Therefore, postmortem wounds don't show signs of inflammation and tend to have a yellowish, bloodless look, even after four days in the water."

Gareth nodded. "Submersion in cold water tends to slow rigor, but this body has still gone through the process. That puts his time of death near to Everard's.

"The ear isn't his only injury either, as you yourself just pointed out." Gwen kept speaking, deciding it was better to have Reginald's ire directed at her than at Gareth. Picking up one of the body's hands, she showed him the fingers. "Do you see this damage to his knuckles and fingernails? This happened before he died, indicating he put up more of a fight than Everard."

"Couldn't he have had a dispute with someone at the inn, or just fallen to the ground? His fight could have been with the very earth."

"It is possible," Gareth said mildly. "Nonetheless, it is a fight he lost."

Commander Reginald bent his head. "I give way to your experience. I must now see to my people." He departed.

Once he'd gone, Gwen looked ruefully at her husband. "I can't say that went well."

"I fear his patience is growing as thin as mine. We are running out of time to find this murderer."

"To that end, can I summarize, just between you and me?"

"I never have a problem with a cogent summary." As he spoke, Gareth again bent over the young man's body.

"To begin, Everard visits Joan and then, having told her he was meeting someone she thought might be a woman, departs for the inn. Unbeknownst to him, Lucan follows him and sees him meeting Brigid. Lucan doesn't know what they talk about, but the innkeeper doubts it was about healing and recalls mention of Richard, the Earl of Pembroke."

Gareth grunted his agreement before picking up the tale. "The next morning, Everard is found dead in Helen's coffin. This young man, who fits the description of Brigid's manservant, for whom she was looking on the road to Aberystwyth the next morning, was killed about the same time. In other words, our murderer was quite busy that night."

"Now for the speculation," Gwen said. "If Brigid sent her manservant after Everard, if only to see he got home safely, and he witnessed Everard's murder, then that would be a reason to murder him too. I note you didn't show Reginald the three separate foxglove blooms we have collected. To have done so might have convinced him the deaths were connected."

"The skewer into the ear connects them. If the murderer had really wanted to put us off his trail, he would have killed the young man by a different method and done a better job hiding the bodies."

"I think he tried," Gwen said. "He hid Everard's body in Helen's coffin and threw this young man—I wish we knew his name—into the river."

"Neither meets my definition of *hiding*."

"In the end, yes. But it was dark, and he was in a hurry. He needed to get home, wherever home might be." She tipped her head. "So, may I speculate again?"

Gareth eyed her. "I'm almost afraid to hear what you have to say."

"How wrong would I be to think that our killer saw Everard talking to Brigid, who is, in fact, a spy as the innkeeper thought, and killed him for it?"

"That makes Everard also a spy for the Earl of Pembroke."

"We know he corresponded with him. We know the earl himself sent a foxglove bloom with his message to Everard. That he worked for the earl would also explain the money in his purse and mattress—no great sum as these things go, but enough for expenses."

"You are assuming Everard lied to John about why he was contacting the earl."

She scoffed. "Of course, he lied. You think so too."

"Do you know what might be worse, Gwen? What if one of our people is responsible because he was trying to prevent Everard from passing information to the Earl of Pembroke? If that's the case, do we really want to catch him?"

"A Welshman!" Gwen hadn't thought that far ahead yet. "We haven't interviewed very many of those. Only the innkeeper and a few of the servants here. And then what about Brigid?"

"As the murderer or the next victim?"

"I don't know. We've come far afield."

Gareth let out a heavy breath. "A murderer killed two people with the same weapon, whatever that weapon may be. Our difficulty lies in tying these deaths to any one person. In the past, I have been less concerned about the *why* of a given murder since my focus could always be on the *who*. But we have no suspects who had both the knowledge and the time to be about in the middle of the night killing these two men. Maybe we need to begin with motive and work backwards from there."

Gwen stared down at the body. "So now we ask the question we had set aside: *who gains the most from these deaths?*"

30

Day Four

Llelo

They had spent what felt like far too much time over the course of the day looking for the red-haired woman who called herself Brigid, stopping at every house and hamlet on the way to Aberystwyth. It had reached a point where Llelo honestly wasn't sure why they kept asking. He and Dai had done it without consultation, both just somehow *knowing* that it was what they were supposed to do, and that their father would have wanted them to do it. Even more, they saw it as *their* responsibility. They had hold of a thread, and they were compelled to tug on it.

Now, having crossed the River Rheidol yet again, as well as the Ystwyth, they approached the elongated plateau upon which Prince Hywel's castle was situated.

Dai had his head down, dragging a bit. Even with their mother's help, they'd underestimated their food requirements for a day on horseback. It was one thing to saunter along beside a wagon, where they could reach into the back for a carrot or a hunk of bread any time they pleased. It was another to be traveling concertedly with an end in mind. There'd been far fewer taverns along the way than they'd expected, given that there'd been practically two in a row just north of Ysbyty Cynfyn. If not for this issue of the riderless horse and the woman, they might have been here hours ago instead of as the sun was setting, with ten miles still to go to Llanrhystud. They wouldn't reach it tonight unless they were willing to ride through the dark.

At one time, Dai might have urged them on, and Llelo might have acquiesced. But they were older now. Both had been to war and knew what it was. Continuing their journey after dark would have been, in a word, *stupid*.

"Maybe some of the Dragons are here," Dai had spied the gatehouse on the hill above them, "or, if we're really lucky, Prince Hywel himself."

Llelo studied the wooden ramparts. The castle wasn't quite the stronghold of some Norman holdings. King Gruffydd of Deheubarth, Cadell's father, had burned the original castle in 1135. Cadwaladr had rebuilt it during his brief stewardship after 1136, and Hywel had burned it himself seven years ago. But here it was again, risen from the ashes. To hold Ceredigion against invaders, they needed this castle by the sea. Llelo couldn't see the water from where he stood, but he could smell it. It was comforting to him, having spent so much of his life in recent years in Gwynedd within a mile of the water.

The approach to the castle was winding, giving the guards watching from the ramparts a good view of any person (or army) arriving long before they reached the gatehouse. The whole time they walked their horses up the long road, Llelo felt a prickling up and down his spine. But once across the ditches that defended the castle, they were admitted without fanfare and found themselves dismounting in a rectangular bailey located outside the ringwork defenses, so not actually within the castle itself yet.

This was where the horses would be kept, let out to pasture in less turbulent times in the sloping fields just to the west of the ramparts. Evening was here, so the castellan, Hywel's foster father, Cadifor, accommodated their mounts in the stables. He had been the captain of Hywel's guard for a short time, after Gareth had become Hywel's steward, but only until a younger replacement could be found. One of his sons was already the captain of King Owain's guard, and another, Aron, was a Dragon. Cadifor had five more sons placed throughout Hywel's retinue, with varying degrees of responsibility.

"Were you able to congratulate Aron on his marriage?" Dai asked in his typical straightforward, and somewhat mischievous, fashion.

Cadifor grinned. "I was glad to do it! He won't do better than a cousin of Ifon of Rhos, and I am anxious for the day I can dandle a grandchild or two on my knee. He should be home with her right now instead of fighting in this blasted war. Damn Cadell and his ambition."

They passed through the first protective ringwork, which housed the main buildings of the castle, including the great hall. Above them on its Norman motte, since it was a Norman who'd originally built the castle, was a wooden tower. Llelo could just make out a man pacing around the small battlement, his eyes watching for enemies. He allowed himself a small sigh of relief to know that at least Aberystwyth remained in Hywel's hands.

"Do you have news to share?" Cadifor lifted a hand to the man who opened the main door to the hall for them. "We have not heard from Hywel in several days."

"Not from Hywel," Llelo said. "We are chasing down a rumor."

Cadifor inspected him. "I sometimes forget that Gwen was Hywel's spy long before she was your mother. I recognize the look in your eyes. Bad news?"

Llelo thought about how to answer that question. Maybe not answering would have been sufficient warning, but he ended up saying, "It isn't good."

Cadifor snorted. "And now you sound like your father. Can you tell me?"

After a glance at Dai, who nodded, Llelo decided he had to speak plainly. "We have heard from a credible source that Cadwaladr has betrayed us with King Cadell. We are riding to Llanrhystud to uncover evidence to prove the rumor true."

Cadifor rubbed his chin, looking less shocked than resigned at Llelo's news. "It has been a fortnight since I heard from Llanrhystud, but it hasn't fallen to Cadell's forces. Of that I am sure."

"It wouldn't have to fall, though, would it? Not if it was already counted as an ally," Dai said.

Cadifor grunted. "If Hywel hadn't forbidden all of us to take care of Cadwaladr years ago once and for all, believe me I would have done it myself."

"Any one of us would have done it," as a member of the Dragons, Dai spoke only the truth, "which is why Hywel felt he had to forbid us overtly."

"What do you need from me?" Cadifor said.

"A bed for the night, food for the journey, and your discretion," Llelo said. "We don't want to appear as if we are anything more than messengers."

"You do look the part." Gesturing towards one of the tables nearest the fire, he added, "Eat; drink; we will talk more when you are sated." He headed off on other duties.

Dai, however, tugged at Llelo's sleeve, pulling him back from the table Cadifor had indicated towards one far less desirable, given its distance from the fireplace. Except for the person who occupied it. "She's here."

The red-haired woman was focused on her trencher, although something about the set of her shoulders gave Llelo warning that she had seen them arrive and speak familiarly with Cadifor. As they approached, her knuckles whitened briefly on her cup, and then she visibly relaxed them. He might not have noticed if it wasn't something he had to make himself do all the time. She was worried about who they might be.

"We've been looking for you all day. Well, really since yesterday." Dai sat himself opposite her, his back to the room since hers was to the wall. Normally the latter position would have been Llelo's preference. Now that he surveyed the layout of the room, however, he realized she was trapped between them and the wall. All to the good.

Maybe she had suddenly realized it too, because her eyes flicked from Dai to Llelo and then to the exits. She could scoot down the bench and try to get out around the long table, but even there, people were in her way.

Dai's greeting had a further effect, in that Brigid moved her hands from her cup to her lap. Although Llelo could no longer see them, the tightening in her upper arm told him she was gripping the hilt of her knife.

"We mean you no harm." Llelo glanced at his brother with something of a warning look. They wanted answers, not hostility. "You have been given hospitality at this castle, and that is something we would never violate." To be less intimidating, Llelo swung one leg over the bench and sat beside his brother, facing sideways with his right elbow on the table. Truly, he had never thought of himself as menacing before this moment.

"Perhaps I should have said first that we have been looking for you because we found your servant's horse cropping the grass beside the road," Dai said. "We know you met with Everard the physician four nights ago at The Castle inn. We have come all this way to ask you what you talked about."

31

Day Four

Dai

That they were at Aberystwyth for Brigid wasn't strictly true. Their initial plan had been simply to break their journey here, but the woman didn't need to know that. She gazed at Dai for a count of three, transferred her gaze to Llelo for another few heartbeats …

… and then she began to laugh.

Dai hated being laughed at, if that's what this was. He tried not to show his anger and just let the woman's laughter subside into chuckles. She was still shaking her head, when she said, "I'm a healer; Everard and I were discussing remedies."

"You were not discussing remedies. You were overheard."

"I don't know what you're talking ab—"

Llelo leaned in now and spoke in a harsh tone. "Before you deny again, perhaps you should know that we are investigating the murder of Physician Everard."

She blinked just once and then settled back against the wall. "Now, I really don't know what you're talking about."

Dai had watched his father sketch an image of this woman in charcoal. He hadn't been able to render her red hair, which (like Godfrid's wife, Cait) Brigid couldn't entirely contain in any kerchief. She was twenty years older than Cait, and time hadn't been kind to her face. She didn't do innocent well.

"We know you work for the Earl of Pembroke." Dai hoped that by giving away more than he himself would have preferred, she would just tell the truth.

But if she was a spy, which they had all concluded she had to be, rather than Everard's lover, as Lucan might have supposed, it would be against her nature. Dai didn't care that she was a woman. As Cadifor had rightly pointed out, Gwen had spied for Hywel for years before she'd married Gareth or adopted Dai. They'd met an incredibly accomplished female spy just a few months ago in Holywell. She had since married Taran, King Owain's steward, and Dai had little doubt that she was putting her considerable skills to work for Gwynedd. Sometimes it might really be best not to know.

But not in this case.

"We have met the earl ourselves and won't hold the fact that you're working for him against you unless you make us." Llelo's eyes were fixed on Brigid's face. "We found a straying horse near that tavern, west of the ford across the Rheidol. It has occurred to us that if you sent your servant after Everard, for whatever reason, and he didn't return, the fact that your man's horse is wandering means you never did find him."

"One might even wonder if you sent him to murder Everard." Dai looked at Llelo and spoke conversationally, as if the thought had just occurred to him (which it had). "And then fled."

"Without his horse?" Brigid's composure was impressive. "You're smarter than that."

Dai bent his head. "My thanks. I think."

"You both wear swords; you're Welsh; and you also obviously know the castellan of this castle well enough to have had an intent conversation as you came in. He then put you at the table closest to the fire, one reserved for men of standing." She studied them more closely now. "You obviously know something of me, but I don't even know your names."

"Dai ap Gareth." Dai motioned with his head to the right. "My brother Sir Llelo."

"Sons of Gareth ap Rhys, the prince's steward?"

"Yes," Dai said.

Instead of looking wary, or afraid, or even concerned, Brigid gave a little harumph and took a sip from her cup. This was the first time she'd taken her hand out of her lap since they'd sat at her table. "Earl Richard has spoken to me of him—and of you." All of a sudden, her tone was infused with laughter again. "And here you are. I think he would be pleased."

"Who are you to him, and why did he mention us?"

"I think you know who I am to him, and he told me about you because I was riding into Welsh territory. He said if I ever found myself in trouble, I should ask to speak to your father."

"You mean if you were captured and exposed as a spy," Dai said.

She narrowed her eyes at him. "Let's just say if my situation became untenable."

"Who was Everard to you?" Llelo asked.

"Someone Earl Richard trusted."

"Had you met with him before the other night?"

"Never." She cleared her throat. "He sent a message to the earl asking for someone to come."

"Why did he need the earl to send someone into Ceredigion in the midst of a war?" Llelo continued to ask the questions. "What couldn't be written in a letter?"

"Everard feared his message would be intercepted. He didn't trust anyone. He even wrote what he was willing to say in code."

"Code?" Llelo looked at Dai, who shrugged. He'd heard of spies doing such a thing, but not here in Wales.

"It was something he'd worked out with the earl. I never saw what was written, only what Earl Richard told me."

A spark of a thought passed through Dai's head, and he allowed it out his mouth. "How was he to trust you if you'd never met him and you weren't privy to the code too?"

She gave him a long look and then delved into her purse to remove a faded foxglove bloom, wrapped, like they all had been, in a cloth. "The earl sent one back with the last letter they exchanged and gave this to me to carry so Everard would know I came from him. Did you find a bloom in that horse's saddle bags?"

"No."

"My servant had one too, just in case something happened to me." She looked a bit rueful. "He wasn't really a servant, though he played the part well. We agreed he should follow Everard, to make sure he reached the commandery safely." She wet her lips. "He never came back, and now you tell me Everard is dead."

"Murdered."

"Will you say how?"

Dai glanced at Llelo, who shrugged and answered, "He was hit on the head to subdue him and then killed with some kind of skewer to the ear."

"Ugly." Brigid shivered. "I can tell from the looks on your faces that you fear Baldwin is dead too."

"If he isn't dead, then where is he?" Dai said. "Would he abandon you?"

"Or his horse?" Llelo asked.

"No to both questions. He was a squire in the earl's household and absolutely loyal."

"So why are you still here?" Llelo said. "Your servant disappeared days ago. What have you been doing since then?"

She pressed her lips together in a way that in a normal person might indicate she didn't want to tell them. Since she was a spy and used to deception, Dai didn't know if he could believe what her face was telling him. Finally, she said, "I rode north for a while."

"Into Gwynedd?" Dai said.

For a moment, her eyes skated away. "Yes."

Dai and Llelo looked at each other, acknowledging their duty to report that Earl Richard had sent a spy into their lands. It was the last thing Hywel would want to hear, but also not something that should have surprised any of them.

"I really did come to Ysbyty Cynfyn to speak to Everard about what he feared was happening there—" She broke off as a servant brought a tray of vegetables, bread, and mutton, as well as a carafe of mead and two more cups.

They waited for him to leave before Brigid shifted in her seat and continued, "Everard had written to the earl that he was concerned about some deaths at the commandery."

Dai and Llelo themselves sat a little straighter to hear it.

Brigid allowed herself a small smile. "Not what you expected?"

Her words were, in fact, the last thing Dai had expected to hear. But it was also exactly what had brought them to Ysbyty Cynfyn too. "What deaths?"

"A handful in all. Several were healthy men dying in their sleep."

"Did he mention the name Iago?"

"He did!" Now it was her turn to straighten. "He had been one of the men made ill by this plague. But he was on the mend. And then he was dead."

"Is that why you used a foxglove flower as an emblem?" Llelo said. "Did Everard think someone was poisoning them?"

She smirked a little. "The earl has used foxglove blooms for his communications since he came into his inheritance. Because of the rash, no reasonable person would carry one around. It was a way for us to recognize others who were working for him." She made a motion with her head. "As regards to your question about how the men died, Everard wasn't sure. If they were poisoned, he didn't know how it was being done."

All of a sudden, Dai was confused. "So why write to the earl at all? What were you expected to do?"

"Me? I was to hear him out and report back."

"And then what?" Llelo said.

"If I thought what he had to say was reasonable, Earl Richard has the standing to take action. He is a patron of the Hospitallers in general and Ysbyty Cynfyn in particular. With the right word in the right circles, a knight of the order could have been sent to look into the matter, without anyone at Ysbyty Cynfyn knowing the request had ultimately come from Everard."

"Were you going to ask for that?" Llelo said. "You never even visited the commandery."

"Everard himself told me he'd changed his mind. All was well, and I wasn't to bother the earl with this."

Llelo frowned. "Do you know what changed for him between when he sent the letter and your meeting with him?"

She shook her head. "I confess, I was a little put out to have come all that way for nothing. Really, I didn't know whether or not I even believed him. But I had nothing to go on and other claims on my time. Obviously, that has all changed with Baldwin's disappearance and Everard's death, which I didn't know about until you told me of it. I will definitely be recommending the earl send someone to Ysbyty Cynfyn!"

"Why didn't Everard just speak to my father, who was right there? Investigating murder is what he does." Dai was more than a little outraged on Gareth's behalf, never mind that they had actually already tried to investigate Iago's death and failed to uncover any wrongdoing. "He's *already* doing it."

"Earl Richard might trust your father, but Everard did not." Then, when Llelo and Dai looked surprised, she tsked under her breath. "Your father is Welsh and serves a Welsh lord. How could Everard have been sure that Prince Hywel wouldn't decide the problems at the commandery were too great to fix and claim its holdings for himself?" Brigid gave a sad shake of her head. "Earl Richard was the only person Everard thought he could trust."

32

Day Five

Llelo

"**W**hat are you doing?" Llelo's eyes narrowed as he watched his brother wad his fine cloak into a ball and put it in his saddlebags.

Then Dai pulled off his boots, shrugged out of his tunic and, as a last, practically sacrilegious act, unbuckled his sword belt and handed it to Llelo. "Keep this safe for me."

By now, Llelo had figured out without Dai having to explain that he was trying to look less like a Dragon and more like a farmer boy. Men-at-arms and knights never went barefoot. Archers would remove their boots on occasion, if the footing was uncertain. Even then, shoes with soft leather soles served a man better than the possibility of stabbing one's heel on a stick or thistle in the wet and dark. Llelo was speaking from experience on that front.

"What am I supposed to do while you enter the castle and put yourself in danger? I'm not waiting here, twiddling my thumbs."

They had found a spot in the woods to the north of the castle, having risen in the gray before dawn in order to get close to Llanrhystud before too much of the morning had passed. They couldn't enter until the gates were opened for the day anyway, and they needed to be able to *see* the castle in order to assess what they were walking into. This spot had given them a good vantage point of the front gate, located on the northwestern side of the castle.

"Rest." Dai smirked at him as only a little brother could. "You were ill not long ago."

"I am recovered." Llelo would have wrestled him to the ground like they were eight and ten if it weren't beneath his dignity.

"Then you shouldn't come because you are a knight and far too recognizable."

"You can't actually be thinking nobody will know you in there! We rode south with these men less than a fortnight ago."

"I am a boy, with a mop of hair and no shoes. Nobody is going to look at me twice."

Llelo had to admit Dai had transformed himself remarkably and, with his facility with accents and languages, could pretend to be almost anyone. Still he wasn't ready to stop arguing. "I have a letter to Cadwaladr from our father, sealed by his own hand. We have every right to enter Llanrhystud. Do you think you can just saunter in there and find evidence? How? What's your excuse for being there? Will you ask for employment for the day?"

"He can saunter in with me." They turned to see Brigid leading her horse out of the woods.

Llelo and Dai had left Aberystwyth early enough that they hadn't looked for her. In truth, it hadn't occurred to Llelo that he should. "What are you doing here?" He found himself whispering, even though there was nobody else about. Or so he hoped, since he hadn't known Brigid was here to overhear either.

"I am riding home. You didn't put me in chains last night, so I thought it best to leave while I could." She gestured towards the castle. "I was intending to stop here on my way. What's curious to me is why you have come here too."

Llelo opened his mouth to speak, but Dai whacked his chest with the back of his hand. "Surely we aren't trusting her. I can handle this myself."

"You could handle it better if you entered leading my horse." Brigid gave him a wry smile. "If I had known your real destination was Llanrhystud I would have offered to help you last night."

Llelo found himself staring at her. "I don't understand."

"I am thinking now that you weren't at Aberystwyth for me at all. The fact that I was there was just a happy coincidence." Her eyes were alight with a strange sort of joy. "Just now, I overheard you say that you're looking for proof that Cadwaladr has allied with Cadell. Maybe I can help."

Llelo should have known better than to think he could outwit a spy for the Earl of Pembroke. He also really didn't want her help. From the look on Dai's face, he didn't either. They knew she was resourceful, however, and Earl Richard was no ally of either Cadell or Cadwaladr, not with the recent raids on Norman holdings, none of which had actually been perpetrated by the men of Gwynedd. *The enemy of my enemy is my friend?*

"Can we keep up with her?" Dai said in an undertone that Brigid pretended not to hear.

"If we do, we would be sleeping with one eye open—if either of us manages to sleep at all."

"We're not asleep now," Brigid said loudly. "Are we going to do this or not?"

Dai turned to look at her. "You've been telling everyone you're a healer. Are you really?"

She patted one of her saddle bags. "I have remedies to prove it."

"I'll give you a good head start before I follow," Llelo said. "We meet right back here by mid-afternoon, whether or not we've discovered anything."

Dai had been reaching up to grasp the leading rope of Brigid's horse. "What are you talking about? You're staying here with my horse and yours."

"I never actually agreed to that." Llelo infused his voice with the heavy weight of extreme patience. "If you think I'm letting you go in there alone with Brigid to get yourself into trouble, you are sorely mistaken. If nothing else, I'm coming in afterwards as myself to get you out of it."

33

Day Five

Gwen

"Are you all right, Desmond?" Gwen peered into the monk's face. "You're looking a little gray."

The funeral of the young man they'd found in the river had taken place as the sun was rising over the hills to the east. As had been the case all week, funerals took place at Ysbyty Cynfyn at non-traditional times and, in this instance, immediately after dawn prayers. The previous evening, Gareth had examined the young man's body the best he could, and then it was necessary to get him in the ground as quickly as possible. While so many days in the water had slowed the body's decay initially, now it had sped up again, and its smell was pungent, to say the least.

"I'm feeling more than a little queasy, actually." He bit his lip. "More and more with every moment that passes."

"Was it the funeral?" Gwen resisted the urge to step back and instead put a hand on his upper arm to steady him. "Have you vomited?"

"Not … yet. It will pass, I'm sure."

She raised her eyebrows. "Have you spoken with my step-mother, Saran, or one of the physicians about this?"

"I have not; after this last week, I really don't want to be more of a bother. My fellow monks put up with enough from me without me needing help again."

That wasn't quite Gwen's perception of the situation. His fellow monks had disliked the extent to which he'd wallowed in his grief, thinking it represented a lack of faith. After his mother's funeral, they had been much more cordial, and he himself had been much improved. She had known Desmond for only a short time, but it was in her mind that he was happy to be fussed over when he was in the mood for it. Although she believed his grief real, he might have controlled himself more if everyone hadn't been so sympathetic, herself included.

"This is different, Desmond. Nobody wants you vomiting on the floor or turning into that fellow Everard brought to the infirmary before he was killed. It's been three days. In all that time, he has barely managed to keep anything down. Nor have the two who've come after him. Someone has had to spoon feed them warm water and honey four times an hour just to keep them alive." She eyed him. "You have been that man a time or two."

"I'll be fine. Something I ate just didn't sit right with me."

Gwen truly hoped that was the case. As she studied him, she reminded herself that suppressed grief could have physical effects on the body. After her mother died when Gwen was ten, she had vomited up the first several meals she'd tried to force down. In retrospect, she hadn't suddenly given in to an ailment. Her heart had been in pain, so her body had been in pain too.

She was just turning away, attempting to imply that she was done fussing over him, when Brother Peter, one of the younger—and entirely hale—monks, skidded to a stop in the entrance to the hospital. "It's Commander Reginald. He is very unwell! You must come with me!"

Gwen looked around for any of the physicians, or her stepmother, but they all seemed to have disappeared. Her only resource was Healer Efa, who was just coming out of the remedy storage room.

She halted beside Gwen to speak to the messenger. "What's wrong with him?"

"He can't stop vomiting."

Gwen glanced at Desmond, whose eyes widened, and then she pointed at him. "You stay here until Bardolf returns. Maybe lie down while you wait."

"Yes, my lady."

"Maybe even put a bowl next to your head. You're definitely greener than you were." Gwen followed Efa and the monk out the door, even though she herself was feeling a bit greenish too.

"Where is everyone else?" Efa asked as they hurried together towards the commander's quarters.

"I don't know. They have been working hard of late, especially in the absence of Brother Everard." Now that Gwen thought about it, it had been upwards of a half-hour since she'd seen any of them, including Saran.

Efa let out a puff of air. "The commander won't like being seen to by two women, but since we are all he has right now, he'll have to put up with it."

Gwen herself wasn't particularly enthused about tending to any vomiting monk, having stayed far away from the ones currently in the infirmary. Being pregnant, she found most anything set her off. But she couldn't refuse to go either, given how ill Reginald sounded. She didn't even have the excuse of seeing to her children, as they were currently being tended by her father and Gareth. Back in Holywell, they'd thought about acquiring another nanny. In the end, after consultation with her parents and elder sons, they'd decided to manage the best they could on the journey with just their family. They hadn't had fantastic luck with their children's nannies so far, culminating with the last one, Marged, who'd married one of Prince Cadwaladr's men.

Marged was past child bearing years, so it would have been theoretically possible for her to have continued as Tangwen and Taran's nanny even while married to Geraint. In practice, however, she could not do both: they could not have tolerated a spy in their household, and Marged could not have helped but be one. Even so, Marged and Geraint had ridden most of the way to Ceredigion with them in Prince Cadwaladr's train and even now might be settled in one of Cadwaladr's castles. Like Llanrhystud. Where Llelo and Dai might be entering even now.

By the time they arrived at the commander's quarters, more monks had gathered. Brother Peter edged through the doorway. "I brought healers! Let us pass!"

Nobody said anything about the identity of those he'd brought. Commander Reginald certainly wasn't in a position to complain, since he was on his knees before a chamber pot, one of his brethren hovering over him.

Efa went straight to him, while Gwen turned entirely around, her hands in the air. "Brothers, if you could leave your commander alone, that would be best. He is ill, as you can see. As soon as we know more of his situation, we will speak to you. Your prayers on his behalf would be of the greatest service now."

Brother Peter departed as well, after a whispered suggestion from Gwen that he might check the herb hut in the garden for the physicians or Saran. Fortunately, all the monks were used to being told what to do and, a moment later, only Warden Geoffrey, Reginald's second-in-command, remained. He was pursing his lips as he stood off to one side. "I don't like this."

"None of us do, including, I'm sure, your commander!" Gwen wasn't being censorious, just stating a fact. "Can you tell me what is so concerning to you, beyond the obvious?"

"I agree the illness is distressing. He's vomiting." Geoffrey gestured for them to move into the corridor, so they wouldn't disturb Efa's quiet conversation with the commander. "A more pressing question is *why* he is ill."

Gwen would have thought that was obvious too, given the ongoing sickness in the infirmary. But because Geoffrey appeared to be a thoughtful man, she accepted that he meant something deeper. "If you don't think this is a regular illness, are you wondering if he's been poisoned?"

"I think he has been poisoned," and before Gwen's mouth could open in shock, he added, "but not in a way that would necessitate an investigation by your husband."

"Then what?" Gwen was really confused now and didn't mind showing it. "One of the monks has been ill since the night Everard died. Two more came in later, but I hadn't heard of any others until just now when Desmond informed me that he was feeling queasy."

"Desmond works in the infirmary, so it would not be unreasonable for him to have tended the sick man and then fallen ill himself. That is not an uncommon effect. But Commander Reginald is rarely in the infirmary, and he does not physick the ill."

Gwen still didn't think that was a compelling argument for why they couldn't have the same illness. They certainly looked similar. While she hesitated to say so, her thoughts must have shown on her face because Geoffrey consented to explain, "I recognize what's happening from a pattern I first saw in the Holy Land. Believe me, I would have run to the herb garden myself for an antidote if there was one. These men aren't ill from a sickness that can be physicked in the same way as others you have encountered."

He was dragging out this explanation far too long, having paused yet again, but she understood from the way his head was wagging back and forth and his lips kept twitching that he was struggling to voice his thoughts adequately—and maybe didn't want to. He finally did anyway: "I believe my commander is suffering from the effects of the withdrawal of Everard's elixir from his diet. Now that Everard is dead, and we have all but run out, he isn't getting as much of it as he needs."

Over the last few days since Everard's death, Gwen had encountered discussion of the elixir and the need to find the recipe. Nobody had mentioned any illness resulting from its absence, however. "Why? What is in it?"

It was Saran who answered, having just entered the corridor through a side door. "Tell her, Geoffrey. Everybody is going to know soon."

He sighed one last time and then finally came out with it: "The elixir's primary ingredient, I'm afraid, is poppy."

34

Day Five

Saran

A half hour earlier ....

Somehow, Saran had been the one to lead the meeting in the herb hut. In large part, this was because she was the only one of them detached enough from the situation to see it clearly. In addition, none of the physicians, even Bardolf, seemed to want to put themselves forward in that manner.

There had been four physicians at Ysbyty Cynfyn. With Everard's loss, there were now three: Bardolf, Thomas, and Gabriel. Bardolf was the head of the infirmary. To all appearances, he remained comfortable in that role. He was keeping everything running smoothly while Thomas and Gabriel, both younger and far less experienced, took on the majority of the patients.

They'd spent the first part of the conversation divvying up the remaining duties and discussing which of the monks currently living among them they could start training as a physician to fill at least some of the gaps left by Everard's loss. Among their brethren was also the animal physician, Brother James. His duties were no less than before, however, and everyone agreed he was better with animals than with people.

Saran had already suggested that they find someone who could be trained for organizational duties, to take that burden off Bardolf. It made sense that the person in charge of the remedy storeroom would know what each of the herbs and remedies were, but with Everard gone, Bardolf was also the most experienced physician. He needed to be teaching, not sitting in a room with a ledger.

"If we can't find Everard's recipe, we won't be able to make more of his elixir anyway, and then where will we be?" Gabriel said. "It's a disaster to try to care for patients without it."

While they'd been talking, Gabriel had been going through the vials and bottles in the herb hut with what looked to Saran like increasing desperation. She continued to be glad that she had stopped Llelo from consuming another dose. "The elixir is, in fact, the next thing I would like to talk about."

Gabriel swung around. "Why? What do you know about it?"

"Gabriel." Bardolf put out a hand to him. "Calm yourself. What has got you so upset?"

"Why is she here at all?" Gabriel made a large gesture with both hands. "She is not one of us. She barely knew Everard. And she's a woman. Who is she to judge?"

Bardolf's eyebrows came together in confusion, but Saran was finally seeing the root of this young man's issues, and probably a number of men's issues. "I see you have been taking Everard's elixir yourself."

"You don't know what you're talking about."

Saran gave a little sigh. "I take it Everard didn't know that you had started on it?"

Gabriel's mouth opened and closed like a landed fish, his sputtering denials only confirming her assessment.

She turned to Thomas. "You have been very quiet. Did you know he was taking it and in what quantity?"

Thomas replied as if she hadn't actually asked a question. "Everard took his recipe to his grave. We must carry on without it."

"And you're fine with that?" Gabriel advanced on him.

He shrugged. "All is as the Lord has decreed."

Saran pursed her lips as she studied him, no more able to read him now than when they first met nearly a fortnight ago. He was very contained, and perhaps that impression was exacerbated by how small he was, only a few inches over five feet, the same as Commander Reginald. This made quite a contrast to Gabriel, who was a good foot taller.

Bardolf was staring at the two men like they'd each grown two heads, and Saran was about to explain what was happening when a young monk came headlong through the doorway. "The commander is ill. He needs you! Your daughter sent me."

Saran didn't correct the young monk about her relationship with Gwen any more than Gwen ever did. She would introduce Saran as her *stepmother* when called for, but otherwise, she treated her as any daughter might. It was a blessing to Saran in her old age that she had joined such a complete family and been made welcome.

They all trooped towards the commander's quarters, Saran in the lead, and when they arrived in the corridor outside his room, she met Geoffrey's eyes. Every one of her concerns that she'd been quietly quashing down since they'd arrived at Ysbyty Cynfyn rose to the fore.

"Poppy," she said, once Geoffrey had said it first.

The other physicians bunched up behind her.

"No." Bardolf was aghast. "He wouldn't."

"He must have," Geoffrey said. "I have wondered for some time at the way the aches and pains of our older monks had diminished under his care. As long as Everard was alive, the withdrawal of the elixir would never have become an issue. They were old, and he was easing their pain."

"But poppy is very dangerous if taken over a long period of time!" Bardolf had his hands up and was making a double gesture to imply everyone needed to stop where they were. "I don't understand what's going on. Are you saying that these men who are vomiting, our commander among them, are dependent upon the juice of the poppy?"

"That is exactly what we are saying," Geoffrey said, while Saran nodded her head in agreement.

"How?"

"Men need air to breathe. Food to eat. Water to drink," Geoffrey said. "Withdraw any one of those and they founder. Poppy has the same effect. If they have been taking it for very long, they need it to live. Vomiting is one of the first signs that they aren't getting enough—that and pain."

Bardolf made another cutting off motion with his hand. "What you're saying is impossible. I am in charge of the stores. I keep careful watch over the quantities of remedies. Everard himself expressed concern to me not a fortnight ago about minimizing the use of his elixir in the infirmary—not because he couldn't make more, but because he was concerned about patients taking the elixir too often and in too large a quantity."

Saran turned to look at Gabriel. "You gave the elixir to my grandson. Was that authorized by Everard?"

For a moment Gabriel's face spasmed. "Of course."

She didn't need to be a real investigator to see that was a lie. "Did Everard discover that you were using too much of the elixir, not only for your patients but for yourself? Is that why you killed him?"

"No! I would never!" Gabriel stepped back, surprise in his face. "That would have served nobody."

Gabriel was afraid of not having enough of the elixir. From his expression, it had never occurred to him to murder Everard over it. As he said, that surely would have stopped it coming. She would need to confirm her impression with Gareth later when he questioned Gabriel himself. For now, his gasping denial sounded genuine to her.

"When did he speak to you of your dependency?" She made sure she didn't inquire *if* he had. She wasn't in the mood for sparring.

Gabriel was too distraught to deny it. "Two days before he died, he caught me skimming from a portion allotted to a patient. I begged him not to dismiss me, and he consented not to tell anyone, that he would work with me to ease me from it."

"He realized it was all his fault, didn't he?" Thomas finally gave his opinion, his upper lip curling in a manner Saran thought she needed to mistrust.

Gabriel didn't notice, having leaned his head against the wall and closed his eyes, the very epitome of misery and despair. "He was our teacher. In dying, he has betrayed us all."

35

Day Five

Dai

They'd continued to discuss the plan of action all the way back to the main road, with Llelo refusing to see reason, Dai arguing for his initial proposal, modified by Brigid's suggestions, and Brigid keeping entirely silent—until she stopped both of them in their tracks with the thought, "Is there some place safe we could leave Dai's horse which would satisfy both of you?"

"This is Cadwaladr's territory," Llelo said. "No place is safe."

"That—" Dai paused, stemming his original surly reaction, "—might not be strictly true."

When Brigid and Llelo turned to him, he shrugged. "I might know someone."

"Who?" they demanded together.

"Tad and I met a Welshman and his wife at the inn on the high road to Aberystwyth, the one where you met Everard, Brigid. He said his father lived just north of Llanrhystud and implied a lack of fervor in his allegiance to Cadwaladr. Maybe it would be worth trying to find him."

"And if it isn't?" Llelo said. "If you're wrong about this man's sentiments?"

"We can pay him for keeping the horse without saying anything more. We are still the sons of Gareth ap Rhys."

"What if he tells Cadwaladr we're here?" Llelo wasn't ready to admit anything.

"How?" Dai said. "Do you think he could beat us to the castle with his news? Or better yet, have a pigeon carry the message?"

Llelo grudgingly admitted that was unlikely and consented to make the attempt, especially after their first inquiry as to the whereabouts of Bleddyn's farm produced immediate results. After a quarter of a mile extra journey, they came to a halt in the yard in front of a substantial house, two stories high, with a stable and barn behind it. Whether because he heard them coming or just a matter of coincidence, Pedr, the man Dai had met at The Castle inn a few days before, along with an older man Dai guessed must be his father, Bleddyn, came around the back of the house.

Bleddyn's eyes were narrowed, but Pedr hesitated only a moment at the sight of the three of them on horseback. Then he strode towards Dai, in no way confused by his tousled look and lack of cloak and boots. "My lord! What are you doing here?"

Dai dismounted and held out his hand. "I didn't know that you'd remember me." They gripped forearms, and Dai introduced Llelo and Brigid and then explained what they needed.

Pedr looked a bit sideways at him. "Am I allowed to ask why you would need to leave your horse at all?"

"That would depend on how you feel about the goings on up at the castle." And then, as a sneer appeared on Bleddyn's face, Dai threw caution to the winds and decided to tell the whole truth. "To be blunt, we serve Prince Hywel, who distrusts his father's brother. He's worried about what's going on within Llanrhystud."

They'd been speaking in Welsh, which of course Bleddyn understood, and at that point his chin jutted out. "Interlopers."

Dai decided he'd better ask straight out what he meant. "Do you mean us?"

"None of you belong here. We had old King Gruffydd, who was a fine man, but then that Norman Clare came in, then Cadwaladr, then Hywel, and back to Cadwaladr again." Bleddyn's face screwed up. "I've not liked any of them, but Cadwaladr is the worst."

"And that is saying something," Pedr said. "My father has said in my hearing that your lord, Hywel, takes after old Gruffydd."

As an accolade, it lacked fervor, but given how Bleddyn felt about everyone who ruled over him, was probably the best they were going to get.

They left Dai's horse.

If this turned out well, everyone was going to admire Dai's foresight in acquiring such an ally. If it went badly, they would tell a different story.

Dai led Brigid, riding her horse, up the long pathway to the front gate of the castle. They'd wasted a good hour, maybe more, with all that deliberating. He didn't like the delay. The intent was to be in and out of the castle before noon. Or sooner, if they could quickly find the evidence they needed. Whatever that might be. He was trying not to think too hard about it, hoping he'd know it when he saw it.

Most Welsh castles were built on high hills, the better to see enemies coming. The Normans tended not to have the same head for heights, situating their castles in such a way that they either could be supplied from the sea or were located on a cliff above a river. Their faith was in water to protect them—or to save them. The Welsh had long experience with trusting their mountains.

"Don't be nervous," Brigid said. "Just duck your head and look like you mean to stay out of trouble."

"I do mean to stay out of trouble," Dai said. "I have done this before, you know. I have been a spy; I have been captured and escaped; I've been to war."

"And you all of sixteen." Her tone was dry.

She'd baited him on purpose, and he'd responded defensively. Upon consideration, she might have done so as a means to stiffen his spine for whatever was to come. If he was angry at her, he would be less afraid. So he hunched his shoulders and started plodding a bit more theatrically, as if he really was a cowed servant.

"How are you today, Iolo?" Brigid raised a hand to the guard at the outer gate.

He bent his head to her in return. "Very well, thank you. Welcome back."

"You've been here before." Dai glanced up at her, kicking himself for not realizing it sooner.

"Many times, though not this year; not since this castle was returned to Cadwaladr. I thought at the time to do so was a mistake, a rare misstep on the part of your king. We'll see if my doubts are proved true."

They were passing through the very large outer bailey, which was sloped upward towards the inner ring of defensive earthworks. Dozens of men were moving about inside, having set up camp within the protective palisade.

"King Owain knows it's a mistake," Dai said, "but it was also the only way to keep Cadwaladr loyal. He needs regular rewards, like a good hound."

She scoffed under her breath, before turning in the saddle to look back the way they'd come. "I'd say Cadwaladr himself isn't here. These men don't give the impression their lord might come upon them at any moment."

"I fear you're right, but not for that reason." Dai wrinkled his nose. "I recognize only one or two faces out of all the men and servants brought from Gwynedd." He was trying to keep his head tipped down while at the same time looking around. Even if they didn't find proof of Cadwaladr's duplicity, he wanted a good tally of Llanrhystud's defenses for his father and Hywel, in case that knowledge was ever needed. "In a way, that makes things worse. What if Llelo was right? All it's going to take is for one person to see through my disguise."

"Nobody is going to be looking for one of Hywel's Dragons in the face of a servant boy, especially my servant boy." Brigid dismounted with Dai's help in front of the inner gatehouse. "Take the horse. See what you can discover. I'll speak to the castellan, and then we'll see where we are."

Dai ducked his head in obedience, as a servant would, and led the horse towards the stabling area. Because the bailey was so large, the stables were commensurate in size. With the fine day, several horses were cropping the grass in the small corral adjacent to it. Dai continued to keep his head down as he led the horse to the entrance. No stable boy ran to take the reins. But then, he reminded himself, none would, since he would be seen as a stable boy himself.

The stables were dark in comparison to the light outside, so at first he didn't know whose sharp voice called to him from the other end of the long row of stalls. "Can you help me with this strap?"

Still blinking, Dai led his horse closer and was almost upon the speaker before he realized who he was. "My-my-my lord—"

"Don't call me that!" The words came a hissing whisper. Prince Rhys was still dressed as he had been, his boots coated in mud to hide their fine quality. "Are you completely mad?"

Dai put a hand on the strap to help tighten it. "Me? What do you think *you're* doing?"

"I arrived as the gates were closing on the night. I should have been gone at first light but I overslept. What's your excuse?"

"I am quite sure you meant us to come here, and I am not nearly as recognizable as you anyway. You're a prince of Deheubarth!"

"As you are clearly aware, everyone looks more at a man's attire than at the man himself. I have been overlooked all my life."

"I very much doubt that."

"You'd be surprised. People see what they want to see."

Dai chose not to argue further, since he was counting on exactly that too, as Rhys had said. "Was our journey for nothing, then? Is Cadwaladr's betrayal no longer a secret?"

"Have you no ability to keep any thought to yourself?" Rhys growled the words at him. "For a Dragon, your discretion is remarkably deficient."

Dai was offended again, since, as he'd said to Brigid, he'd been put into far worse situations than this and come out victorious. But he would get nowhere with Rhys being offended. "You spoke plainly when we saw you last. If I am to believe a word you say, I need you to be clear again."

Rhys bent his head. "I have not betrayed you."

"Cadwaladr could turn on your brother as easily as he has already turned on his own." Dai felt able to say that because he'd seen Rhys's shame—as well as his determination. "By telling us the truth, you may, in the end, have saved him. So again I ask, why are you here?"

Rhys gazed at him through a dozen heartbeats. They were still alone, which Dai realized now was because everyone else was caring for horses put to pasture outside the walls for the day. A number of animals still remained inside, so once the stablemen came to retrieve them, this conversation would need to end. Rhys understood they were running out of time too. "I did not ride into Ceredigion just to see your father. My brother sent me here as a messenger, with a letter to Cadwaladr, though in the end I had to give it to my cousin."

"What cousin are we talking about?"

"Cadfan."

Dai scoffed. "He's twelve years old. Why would you have to speak to him?"

"Because it is he who rules here."

Dai took one step closer and lowered his voice even more. "Are you in danger, my lord?"

"Trust you to think of me as much or more than yourself."

"I'll be fine."

"Like father; like son."

"I don't know what that means. Gareth and I do not share blood."

"You share everything that matters." Rhys's horse was finally ready, but he delayed mounting to say, "It is you who are in danger. You don't know Cadfan."

"He's a boy."

"My brother sent me here in disguise. What's more, he left it up to me whether I would reveal myself, even to Cadwaladr. And I chose not to."

"He wanted to protect you. He doesn't trust Cadwaladr either."

"Of course, he doesn't. My brother is not a fool. It is, however, why he had to write a letter, even though he was sending me, and risk it falling into the wrong hands. As soon as I arrived in Llanrhystud, I was glad of it. While Cadfan has the height and voice of a grown man, he acts like you would expect the son of Cadwaladr to act, with the morals of a child. To let my cousin know who I really am would have been … unwise." Rhys mounted his horse.

That was not a piece of news Dai wanted to hear, not with Llelo riding at any moment into the castle. He gazed up at Rhys, suddenly anxious that he not leave just yet. "And Cadwaladr? Where has he gone?"

"I do not know, and even if I did, I could not say." Rhys leaned down to him, and for a moment his eyes held a mischievous look. "But that proof you're looking for? You'll find it in the letter I brought."

36

Day Five

Llelo

The last thing Llelo had expected to see on his way up the road towards the castle was the face of Prince Rhys, intent with effort, bearing down on him. Llelo himself was riding sedately in the opposite direction. Their eyes met in acknowledgment, just for a moment, and then Rhys was past him, with no further indication that they knew each other.

But since it was Rhys who had set them on this path in the first place, Llelo was suddenly having second and third thoughts about this course of action. *Was this a trap, an elaborate scheme to further drive a wedge between King Owain and Cadwaladr?* On one hand, to deceive them would be out of character for Rhys, but on the other, a great deal could change in the years between fifteen and eighteen. Rhys *was* second in line to the throne of Deheubarth. The entire trip to Ysbyty Cynfyn, including his confession of betrayal and his affection for Gwen, could have been a ruse.

It was too late to turn around now. The men manning the gate had seen him. And Dai and Brigid were already inside.

Squaring his shoulders, Llelo trotted his horse the remaining yards to the castle entrance and announced himself to the guard who blocked his way, "I am Llelo ap Gareth ap Rhys, who is steward to Prince Hywel of Gwynedd and Ceredigion. I have a letter for your master."

The man bent his head. "Of course. This way, my lord." Then he gestured for one of his compatriots to take his place in front of the gate while he led Llelo into the outer bailey.

At the entrance to the stable, Llelo was somehow unsurprised to find Dai accepting the reins Llelo threw him. They had time for only a short conversation, consisting of Dai saying, *Cadwaladr isn't here and nor is anyone else, not even Marged,* and Llelo answering, *Thank goodness.*

While Llelo had intended to ask for Prince Cadwaladr at the gate, he had changed his little speech at the last moment. Cadwaladr's banner streamed from one of the towers, but his personal arms were not atop the other one. They'd all been so caught up in their planning, they had failed to notice earlier.

Llelo allowed himself an easing of the tension in his shoulders. He had not been worried about being recognized by any of Cadwaladr's men, but he had feared for Dai. He was hoping now that not being personally known would make it easier to elicit the information they needed from those retainers who remained. They would know who Llelo was, and likely distrust him, but not with the passion of those in Cadwaladr's immediate circle.

It was Dai's last words, however, that had Llelo's jaw tightening again at the enormity of the task before them: *Cadfan rules here. Rhys gave him a letter from King Cadell. We need to find it. Prince Rhys says it has the proof we need.*

There was nothing Llelo could do about his position now, other than carry through with the charade he'd started. Dai hadn't been able to tell him where Brigid had got to. He at first assumed she was speaking to people in the kitchen or the infirmary, if the castle had one.

But as it turned out, she was the only other person in the receiving room with Cadwaladr's son when Llelo was ushered inside. Llelo himself had been forced to wait a quarter of an hour in the corridor on the other side of the door. Initially, he had assumed the worst, namely that this was a chance for Cadfan to exert his power over the son of the man his father hated most in the world.

Or, if Llelo were being charitable, given that Cadfan was twelve, it also could have been thoughtlessness.

As it turned out, it was neither.

"There!" Brigid said in French. "Is that better?"

She was sitting on a stool in front and slightly to the right of Cadfan, who occupied what passed for a throne at this castle, his back to a roaring fire. Llelo's eyes went instantly to the scrolls, ledgers, and papers of every kind that were piled on a long table in front of a wall of shelves containing even more papers. Cadwaladr had wasted no time making Llanrhystud the seat of his newly acquired lands in Ceredigion. What they needed was on that table. It was just a matter of finding it.

Just.

The room itself wasn't large, not like the great hall Llelo had just left, perhaps fourteen feet by sixteen. It could have held a dozen counselors comfortably, but at the moment held only the three of them.

Cadfan held up his index finger and studied it, before speaking in a man's voice, also in French. Llelo reminded himself that the boy's mother was the daughter of the same Earl Clare who'd established Ysbyty Cynfyn. Consequently, he'd spent most of his life outside of Wales, with his mother's family. He might not even be fluent in Welsh. "Yes. Much obliged. You are welcome at Llanrhystud any time you need a place to break your journey."

Then Cadfan's eyes went to Llelo, and he stood to greet him.

Llelo was wholly unprepared not only for Cadfan's voice, but for his physical form. He was taller than Llelo, well over six feet, and not skinny either. His shirt had been rolled up to the elbow for Brigid to tend to him, revealing a muscular forearm thicker than Llelo's own. His face was the only part of him that was child-like, soft and round.

"Why are you here?" In that moment, Cadfan's expression transformed from that of childish relief at having a splinter removed from his finger to a look of such loathing Llelo had to stop himself from taking a step back. There was an outsized anger there, and a hatred that could not really have been directed at Llelo himself but at his father and everything Llelo represented. In a way, it was a relief that Cadfan appeared incapable of dissembling.

"I have brought a letter for your father from my father." Llelo took a step forward as he held it out.

"My father isn't here."

"Do you know where I might find him?"

Cadfan's face took on a weasel-like expression. "No."

"Who rules here? Perhaps I should be speaking to him."

Llelo could not have chosen a sentence more likely to arouse Cadfan's ire. His face reddened, and he glared at Llelo, too young to realize that Llelo had asked the question intentionally to get exactly this response. "*I* rule here while my father is gone. Give it to me." He held out his hand, but didn't move himself, instead requiring Llelo to walk towards him.

Llelo instructed himself not to respond similarly, that he had made Cadfan angry deliberately to engender a reaction. He needed to know where he stood, and now he did. Still, even as he placed the letter in Cadfan's hand, he said, "Surely you have an elder adviser your father has left with you, someone like Geraint, perhaps?"

"I do not need advice; nor do I want it. It is enough that the captain of the guard commands the men when I cannot."

It seemed an extraordinary situation for a twelve-year-old to be in.

"How long has your father been gone?" Brigid had risen to her feet as well.

"Two days. He will return tomorrow, though—" Cadfan returned his gaze to Llelo, "I wouldn't suggest you stay." Then he handed the letter to Brigid, unread, while at the same time pointing towards the table with its stacks of similar documents. "Put it over there, if you would."

He was polite to her, at least, and Llelo caught the grim look she sent him as she obeyed. He didn't know if Brigid had seen Rhys. If she hadn't, she wouldn't know that he'd brought a letter too. It might even be the most obvious one, right on top.

Llelo tried not to look at it as he said to Cadfan, "Has he gone to support Prince Hywel's defenses against Cadell at the River Elwy?" He'd said Hywel's name to keep Cadfan distracted, and it worked.

With one hand gripping the hilt of the sword, which Llelo couldn't imagine he had actually earned, Cadfan glared at him. "If you don't know, I won't tell you. You could be a spy for our enemies."

Llelo just managed to swallow down his laugh. "My father—"

But before he could finish his retort, the door to the receiving room was flung open, and two men marched a somewhat struggling Dai between them, who they proceeded to fling face down onto the floor. One of them said, in French, "We found him sneaking about in the stables, my lord!"

It was only then that the man who'd spoken realized Cadfan wasn't alone in the room. His eyes went to Llelo's face. Astonished, he pointed. "He shouldn't be here either. That's Lelo (he pronounced the name without the seemingly difficult /sh/ sound), son of Gareth ap Reese!" He toed Dai's thigh. "This is his brother! I know them from when we took Wiston three years ago."

Cadwaladr hadn't been at Wiston; nor had Cadfan.

But Cadell had. This had to be one of his men.

As Dai pushed to his hands and knees, blood dripping from the corner of his mouth where one of the guards had punched him, Cadfan took a few steps forward. "What is happening here? Is this true?"

"What have you done to him!" In high dudgeon—or doing a good job of feigning it—Brigid went to Dai and patted him down, as if looking for more wounds. "All Welsh boys look alike. You know that, my lord. This boy is my servant, whereas he—" she punctuated her words with a stab of a finger in Llelo's direction, "is someone I have never met before. If he is truly Llelo ap Gareth, he was knighted last year by the hand of Prince Henry himself. You can't touch him."

Dai then bobbed his head in a servile manner and spoke all of a sudden with a southern Welsh accent, in the whine of the truly aggrieved, "My apologies, my lord. But I don't understand what's going on. My name is Aron. I don't know this man."

Llelo had to admire Brigid's and Dai's quick thinking, even if he was internally cursing their mistake in not following his original plan for him and Dai to ride into the castle openly together. In so doing, they could have avoided this debacle.

While the guard sputtered his protest and Cadfan looked confused, Brigid's focus was on getting Dai out of the room. "Prepare my horse. We should be on our way."

"I should go too. Good day to you all and remember me to your father." Llelo spoke these last words over his shoulder, probably more tongue-in-cheek than was wise, but also the polite thing to say and something that Cadfan couldn't react to with his two guards in the room.

Llelo was out the door a moment later, Dai on his heels, pretending not to know him. Meanwhile, he could hear Brigid making her own goodbyes and then her hurrying footsteps coming after them. By the time she caught up, Dai had already disappeared inside the stables to get her horse. Dai had left Llelo's horse tied to the hitching post outside.

There, Llelo lingered a bit, checking his gear. He wanted to make sure Dai was able to lead Brigid on her horse out the main gate of the castle without pursuit. Once Llelo followed, all the way down the long road, he strained to hear a shouted command for him to stop, and the space between his shoulder blades itched, as if waiting for an arrow to strike.

Only once they were among the trees did the three of them gather again, safe from watching eyes.

Dai was feeling about within his shirt. "What did you give me?"

"A letter." Brigid was preening. "From Cadell to Cadwaladr."

"She slipped it under my shirt when she came to defend me," Dai explained to Llelo as he pulled it out. "It was a job tucking it into my waistband so it wouldn't fall onto the floor. How did you know what to look for?"

"Cadfan told me."

"He told you that his father had allied with Cadell?" Llelo asked.

"Of course not. He isn't quite that stupid. But he couldn't help boasting of his authority and how important he had become. The perfect opportunity came when you gave Cadfan your father's letter,

Llelo, and then he gave it to me. With all those papers scattered on the table, I would have grabbed any one of them and hoped for the best, but the one with Cadell's seal was right on top."

"Once I had it in my possession, my goal was to get you two out of that room as quickly as I could—along with the letter. I feared Cadfan would make me stay, and I didn't want to risk keeping it on me, which was why I gave it to Dai."

"You did amazingly." Dai had unfolded the paper and now his eyes moved back and forth as he read. "It says, in a nutshell, *I will send you the men you need to hold Llanrhystud against Hywel.*"

"So you read too?" Brigid gave a little snort. "I'm impressed. Maybe Everard should have entrusted his investigation to your father after all."

"We will get to the bottom of it, one way or the other." Llelo's tone was grim as they set out for the farmer's croft where they'd left Dai's horse. He knew as well as the other two that this letter was going to ignite Gwynedd. It was a wonder it hadn't burned Dai just to have it touching his skin. "You can tell that to Earl Richard when you see him."

"I shall. In due course. First, however, I think I'll come with you to Ysbyty Cynfyn. I would very much like to meet this father of yours. I'm thinking we have a great deal still to talk about."

37

Day Six

Gareth

As he entered the infirmary the next morning, Gareth was surprised to see Desmond on his feet, tottering among those who were sick, bringing each a bit of food if they could manage to keep anything down. "You're out of bed?"

Desmond looked up, and though his face was paler than it should be, he managed a welcoming smile. "I thought Everard was helping me. Turns out, maybe not. But I'm struggling on."

Commander Reginald had insisted on joining his fellows in the infirmary, rather than forcing the healers and caregivers to travel constantly between the infirmary and his quarters. After Geoffrey's revelation about Reginald's need for Everard's elixir, the healers had gone through their dwindling stores. They had known already that there was none left in the herb hut in the garden and, as they had feared, they had only a single small vial in the infirmary storeroom.

Unfortunately, it was so diluted by Gabriel's repeated skimming that there was hardly any poppy left in the mixture at all. This was how Gabriel had been hiding his dependency for so long, taking what he needed from what was there and replacing it with wine so neither Bardolf nor Everard would know what he was doing.

Poppy juice was an ancient remedy. And, as Bardolf and Geoffrey had each ranted in turn to Gareth, known to be extremely dangerous. That was the reason *dwale*, in which poppy was the main ingredient as well, was so carefully husbanded, not to mention made to taste so vile that few could tolerate more than a few doses, no matter their degree of pain. They did have one small jar of pure poppy juice remaining, as well as a similar portion of *dwale*, through which they could ease these men's symptoms for a few more doses.

Bardolf had thus gone to each of the men who'd been vomiting, of which there had suddenly been two more, plus Desmond, and inquired as to whether they'd been taking Everard's elixir. All seven admitted they had, and all seven had fallen asleep under a renewed small dose.

In addition, Efa had volunteered to ride to Llys Arthur. Lucan had poppies growing in his garden now, but the plants were months from harvest. They hoped he could make more poppy syrup from what he had left over from the previous year, while still leaving him with sufficient quantity to succor Joan.

Efa had departed as darkness was coming on last night, and Gareth had been keeping half an eye on the front gate all morning in the hope of her imminent return.

As was usually the case with these investigations, Gareth wished he could have known the victim better. He certainly wished he could have asked Everard a few pertinent questions. Of greater importance for the long-term, and a great fear in everyone's hearts, was how long it might take to wean the men here off of the elixir entirely. Maybe, if Gabriel was to be believed, that had been a concern close to Everard's heart in his last days too. If so, it was a concern he had shared with nobody else.

Gareth settled next to Commander Reginald's bed. He had woken a few moments earlier and appeared to be resting comfortably for now. "How long have you been taking Everard's elixir?"

Reginald didn't have the strength to resist Gareth's steady gaze. "About a year."

"Why did you take it the first time?"

"Does it matter?"

"I need to know how this all started."

"I fell on a patch of ice and broke my wrist. It looked fine from the outside, but Everard could tell it was fractured. Certainly the pain indicated it was. He splinted it, and it healed, but many nights I couldn't sleep for the pain, both from my wrist and from my lower back, which had also been hurt in the fall. That's when I started taking it."

"And then what?"

Throughout this recitation, Reginald had been looking directly at Gareth, answering easily—or as easily as seemed possible in his current state. But now, he glanced away, not as if he was remembering a past event, but as if he couldn't look Gareth in the eyes. "He gave me more."

"Everard himself gave you more?" He asked this question because Gabriel, by his own admission, had been skimming to get his doses. Everard hadn't known about those. If he had, he certainly wouldn't have approved them.

He returned his gaze to meet Gareth's. "Yes."

"All right." Gareth patted Reginald's hand and stood up. "Feel better, Father."

Reginald subsided into his bed and closed his eyes.

Bardolf had been standing a few feet away, observing their exchange. Now he said in a low but heated tone, "How could Everard have done such a thing? I thought he was my friend. And a good doctor!"

"I do believe he was your friend, and he isn't entirely to blame for what has happened here." Gareth gestured that they should walk out of the hospital and onto the path that led to the gatehouse. He didn't want anyone else to overhear.

"What do you mean?" Bardolf came with him, but his voice remained full of anger, still not understanding the nature of the situation. Not that Gareth did completely either. Not yet. "Did Reginald take the elixir or not?"

"He did take it. And at first it was Everard who gave it to him. But afterwards, my sense is that Everard would have refused him."

"So he was skimming from the doses like Gabriel? How? I would have noticed him coming to the infirmary that often. It was not his custom."

"I believe you." Gareth could appreciate why comprehension was difficult. He was still struggling to get his head around the order of events himself. "Everard did supply this hospital with his elixir, on which several, if not many, of the monks became dependent. But he did not keep supplying them. That's why I am wondering if your commander was even taking *Everard's* elixir."

"If not Everard's, then whose—" Bardolf broke off, his eyes widening.

Gareth nodded. "I will question the others as soon as I can. Until then, keep them separated. I don't want them coordinating their stories. If your commander can lie to my face, I have to wonder how many other lies I've been told this week. How many in this community have been lying to me all along?"

38

Day Six

Gwen

Gwen's stepmother was both an outsider and one of the most organized people Gwen had ever known, so it was probably no surprise that she had become the one person Bardolf trusted enough to go once again through the herb hut. It wasn't just a few patients who were sick now. It was the commander himself. And Gabriel. And Desmond!

They needed to find Everard's recipe or, barring that, more poppy. So far, Saran had placed each jar, vial, and pot on the large worktable in the center of the room. As it was eight feet long and four feet wide, there was plenty of room for most everything. Already her back was tired from bending over, trying to see what was in each container.

Once inspected, each could be returned to a shelf. In Gwen's experience, organization was usually done by ailment, so remedies for the stomach were on one shelf, heart on another, head elsewhere, and so on. The drawback to this method was that many herbs could physick multiple ailments. An experienced healer, who had organized the workshop him or herself, would know where everything was, but a stranger would struggle.

As Saran and Gwen had done.

Everard's workshop was not organized in the traditional way. It had taken Saran some time to discern that Everard had sorted his herbs and remedies alphabetically by their Latin names, which he would have learned during his studies before coming to Wales.

"Did you already know the Latin names of all these herbs?" Gwen asked, having now emptied all the shelves.

"Sadly, no."

"So how are we to put them back in a way that anyone can find what they need?"

"Everything is labeled, and I have kept careful notes on how Everard left things." Saran held up her ledger, all but identical to Gwen's own, in which she wrote observations and treatments. Gareth had a similar ledger for investigations, which Gwen mostly left to him. If he wanted assistance in describing something that had happened, she was always ready to help.

"I don't have to ask why the physicians aren't taking part in this themselves," Gwen said dryly. "While they are anxious for the recipe or the elixir, it's also a lot of work!"

"They have quite enough to do without doing this. Besides, Bardolf assured me that he could never find anything in here before, so any progress I make can only be helpful."

"He likes you."

Saran laughed. "I think he appreciates my willingness to do what is needed without complaint. He knows that I may have more experience with healing than any of the monks here, barring perhaps Everard."

"Who is no longer with us."

"Just so." Saran made a motion with her head. "It is my impression that the monks who worked with Everard were more than a little intimidated by him and, until they became desperate, were reluctant to touch anything inside this hut. This was *his* kingdom, which he ruled absolutely. Even with him dead, they have felt like they're trespassing. Only desperation had Gabriel going through the vials and bottles yesterday during our meeting."

Gwen set a bowl of rose petals next to a vial of a dark liquid labeled *Foeniculum,* under which Saran had written in a fine hand *fennel.* It was often used to aid digestion. "I assume that his ledgers, both here and in the remedy storeroom, show no sign of the elixir recipe everyone is looking for?"

"No. Believe me, we have all tried to find it." Saran flipped open Everard's ledger to show it to Gwen. Truly Bardolf had been right when he'd told Llelo that they had an amazing family. Saran had learned to read long before she'd married Meilyr. But Gwen knew, because she knew her father, that if Saran hadn't known how by then, she would have been made to learn. "It's the third one we're looking for."

"Couldn't you just make more poppy syrup?"

"I could, but our stores of poppy heads are gone. Lucan's supply, if he has one, is our only option."

The ledger wasn't on the shelves with the herbs, so Gwen was well on her way to deciding that Everard had hidden it deliberately. If she was right about that (and if it existed at all), she thus needed to think about possible hiding places.

While the walls of the hut appeared to be a single board-width thick, they had found secret compartments before where they'd least expected them. It wasn't long before Gwen was crawling on her hands and knees on the wooden floor, tapping each board, trying to get a sense of what was underneath.

"Everard wasn't young," Saran commented as she watched her out of the corner of her eye. "I don't think you can understand yet, even pregnant as you are, but I can tell you right now he wasn't crawling on his knees every day to get to his journal. He would have wanted to keep it more accessible."

"That's why he should have hidden it in his bed chamber." Gwen sat back on her heels. "It wasn't there."

"Maybe it was. The intruder could have found it and thought that was all there was to find. If so, you are wasting your time."

"That's what I thought I was doing when we found the rock used to bludgeon him in the church."

"Keeping looking, then." Saran went back to her work. "He wouldn't have put it between the floor and the earth either because he wouldn't have wanted it to get wet."

"Not the floor; not the ceiling, which is open to the thatch." Gwen made a gesture that encompassed the hut as a whole. It was some twelve feet square and sturdily built. "With the weather what it is, the roof has the same problem as the floor."

In truth, Gwen was surprised that the hut had a wooden floor at all, since she would have thought a dirt floor would have been more utilitarian, soaking up spills and avoiding the little burned patches she could see dotted here and there. In that case, Everard could have wrapped the book in oilskin and buried it in the ground. That would not have been accessible either, however.

Still on the floor, Gwen thought back through everything they'd learned so far about Everard.

He was kind.

He liked to laugh.

He hated to see anyone in pain.

He also liked nice things, even as he maintained the trappings of a good monk.

With his wealth, he could have paid for improvements to his fiefdom and not told anyone about it. Out loud, she said, "The walls are thin enough to indicate that nothing can be hidden in them. Otherwise I see shelves and more shelves, a large worktable, and—"

She cut herself off, curling up over her knees and, in as smooth a motion as possible for a pregnant woman, rolled onto her back, putting her face up underneath the large table. The table had been constructed with support boards running around all four sides below the tabletop. Just behind one of the boards on a long side, about the length of her forearm towards the middle of the table, was a shelf. It had been suspended in such a way that nobody would ever notice it, even if they squatted to the floor, unless they were looking, as Gwen had finally done.

"I found it!" A corner of a book was sticking out over the edge of the shelf. She grabbed it and then worked her way out from underneath the table. It was harder getting out than it had been getting in. Levering herself awkwardly to her feet with the help of the table, she handed the journal triumphantly to Saran.

Saran opened the first page, and then quickly flipped through the rest. Not standing on ceremony, Gwen looked over her shoulder. She already knew from the ledgers he'd left that Everard wrote with a fine hand and drew nearly as well as Gareth. In those books, he'd catalogued a huge number of herbs, each with their Latin name and accompanied by a list of ingredients as well as symptoms the potion cured, all in French.

This ledger, by contrast, contained line after line of tiny writing, in what appeared to be a daily journal. The letters were so small Gwen had to peer closely to make them out. Initially, the entries were a matter of a paragraph or two and not illuminating, being literally about what he'd eaten and how many patients he'd seen. Interspersed, every so often, not on every page but every few pages, were short strings of numbers.

"Are these accounts?" Gwen tried to make sense of an opening combination that read, 1 31 3 14. This was followed by 3 15 23 5.

"I have no idea." Saran took a few steps to stand in the doorway of the hut, giving them both more light by which to read. "If they are, I have no idea what he's counting."

Gwen stared at another string for so long her eyes crossed. "Could it be a code that only makes sense to you if you're Everard?"

Saran closed the ledger with a snap and handed it to Gwen. "Go be Everard. Read the book and decipher the code. Find out what he was hiding—and the recipe if it's in there to be found."

Gwen blinked. "Me?"

"You have seen codes before. I suspect, you have used them."

"Well, yes, but—"

"The investigation takes precedence over this mess." Saran waved a hand to indicate the hut. "You're the spy, *cariad.* I'll be occupied here for some time to come. Rope in your father while you're at it. He needs entertainment, and Everard's journal should keep you both busy for a good long while."

39

Day Six

Meilyr

Meilyr had been entertaining Taran with chords on his crwth, a stringed instrument, when his daughter had dropped Everard's book into his lap, literally and figuratively. That was hours ago now, and while he had worked his way through many pages of the physician's tiny writing, he was starting to doubt his own abilities regarding the code.

Gwen had shared the book in part because she valued his intelligence, but it was surely also because she was afraid for him. He had been very ill and was still not entirely well, not like Gareth, Llelo, or—praise the Lord—little Taran, who were up and about as if they'd never been ill at all. Meilyr, by contrast, could still feel the weight on his chest of whatever had clouded his lungs. He couldn't sing yet either, and he was starting to be afraid that he might never be able to sing again.

Gwen had dismissed that fear, but she had also kept coming his way a constant stream of warm drink, whether an herbal infusion cooked up by Saran or very watered down mead. He had learned to keep an eye on his consumption of alcohol, and none of them wanted a relapse into dependency. What he hadn't said to her as he accepted another warm beverage, was that, at the moment, he couldn't taste anything anyway.

"Let's go over this again." Gwen had a piece of paper in front of her, separated from any of the papers in Everard's journal. She had been painstakingly copying the numbers from the book, trying to turn them into letters and then manipulate them so they made sense.

They'd already tried substituting them alphabetically and reading them from right to left instead of left to right. Once they figured out with what letters the numbers were supposed to correspond, they would be able to determine in what language Everard had written. Meilyr knew it wouldn't be Welsh, but he was hoping for French or Latin, rather than Greek.

That was, of course, if the numbers were supposed to coincide with letters at all and weren't some code of their own having to do with, as Gwen had first thought, accounts.

"I honestly have never seen anything like this." Meilyr took Gwen's pen from her hand and tried a few changes of his own. The journal, which so far they had not shared with Bardolf (Meilyr chose not to feel more than a twinge of guilt at that lapse), had made Everard seem both more relatable and more intelligent, even if also obsessed with secrecy. It wasn't every man who could in the same book write about his bathroom habits while also expressing himself in an impenetrable code. Meilyr truly hoped the code, once deciphered, wasn't about the workings of Everard's innards too. "Could Everard have been a musician?"

Gwen looked at him a bit sideways. "I suppose, but not that I have heard. Why?"

"Well, these could be finger positions corresponding with notes."

"I don't recall a forty-third finger position anywhere."

"No, but what if Everard meant the fourth and then the third."

"Like with the music the monks sing here, using that song sheet in the shape of a hand with every note laid out between one and fourteen." Gwen frowned. "That would limit what you could say by the letters available."

Meilyr himself had a copy of the sheet in question amongst his papers, and they both studied it. "It just repeats *A* through *G* over and over again."

"That's true, Tad, but you may be on to something. The key wouldn't have to come from music, would it? Where else can we find numbers and letters together?"

Meilyr gave a little snort. "The Bible."

Gwen frowned. "Do you mean when it talks about the ages of Abraham and Sarah?"

Meilyr laughed. "No, I mean every passage has a number. John 3:16, for example."

Gwen sat up a little straighter. "Didn't Gareth say Everard had a book of the gospels in his room?"

Before Meilyr could protest that he had one too, she was gone, racing out the door. She must have run all the way to the warming room where Gareth was back to speaking with every monk in the monastery today. Over the course of the morning, he had gone from one vomiting man to another, asking them about how they had begun their descent into dependency. Much like Commander Reginald, each had claimed Everard had started them off on it, which on the whole Meilyr believed, and that he'd encouraged their dependency.

Gareth was convinced they were all lying, and that Lucan was involved somehow.

Then Gwen returned with the book, huffing as she entered the room. "I didn't even have to ask where he'd put it. Gareth had it on him. He's been carrying it around this whole time!"

Then Gareth himself loomed in the doorway. "I don't know what you're doing, but it's obviously important."

"It has to do with deciphering Everard's code." Gwen handed the Book of the Gospels to Meilyr. "We think the numbers relate to a passage."

Gareth lifted Taran into his arms. The little boy had been fussing for the last quarter of an hour about being hungry.

Relieved of child duty, Meilyr set to work. To his mind, the first number had to indicate a gospel, of which there were only four. Then came the chapter within the book, then the passage, and then the word within the passage. He read each number out loud before writing the word that corresponded.

Thus, a number series that went 1 31 3 14 referred to book one (Matthew), chapter thirty-one, verse three, word fourteen. Or, if Everard had been trickier, it could be book one, chapter three, verse thirteen, word fourteen. Or maybe even book one, chapter three, verse thirteen, word one, *letter four*. It was all still trial and error, and was going to take time before they could craft a message that made any kind of sense.

Now Gareth shifted to sit with Taran on the table next to Meilyr, bouncing the boy on his knee. "Why would Everard write in such an elaborate code?"

"To keep a secret," Meilyr said absently, still laboring away—and truly hoping against hope that they'd got *something* right this time.

Then he reared back as all of a sudden the next three words appeared as if by magic in front of him: *finger, fox,* and *flower.* The first was mentioned in John, the next in Luke, and the third in Matthew. *Digitalis,* which was the Latin word for *foxglove,* meant *finger-like.*

"Keep a fox glove flower." Gwen looked over his shoulder at what he'd written. "Are we looking at a recipe, advice—or a warning?"

Gareth made a motion with his hand. "Keep on with it. There's lots more there." He stood up, Taran still in his arms.

"Where are you going?" Meilyr asked. "Don't you want to see how this turns out?"

"More than anything, but you won't be grateful for me hovering over you, nor having hungry children underfoot. Gwen and I will take the young ones away so you can keep working. If Everard was sending secret messages, little can be more important at this point than what they said and to whom he was sending them."

40

Day Six

Gwen

This was a moment Gwen would remember for the rest of her life.

Some might think the yard in front of the guesthouse was a strange place for revelations but, to Gwen's mind, it wasn't inappropriate, given the way their investigation had gone so far (and, to be fair, the way their investigations usually went).

The first element was perhaps the most outwardly innocuous, as it arrived in the form of the same gravedigger, Donald, who had waited so patiently days ago at the burial of Desmond's mother, Helen, and then afterwards, at Everard's. He loped to where Gwen and Gareth were standing on the cobbles in front of the gatehouse, saying goodbye. Taran and Tangwen were racing each other from one end of the courtyard to the other.

Gareth had tasked himself with riding to Llys Arthur because Healer Efa had still not returned from her mission to collect more poppy juice. They needed to find out why that was. And they needed the poppy juice. Gareth was hoping against hope that he wasn't about to find Efa's body too. Or Joan's.

"Before he fell ill Commander Reginald asked me to give this to you, but I confess I forgot until now when I found it again among my tools." What Donald held was an iron garden stake, eight inches long, with a sharp point on one end and a spiral ring on the other.

"Where did he find it?" Gareth accepted the stake like the gift from heaven it was.

"In the dirt between the grave of Helen and that of the young man without a name we just buried. Even when he spoke to me, I think the commander already wasn't feeling well, and with every-thing that happened yesterday, I just forgot."

Gareth turned the garden stake over in his hands. It was a formidable weapon,

Donald leaned closer. "Is this what killed Everard?"

"Perhaps."

It was a good thing Gwen wasn't answering because she would have said *definitely yes!* She had no trouble imagining the point being driven into Everard's ear.

"I've never heard of anyone killing with a garden stake." Don-ald motioned towards the spiral on the end. "What's that for?"

"So the small plants can grow up through it without being bent by the wind." Gwen said. "We have many similar to it in the herb garden here, though I wouldn't have said they are exactly the same."

"I know where I've seen one just like it." Gareth interrupted her with an unusual abruptness. "This one is identical to those Lucan uses in his garden."

Then the second piece of revelation arrived in the form of a woman's voice calling from the entrance to the commandery as her horse's hooves clattered on the flagstones at the gatehouse. "He's gone! He's gone! My brother is gone."

They turned to see Joan, windswept, weak, and near to falling off her horse, now that she'd actually reached the commandery and relieved herself of her urgent message.

Gareth ran to help Brother Mark and ended up carrying Joan himself. Rather than going to the infirmary, with its plethora of vomiting men, he headed towards the guesthouse, Gwen running ahead of him to get the door.

"I can walk." Joan struggled in his arms. "I'm fine."

"You are clearly not fine. You shouldn't be here at all!" Gareth had a grim determination in his voice indicating he was masking his real emotion, which was fear—and perhaps grief.

"I had to come. Lucan is gone and that healer, Efa, with him."

41

Day Six

Gareth

Once in the common room, Gwen settled Taran and Tangwen at the table with slices of fresh bread and butter to distract them. Meanwhile, Gareth placed Joan in the one suitable chair near the fire, with cushions against which she could rest. She had flat-out refused a bed.

She did accept a cup of warm mead and took a tentative sip. Finally, she was able to relax against the cushions and let out a trembling breath. Saran approached to sit on a low stool before her. Taking her hand, she felt her pulse, which Gareth could tell even from a distance was racing.

"Are you in pain?" Saran asked.

Joan, of everyone who lived in and around the commandery, was the one person for whom a poppy remedy was legitimately required.

"Of course, but it isn't too bad." Joan took another sip of mead. "I had to come."

"I was just on my way to you." Gareth's voice was full of regret.

She looked up at him. "I believe you, but I couldn't know that, and I knew you needed the information I had. After Efa arrived yesterday, she and Lucan spent hours in his workshop. All night, really. He refused to tell me what he was doing. I think he even gave me an extra dose of poppy in my wine because I fell asleep early and didn't wake until he entered my room again at noon to say he was leaving. He said the monks at the commandery needed a poppy recipe he'd learned from Everard. He told me where he'd put it and included a quantity of the elixir so I could arrange for it to be sent. I actually brought both with me in my bags."

At that, Gwen put a hand on Saran's shoulder, indicating she would take her place, so Saran could get the potion to those who needed it. It wasn't ideal to keep everyone dosed, and they would have to be weaned off it, but that would happen more easily if they took the time to do it, rather than simply running out.

Joan began to weep. "Before he left, Lucan confessed he had been selling his elixir to the men in the commandery, long before Everard died."

"Did he admit to murdering Everard?" Gareth's tone couldn't have been more urgent.

"I did ask him that. I had to! But he said it wasn't him." She made a motion with her head from side to side and even that seemed to give her some pain. "Besides, I knew already that he hadn't. He couldn't possibly have ridden all the way to Ysbyty Cynfyn and back that evening."

"He went to the inn," Gareth said.

"And then he came straight home."

"You said you'd been sleeping," Gwen said. "You know how the poppy acts to confuse. He may have counted on it."

"And then we have this." Gareth brought out the garden stake. "It was found next to Helen's grave. It's one of Lucan's."

Joan had already reared back at the sight of it, indicating she knew what it was.

"We believe it to be the murder weapon," Gareth added. "Lucan must have left it in the coffin, not realizing it wouldn't be buried with Helen. When the coffin overturned next to the grave, it fell into the dirt along with the body."

"That isn't the only explanation." Joan's voice was weak, but she still managed to convey her indignation. "He often shares his plants with the commandery. The herb garden here must have dozens of these because they don't get returned to him. Lucan would never kill Everard. Never!"

Gwen forced herself to speak gently. "Perhaps they had a falling out over the poppy remedy. We know from Gabriel that Everard had learned he was taking it. Maybe he discovered that others were too and that Lucan was supplying them. But Lucan was making too much money to give it up."

"Murdering another man over coin is the oldest crime there is." Gareth meant that literally, as the murder of Abel by Cain had been over their father's inheritance.

Joan kept shaking her head. "I don't believe it. Lucan would never hurt anyone. He started making the poppy remedy in the first place because he hated to see me in pain. Besides, his whole life he has fainted at the sight of blood. It was one of the things that made other men so disdainful of him, including my father and brother—and my husband! He pricks his finger on a rose bush and has to lie down. He told me when you were visiting that he cut himself with a knife while chopping a root and embarrassed himself in front of your son."

"Maybe that's why he used the stake as his murder weapon," Gareth said. "There was very little blood involved. Any inhibition can be overcome if a man is desperate enough."

"I don't believe it." Joan closed her eyes. "I won't believe it. You have him all wrong."

"Joan?" Gwen leaned forward, her hand on the arm of the chair. "Are you all right?"

"I just need to sleep for a moment." And, within a dozen heartbeats, though her chest continued to rise and fall, Joan was no longer responsive.

42

Day Six

Meilyr

Meilyr had been doing a great deal of thinking on his own. He wasn't one to take part in Gwen's investigations beyond what she asked of him. He was a bard, and he was an old man. Murder was a young man's game; solving murder even more so.

But Everard's journal was a different matter. It was he who had taught her and Hywel to read all those years ago. He himself had been fascinated by patterns since he was a small child. What was music but the same notes put into different patterns? There was little he loved more than writing a new song, second only to performing it. The code in Everard's ledger was nothing more than a pattern. But even having discovered the key, it had been hours of work to decipher it all.

Now he put up a hand to draw Gareth and Gwen from the sleeping woman. "Everard did regret making the elixir."

They swung around to look at him, a bit of hope showing in their faces. It had been six days since the discovery of Everard's body. By now, they knew far more about the running of the commandery and the whereabouts of a wide variety of people associated with it than they had when they'd started. And while Lucan sounded like the best candidate for murderer they'd encountered so far, Meilyr felt in his belly that this wasn't the whole story.

"Everard began his sojourn here with the best of intentions." Meilyr gestured to the journal before him. "By his own hand before his death he admitted he knew what was going on at the commandery. At first he didn't know its source, and it infuriated him, especially because it had been he who, for one ailment or another, had started many on his special elixir in the first place."

"Did you find the recipe?" Gwen asked.

"Not yet, but see here—" he tipped up the book, "—a page has been ripped out, by Everard, or someone else, I couldn't say. It looks like he learned within a few days of his death what we now know: Commander Reginald had developed a need for the elixir and had started working with Lucan to augment the supply coming into the commandery. Lucan's potion was different from Everard's, however, since no matter their closeness, Everard hadn't shared his recipe. Everard feared Lucan's was the more potent.

"But here's the real news for you: in the days before he died, Everard confronted Lucan about supplying the commandery, and Lucan confessed his part in it. Everard writes further that he regretted his request to Earl Richard, since he'd made it before he'd discovered the truth about the overuse of the elixir at the commandery. He feared an outsider would expose what was happening, and the commandery would be censured—or even dissolved. To avert that disaster, he and Lucan discussed how to begin weaning the men off the elixir, which Lucan claimed he'd had no idea could create such a dependency."

"When exactly was this?" Gwen took a step forward.

Meilyr made a motion with his fingers. "There's no date, but it's here, at the very end."

"We don't believe Lucan, though, do we?" Gareth looked over at Gwen. "That Everard points the finger at Lucan is all the more reason to think he's the murderer. He wanted to stop all this from coming out."

Meilyr held up a hand again for their attention. "Everard also suspected some deaths in the commandery were related to the trade, and that Commander Reginald himself, because he feared losing his dosing, was covering up those deaths."

"When Earl Richard sent me here, he knew only a small part of that." Into the room stepped a red-haired woman, speaking Welsh, who could only be the mysterious Brigid. "Everard *had* written to the earl about some suspicious deaths. I came because of them. But the night I met with him, he told me he'd got it wrong, and there was nothing to worry about."

Behind her came Meilyr's grandsons. Llelo went immediately to Meilyr and put a hand on his shoulder. "Brigid named Nain's brother, Iago, as one of those who died under suspicious circumstances."

Gwen had both hands to her cheeks. "So if Commander Reginald was covering up the deaths in the infirmary—potentially the very ones Iago was concerned about—and Lucan murdered Everard—"

"Except that I didn't." Lucan himself shouldered his way through the doorway, brushing past Dai and making straight for his sister.

Meilyr said in an undertone to Llelo, "The next time we have a private conversation, we should either have it out in the open so we can see people coming, or post a guard."

Gareth blocked Lucan's progress across the room. "Don't come any closer. We know about your trade in the poppy remedy. We know you murdered Everard."

"I admit to the former, but never the latter." Lucan's tone was commanding. If he maintained his innocence, as a nobleman, no court would convict him.

"It was your garden stake used to murder him," Gareth said.

"Those are everywhere, and you know it. Although elements of my activities may have been unwise, I did what I did with the best of intentions, to help my sister and those suffering as she does."

Behind Gareth, Joan stirred but, despite the intensity of the conversation going on around her, she didn't wake.

"You hid what you were doing from Everard," Gwen said.

Lucan bent his head. "When it became clear how many men were in need of the elixir, how many men *Everard* had started on it, I kept it coming. That I won't deny, even if I now feel nothing but sorrow at my actions."

He did sound genuinely contrite, and Meilyr could see how this mistake could have been made. Poppy appeared to be a far more powerful remedy than alcohol. No man would ever fall under its spell by choice.

Lucan continued in a steady voice: "You need to know that it was Commander Reginald himself who came to me in the first place, asking me to make the elixir and offering to pay me for it. As the money he paid me came from my sister's own silver mine in the first place, I felt I was just getting it back." He paused. "And then Everard told me how the men at the commandery had grown to need my elixir. It had to stop. The next time he came to visit Joan, I gave him everything I had prepared, except for a portion for my sister. I had hardly anything left! And what I did have left, I have now given you."

"When did you give your elixir to Everard?" Gareth said.

"On the day he died." For the first time, Lucan looked ashamed. "Before Everard told me, I didn't realize what was happening; I swear it!"

"We have only your word for this," Gwen said. "Nobody has been able to find the elixir you claim you gave him. You could even be telling the truth about giving it to him, but neglecting to mention you took it back after you killed him."

"I told you, I didn't kill him! I had nothing to do with his death. It wasn't as if I was trying to hide what I was doing anymore. Commander Reginald already knew. Everyone who had any power over me knew."

"You would have had no reason to kill Everard ... if that was all there was to it." Meilyr held up Everard's ledger. "But we know from Everard's own hand, not to mention what you just admitted, that the trade was going to end. You were going to lose your income."

Lucan swallowed.

Gwen found herself frowning. "That's true … so, once Everard was dead, there should have been no impediment to continuing. You should have kept the doses coming, maybe even more so than before. Why didn't you?"

Everyone watched Lucan, Meilyr himself holding his breath. He hadn't often been part of Gareth and Gwen's investigations at the moment they came to a head. He was, in a word, *fascinated.*

"Because what I am saying is true." All of a sudden, Lucan didn't appear defensive, or angry, or outraged. If anything, his shoulders slumped in despondence. "I was only trying to help people. I gave Everard everything I had. And once I realized the damage I'd done, I couldn't just start up again as if nothing had happened. I swore to him I wouldn't make any more. And I didn't, not until Efa came yesterday and told me that what I'd given Everard had never reached the commandery."

Gareth turned to Brigid, who'd been looking on in silence as they'd interrogated Lucan. "Did Everard say anything about any of this to you in the inn?"

"Not exactly. But what he did say now makes better sense." She shook her head wonderingly. "He told me he'd just come from visiting a sick patient whose brother had been growing poppies, trying to replicate his elixir. He didn't see the need to bring it to anyone else's attention, since growing poppies wasn't against the law of any land."

"Did he mention that he'd brought that supply away with him?" Gareth asked.

"Oh, yes. He was in high good spirits because he couldn't wait to add it to the commandery's stores."

43

Day Six

Gwen

Lucan was finally allowed to go to his sister. As he sat heavily on the stool, he asked, "So, where did it go?"

"We don't know," Gwen said, "though honestly we hadn't known to look until now."

Lucan gave a shake of his head. "I don't have any more elixir to give you. If you can't find it, we'll have to wait until this current crop of poppies ripens." He bit his lip as he looked at Joan, who was still asleep. "I will not give up what I've saved for her."

"We wouldn't ask you to." Gwen studied his slumped form. "You were actually going to leave her?"

"Of course not! Why would you think that?"

"Joan thought you had."

"She misunderstood." He was displaying none of the usual twitches and tics that indicated lying. He believed in what he was saying. "I was going to get Efa away, some place safe, and then return."

"So what happened?" Gareth asked.

"I hadn't ridden more than a mile down the road from the manor when I realized I couldn't leave Joan, even for a day. We returned to find she had already ridden away. One of the servants told me she'd come here, so I followed."

"And Efa?" Gwen said.

"She stayed at the manor, afraid to ever set foot in Ysbyty Cynfyn again."

"I don't understand," Gwen said. "Why was she your concern, rather than your sister?"

Lucan's mouth fell open as he looked around the room at everyone's intent faces. "She—" He stopped. "You don't know?"

All of a sudden, Gwen did. "Efa was your go-between, wasn't she? She was the one who carried the supply of elixir from Llys Arthur to the commandery." She paused as she looked at Lucan curiously. "Is she the one who gave the commander the idea to come to you in the first place?"

Lucan couldn't have been more deflated. "Neither of us meant any harm. Don't blame her. This is my fault."

"How do we know that this now is the real truth?" Gareth said. "Maybe what you're doing, more than anything, is protecting Efa."

"I told you what she did, didn't I? And what I did. I haven't made a secret of the fact that we are together!"

"Maybe you murdered Everard together," Gwen said. "She couldn't have lifted his body into the coffin, but she is perfectly capable of skewering a man. And then when she told you what she'd done, you helped hide him."

Lucan gaped at Gwen. "You have us all wrong—" he swallowed hard, "—if you must know, when I returned from The Castle inn that night, Efa was in my chamber."

Gwen didn't think much of Lucan providing Efa's alibi, when Efa herself had given Gwen a different one. For now, however, this was definitive. And plausible, truth be told. Too much had to have been happening at the same time for Efa to have managed it all. "Ideally, she could confirm that. When I questioned her, she told me she was sitting with an ill man."

"She was protecting me."

"And now you're protecting her." Gwen might have thought this was romantic if it also hadn't obstructed their investigation.

Brigid had been standing off to one side, her arms folded across her chest. "So if Lucan didn't murder Everard, who did? Are we really considering this Efa person? Why would she do that?"

"For the same reason Lucan might—money. I am completely willing to believe she would murder two men if it served her interests." Gwen put out a hand. "And I say that with complete admiration."

Lucan, however, had latched onto a different aspect what Gwen had said. "*Two men*? Somebody else is dead?"

His surprise appeared genuine, and if the rest of the conversation hadn't convinced Gwen of Lucan's innocence, she was coming to believe it now.

Not that he was *innocent*. Just innocent of murder.

Brigid's face held surprise too, as did that of Gwen's sons. They had all walked into the room in mid-sentence. It had been dramatic, certainly, but it had also limited their understanding of the recent course of the investigation. They couldn't know about the body found in the river.

Joan was finally awake too. Even her exhaustion and illness couldn't forever mask the commotion in the guesthouse common room. Thus, Gwen and Gareth were able to relate to everyone all at once the discovery of the body of the young man. Although he was buried, his horse was safe in the commandery's stables. Brigid would know if it had been his.

Then Llelo and Dai explained how they'd met Brigid, though they stopped short of a full explanation of their journey, making it sound as if they'd been sent after her from the start. The treachery of Cadwaladr was not for the ears of anyone but those who'd encountered Rhys.

"Baldwin." Brigid blinked back tears. "His name was Baldwin, and he wasn't really a servant at all, more a friend and certainly someone trusted by the Earl of Pembroke. He really was murdered alongside Everard?"

"So it seems. The method was the same." Gareth drew her attention to the garden stake he'd left on the common room table. "Did Everard indicate he was worried about being followed?"

"Not at all," Brigid said. "In truth, part of me didn't really believe him when he said he'd raised the alarm unduly. If not for his cheerful manner, I would have wondered if someone hadn't got to him first and frightened him into not talking. That lingering doubt is the reason I sent Baldwin after him."

"There's nothing more in the diary," Meilyr said. "His focus was on his commandery and what the elixir had done to it."

"I spent less time with the journal than my father, but I didn't find anything in my reading either." Gwen glanced at Brigid. "Did he say if he'd spoken to anyone else about his concerns?"

Brigid shook her head. "He specifically said he hadn't. And certainly, if he still thought Commander Reginald was covering up deaths in the infirmary, he wouldn't have had anyone to talk *to*."

They all thought about that for a moment, and then Gwen said, "In truth, I had dismissed out of hand the possibility that Commander Reginald could have murdered Everard, simply because of his size. He is shorter than I am, and slender. He could not have lifted Everard into that coffin by himself."

"His thinness is partly a result of the poppy. It suppresses the appetite." Lucan still held his sister's hand. "Something else that is my fault."

"Is that why none of the men who are ill are mighty creatures?" Llelo's voice was infused with horror. "I was dosed with it too!"

"It doesn't work that quickly." Lucan put out a hand to him. "Its continual use is what degrades the body over time."

"Regardless, I wouldn't have said any of the users would have had the strength to lift Everard's dead body into the coffin, even if they were desperate to stop him from cutting off their supply of the elixir," Gareth said. "And that's only if he'd told them he was going to do it. Alternatively, none could have wrestled the coffin with Helen's dead body inside it to the floor and then lifted it back onto the saw-horses once it contained both bodies."

"Not alone, anyway," Dai said.

Gareth made a rueful face. "That first day, right after the discovery of Everard's body, Warden Geoffrey told us that every man in the commandery was accounted for after Compline except for Everard. That was why Commander Reginald could suppose the murderer came from outside the commandery, and one reason I looked to Lucan in the first place." He made a gesture in the direction of the man himself. "That, your size, and the poppies."

"He didn't do it." Joan was still insistent.

Gwen wanted to throw up her hands at the way they'd come full circle yet again.

Except ...

She and her husband looked at each other, and she saw the moment the same thought she'd just had occurred to him too.

He spoke slowly. "Everyone was accounted for during the time of the murder ..."

"... because Geoffrey accounted for them." Gwen finished the thought.

"Unless—" Llelo sucked in a breath, "—unless he knew who'd done it and was protecting the culprit."

Dai scoffed. "Unless *he* did it."

44

Day Six

Gareth

areth and Gwen halted in the doorway of the infirmary, neither wanting to move to where Warden Geoffrey was sitting with Commander Reginald. Physician Gabriel was also bent over a patient's bed. His dependency on the elixir truly appeared to be unrelated to everyone else's. As a physician, he had been able to get what he needed by skimming from the hospital supply. It only went to show yet again how dangerous poppy could be.

Their hesitation was partly out of a desire not to disrupt the functioning of the infirmary and partly because they had engendered Geoffrey's guilt out of whole cloth. That still didn't mean he wasn't the one man among all those they'd encountered who had the means, the ability, and the time to have been wandering the commandery late at night.

As they waited for Geoffrey to notice them, Gareth internally reviewed his conversation with Gwen as they'd walked from the guesthouse to the infirmary.

"Geoffrey seemed genuinely surprised to realize Reginald had been taking the poppy remedy," Gwen had said. "He fooled me completely."

Gareth had genuinely *liked* Geoffrey. He respected him. He didn't want him to have murdered anyone. "People have an amazing capacity to lie when their lives are on the line. Men can convince themselves of almost anything."

"Almost? I don't think you have to qualify that statement."

Finally, Geoffrey glanced over at them. When they didn't attempt to speak to him, but also didn't move from the doorway, he turned his head to look at them more directly, gazing into Gareth's face for a dozen heartbeats. Then he leaned forward to kiss Reginald's forehead and said a few words Gareth couldn't hear. Holding up one finger in their direction, telling them to wait, he strode towards the remedy room and disappeared inside. Since it had no windows and no other way in or out, Gareth didn't begrudge him a moment to speak to whomever was inside. That person replied in a tone low enough for Gareth to know he was speaking but not to hear his words. A moment later, Geoffrey exited carrying a cup, which he left on Reginald's side table.

Only then did he make his way across the infirmary to Gareth. Stopping in front of him, he said, "You know."

"We do." Then Gareth motioned with his head that they should leave the infirmary. Like so many conversations this week, this one was not to be had in front of anyone other than those he and Gwen had already chosen—namely Brigid and Saran, who by now would be waiting for them in the healer's hut. Brigid was not a natural ally, but Gareth saw the benefit of having a servant of the Earl of Pembroke as witness.

When Geoffrey stepped inside the hut and took in the faces of the women, his face showed genuine regret, before it smoothed to one of impassivity. "First and foremost, you must all be wondering *why*."

"We know the *how*." Gwen indicated the skewer on the central table, brought from the guesthouse by Brigid.

"Ah." Geoffrey bobbed a nod. "You found it." Then he frowned. "Odd that it sent you to me, though. I'm no gardener."

"We have spoken with Lucan," Gareth said. "His whereabouts are accounted for that evening. Yours are not."

"And you believed him even though he's the right size and build to have lifted Everard's weight, *and* he resented the affection his sister felt for Everard?" Geoffrey asked his question like it was obvious, and they would have been remiss in not noting it. "Why don't you believe Lucan killed Everard? With her marriage, Lucan would lose his position."

"What are you talking about?" Gareth shook his head like a fly was buzzing around it. "Everard wasn't going to marry Joan."

"Of course, he was."

"Not according to Joan," Gareth said.

"Why would she admit to it, now that he's dead?" Geoffrey snorted. "He told me himself how much he loved her."

"When was this?" Gwen asked.

"Before his death, obviously. In confession." For the first time, in the casual way Geoffrey violated the sanctity of the confessional, Gareth saw the man who'd murdered Everard. "He told me he doubted his vocation—not as a physician, mind you, but as a monk. He and Joan had grown close over the past year. He wanted to marry her and make however long she had left a joy. I had to protect the commandery from such a disaster." He made a gesture to encompass the hut but probably meant the commandery as a whole. "If Everard had married Joan, he would have become the landed nobleman of his birth."

Though Gareth still felt like staring, he managed to wrestle his expression back into that of an impartial investigator. "She couldn't have given him a child."

Geoffrey dismissed the idea with a wave of his hand. "He would have ruled from Llys Arthur for the rest of his natural life and deprived the commandery of considerable wealth, especially with the discovery of that new vein of silver." He stated this as if it too was an obvious fact.

"Remind me." Gareth decided to pretend he knew what Geoffrey was talking about. "When was it found?"

Geoffrey shrugged. "The evening before."

By that, he meant *the evening before I murdered Everard.* Even with his matter-of-fact manner, Geoffrey couldn't bring himself to actually say the words.

He did continue unprompted, however: "Our foreman was full of the news. He couldn't wait to tell me. Commander Reginald was ecstatic. But then, he didn't know what I knew about Everard's plans."

Saran had been rocking back and forth on the balls of her feet, as if impatient with this entire conversation, and finally stepped in. "Are you saying that your grievance against Everard had nothing to do with the poppy trade?"

Geoffrey allowed himself a grunt of deep disgust. "Idiot that I was; naïve fool that I was; I didn't know about any of that until yesterday. I wasn't sorry to learn what had been going on, of course, since it made Lucan even more likely to have murdered Everard. My choice to use his gardening stake became even more perfect."

"And my servant, Baldwin?" Brigid spoke for the first time.

Geoffrey's face again showed real regret. "He came into the church as I was putting Everard's body in the coffin. There wasn't room for three bodies in there, so I dumped him in the river upstream and set the horse free. I had a job getting back to the commandery in time for Matins."

"Was it your plan all along to murder Everard when he returned from Joan's manor that night?" Gwen said.

"I hadn't thought it was an option until he told Desmond he would stand vigil over his mother. With that, I knew my opportunity had come. He must have been feeling guilty about leaving the order and taking Llys Arthur with him." This was a true confession, before witnesses. He was not contrite, but now that his crimes had been exposed, he'd become positively chatty. "For the good of the Order."

"For the good of the Order?" Gareth knew his anger served no purpose, but he couldn't stop it from rising to the fore. "That very night, Everard was carrying the rest of the elixir Lucan had made to succor those here at the commandery."

"I don't know anything about that. He didn't have it with him in the church."

"Everard met with me at the tavern before he returned to Ysbyty Cynfyn," Brigid said. "He had asked Earl Richard to send someone here because he was concerned about unexplained deaths at the commandery that he feared your commander had covered up."

"By his own hand, he has admitted to feeling ashamed at bringing his elixir into Ysbyty Cynfyn," Gwen said. "Likely *that* is why he chose to stand vigil, not because he'd asked Joan to marry him."

"I have questioned Joan at length as well." Gareth was watching Geoffrey's expression closely. "She has given no indication she intended to marry Everard, no matter how you think he felt about her. You killed him for nothing."

Up until that point, Gareth wasn't sure they were getting through to Geoffrey, whose expression remained impassive. But then he swept a trembling hand across his brow and leaned his shoulder into one of the beams that supported the roof of the hut.

Saran had been standing on the far side of the table with Brigid but now came around it. Putting a hand on each of his arms, she looked into his eyes. "What did you take?"

"What I had to." He slid to the floor, and then his expression slackened. "So this is what death feels like? I have always wondered. Nothing you can do. Better this way."

He closed his eyes. Hardly ten heartbeats later, he stopped breathing entirely.

And then Gwen remembered the cup he'd given to Commander Reginald.

45

Day Six

Gwen

Gwen swung around the doorframe into the infirmary, feeling incredibly grateful they'd had the foresight to invite Saran and Brigid to their interrogation of Geoffrey. Otherwise, they could have been accused of inventing his confession. If she could have done this over, she would have included a witness from the commandery itself, like Bardolf.

As Gwen bent over the cup at Reginald's bedside, Saran huffed up too. Both breathed a sigh of relief to see the cup still full.

Leaving Saran beside Reginald, Gwen next ran to the remedy storage room. Skidding to a halt in the doorway, she said Bardolf, who as usual was sitting at his desk, "What did Geoffrey say to you when he came in here earlier?"

Bardolf gaped at her. "I don't know what you're talking about. Geoffrey wasn't here."

"He was. He had been sitting with Commander Reginald, and then he entered this room to collect a remedy to give to him. He spoke to you while he was doing it."

"I arrived only a few moments ago, so it wasn't me to whom he spoke."

"Where have you been?" It was rude to ask Bardolf that so abruptly. She couldn't help herself and willed him to give her a reasonable explanation. She liked him. But then, she had liked Geoffrey too.

"Your son—" Bardolf was flustered enough to wave one hand in the air above his head as he tried to recall the name, "—Llelo found me outside the chapter house and asked that I have a look at Lady Joan, who is resting in the common room. Of course, I went right away."

"Who would have been inside the remedy room if not you? To whom could Geoffrey have spoken?"

"I don't know. The room isn't locked. My physicians and helpers are in and out of here all day long and during the night too. They know not to touch remedies other than those specifically designated for a given patient." He turned the ledger around to show her. "See! They make a mark to indicate what they've taken."

Gwen had learned of this system days ago. She put her finger on the recent entries, reading down them. While she did so, Bardolf added, "As you can see, Geoffrey made no mark, and whomever he spoke to didn't either. Do you know what he took?"

"No." She looked up at him, realizing she hadn't yet given him the worse news. "He wouldn't say, but whatever it was, it killed him."

"It did what? What did you say?" It was like he hadn't heard her or, if he had, was unable to encompass her meaning.

She put a hand on his arm. "Geoffrey confessed to murdering Everard and the young man found in the river, and then he killed himself right in front of us."

Bardolf reared back so hard in his chair he almost flung himself into the wall behind him. "No!"

"I'm sorry, but it's true. Saran and Brigid, who as it turns out is a representative of the Earl of Pembroke, were there as witnesses."

Bardolf had both hands over his mouth, his eyes wide above them. "Geoffrey? But *why*?" The question came out a wail.

Instead of giving him Geoffrey's answer, which might not make sense to him any more than it had to Gwen, she said, "As I said, Geoffrey also brought a remedy to Commander Reginald before he came with us."

Only now did that mean something to Bardolf. He surged from his chair and bolted from the room. By the time Gwen came after him, he was already in close consultation with Saran.

Gwen had done what she could for now, so while they talked, she surveyed the men in the other beds. Most were asleep, although some were curled up in a way that indicated they were in pain. Everard had died for the wrong reasons, but she couldn't deny that his elixir—and its aftermath—had left a path of destruction in its wake potentially as harmful as Geoffrey's.

When Bardolf had burst into the infirmary, Thomas, the more taciturn of the two young doctors, had looked up from where he was seeing to one of the patients. Rather than go to the commander's bedside, he made his way to Gwen. "What's going on?"

She saw no point in hiding the truth, since Bardolf already knew it. "Geoffrey confessed to murdering Everard. Before we spoke to him, he ingested a remedy that killed him. We fear he also poisoned your commander."

These were too many revelations at once but, characteristically, Thomas took them all in stride. He merely let out a puff of air. "So, Geoffrey's dead. Will the consequences of Everard's elixir never end?"

"What do you mean by that?"

He gestured in the direction of the outer door. "Efa passed through the infirmary to say that several in the village are ill too. She took a supply of what Lucan created for us to ease them through their pain."

"*Efa* was here?"

"A bit ago." His manner told her he thought nothing of this fact. Of course, he hadn't been present in the common room, so he had no reason to wonder at her role in any of this.

Gwen, however, knew a last thread to tug when it came her way. "Come with me!" She swung around. "It might not be too late to catch her!"

46

Day Six

Gareth

Gareth would have gone to the infirmary, but someone had to stay with Geoffrey's body. Somehow he felt that person had to be him. The issue of the deaths there and the commander's role in them would definitely not be resolved if Geoffrey had poisoned him too, but Gwen was a more than capable investigator herself. She knew what to do, and she was with Saran, after all.

That left him alone with Brigid, who had taken a hemp sheet from a shelf and covered Geoffrey's body with it. "I enjoyed your sons' company. They are quite accomplished."

Maybe that was an odd thing to say while standing over the body of a murderer, but he could see how the series of events up until now would lead her mind down that path. Besides, none of them were going anywhere, and he was interested in what she had to say. "Thank you."

"Not many men could take the orphaned sons of a wool merchant and turn them into knights."

"Much of what and who they are is their own doing."

"I believe that, as much as every man is responsible for his own soul, but you shaped the clay."

Gareth knew he deserved some credit for how his sons were turning out, if only for having the wisdom to take them in and love them as they had never been loved by their birth father. But he'd rather change the subject. "Tell me of Llanrhystud."

"You'll have to forgive your sons for telling me the truth. They are very good, really. Far better than many men older than they, but I kept asking—pressing on them—and they chose to trust me."

"Why do you think that was?" He was digressing, but it seemed relevant.

"Because I am trustworthy," she gave him a small smile, "when it suits me to be."

"Why did it suit you in this instance?" It had been her idea to talk to him, but this was turning into an interrogation with an oddly recalcitrant witness.

"Because Everard seemed like a good man, genuinely concerned about what was happening at his commandery, and Baldwin was missing. Those boys were lucky to find the horse and me, which means I would have been a fool to abandon *them*."

"Even when they went to Llanrhystud?" At last, back to the main point, though really, he was quite certain by now that the preamble might end up being of equal value in the long run.

"It was on my way too, or so I thought at the time, seeing as how it was south of Aberystwyth. And then I made their plan better, and we both got what we wanted." Again, she stopped with the thought not fully expressed.

Gareth had to prompt her. "Which was what? What did you get out of it?"

"Insight into the workings of Ceredigion. Cadwaladr has betrayed your prince, that's clear. I don't know how you knew that he might have, but the letter I acquired at the castle would be enough confirmation for me."

Gareth found his breath catching in his throat. He really should have cornered Llelo on his way out of the common room before having any kind of real conversation with Brigid. He knew she was a spy for the Earl of Pembroke, but not much else. "There's a letter? Do you have it?"

"Your sons read it, which is yet another sign that they are more capable than the typical man." She held out the document. "Llelo wanted to keep it on his person, but I saw it as leverage for my own safety and took it back."

"And yet, you're giving it to me now?"

"I think Earl Richard would agree that an ascendant Cadell is more of a threat to Pembroke than Hywel will ever be."

"Why do you say that?" The letter had been folded into a square, King Cadell's seal broken by whomever had read it first.

She tsked at his ignorance, or maybe at his naïveté. "Because he is of Gwynedd, and cares little about the lands here."

Gareth might have taken offense, but she spoke no less than the truth. It was also hard to feel aggrieved with the letter in his hand. King Owain controlled the entire north and had always wanted to stretch his influence into Deheubarth and Powys too. With one sister married to the King of Powys and another to the King of Deheubarth, at one time it might have been possible. But both Gwenllian and Gruffydd were dead, and Susanna estranged from Madog, who was a snake. Thus, these days, there was little chance of conquering either kingdom. Brigid was right too that few rulers had ever conquered the whole of Wales. Each cared for his own patch of earth and little else.

For now, it was enough for Gareth to hold proof that Cadwaladr and Cadell were conspiring. He could have turned a cartwheel, but instead silently punched the air. Brigid looked on, pleased, as she should be. He eyed her. "What do you require in return?"

Because, of course, nothing with spies ever came free.

"I know better than to ask for something you can't give. Only that your prince be willing to speak with my earl."

"Are you suggesting an alliance against Cadell?"

She tipped her head. "Is that so far-fetched? Cadell is attacking Hywel's holdings. He wants all of Ceredigion for himself, and that means pushing Hywel out. The earl has men and influence. He can help."

Gareth bit his lip. "I will bring the offer. I make no promises."

She bent her head. "That is all that I could ask."

47

Day Six

Gwen

"I don't understand. Why do you need her?" Even without his plaintive query, it had been obvious to Gwen that Thomas hadn't wanted to come with her. But as he was the one who had told Gwen about Efa, he was stuck with her now.

"She carried the elixir to the commandery for Lucan, and although we now know that Geoffrey murdered Everard, she lied to me about her movements that night. I want to talk to her about that."

Thomas lifted the hem of his robe to hustle after Gwen, since in a matter of moments she was out of the infirmary and heading down the hill towards the village on the other side of the road. Her pregnant belly was hindering her speed a bit, but she wasn't so large as yet that she couldn't manage a fast walk. The baby kicked a few times, shifting about at the activity.

"Is that little bit of information really worth running all this way?"

Gwen glanced over at him. He hadn't ever been cheerful in her presence, but he was being even more dampening than usual. "Don't you want to know what really happened?"

"Isn't it bad enough that Geoffrey is dead?"

It *was* bad enough, but not so much so that Gwen was going to forgo this one last thread to tie off, and she told him so.

He grunted. "Just to clarify, Geoffrey murdered Everard as well as the young man we found in the river because he was worried Everard was going to marry Joan and we'd lose Llys Arthur?"

"Yes." By now, they'd reached the village, and she put out a hand to stop Thomas from speaking further. A woman carrying an empty bucket to the village well crossed in front of them. "Can you tell me where I might fight Healer Efa?"

"I haven't seen her today. I didn't know she was here."

Gwen stood momentarily flummoxed at the woman's unconcerned manner. "Who is ill in the village?"

"Nobody. Well—" the woman immediately qualified the thought, "—Branwen's boy was up in the night with teething, but she managed to quiet him down after a bit. Why?"

Gwen swung around to see Thomas backing away. "I thought you said you saw Efa—"

"I must have been mistaken." He turned and got perhaps thirty feet, almost to the entrance to the village, when he pulled up short at the sight of Dai standing in the center of the road.

"Shall I stop him, Mam?"

"If you would, *cariad.*" Gwen herself was not going to run after him. Maybe if she hadn't been so distracted by everything else going on, she would have noticed when Thomas repeated too much of their investigation back at her, elements of which there was no way he should have known unless Geoffrey himself had told him.

Thomas was no soldier. Once caught, he gave no trouble, and Dai hauled him back up to the commandery.

As they walked, Gwen asked her son, "Were you looking for me?"

"I was on my way to find you when I saw you run down the hill with Thomas."

"Why did you need me?"

"Efa really is here. She came while you were busy in the infirmary and confirmed everything Lucan said."

Gwen stopped in the middle of the road to stare first at her son, and then at Thomas. "She never was in the remedy room, was she?"

Thomas looked sullen. "No."

"Why did you tell me she had been?"

"When you said Geoffrey was dead and that he'd spoken to someone in the remedy room, I panicked. I couldn't say it was me. She was the first name I thought of, particularly because she wasn't here."

Gwen turned back to Dai. "Efa really confirmed everything?"

Dai shrugged. "She loves Lucan, and he loves her."

Gwen found laughter bubbling up in her throat. "It's a happy ending for someone, anyway." Then she sobered as she looked at Thomas, still in Dai's grip. "But I think not for you."

When they arrived back in the courtyard, Gareth and Brigid were just leaving the healer's hut with Geoffrey's body, which would go to the laying-out room. This time, Gareth would not need to examine it. They knew Geoffrey had died by his own hand, even if they weren't entirely sure what he'd taken. If they were really curious, they could have Bardolf or Saran examine him for signs of the poison.

"We have more to discover, apparently." Gwen came to stand beside her husband. She felt as if they'd come full circle to be once again by the gatehouse.

Gareth pinned Thomas with his gaze. "What did he do?"

Without warning, Thomas practically folded in on himself. "How did you know I was involved?"

Gwen studied him, trying to assess what leverage she could use to get him to reveal his role in the events of the week. "I didn't tell you why Geoffrey killed Everard, only that he had. You knew the reason anyway. How?"

Thomas twisted his hands together. He didn't want to say, and whether because Gwen was unyielding, or because her husband and Dai were looming over him, their hands on their sword hilts, he capitulated. "Geoffrey told me."

"He told you he murdered Everard?" Inside, Gwen was aghast, but she did her best to remain matter-of-fact in tone.

"Of course not. Only that he was concerned about the commandery's future. He asked me to keep an eye on you."

That sounded like the truth, as far as it went, but this puddle of fear in front of her was a far cry from the cold intelligence he'd displayed up until today. Saran had described his behavior at the healers' meeting. Gwen couldn't decide if he was playing on their sympathies, or this was yet another face of the real Thomas.

"He tasked you with spying on us, you mean," Gareth said.

Thomas writhed a bit more. "Yes. I have a talent for being overlooked."

"Oddly, Prince Rhys said the same thing to me," Dai said softly, under his breath in Welsh.

Gwen ignored her son. "So it was you who searched Everard's room after he died."

Because she sounded certain, Thomas didn't bother to deny it. "We needed to stop you from learning anything more about Everard's activities. We couldn't find his journal any more than you could. We did need the recipe for his elixir, and any sign of whatever else he'd been planning." He gave a little snort that was more like the old Thomas. "I should have known better than to look there. The stables were much more productive."

He didn't seem to realize he had just incriminated himself.

"What exactly did you find there, if not the journal?" Gwen didn't mention that she herself had, in fact, found Everard's journal, and it had been as instrumental as Thomas supposed in explaining what Everard had been thinking.

Thomas let out another scoff, as if they should already know the answer. "That's where Everard put the elixir he brought from Lucan's manor."

Gareth took a step forward. "You found it? When?"

"An hour ago. Nobody bothered to search there because they assumed Everard would have put whatever Lucan gave him in the herb hut with the rest of the remedies. But he wouldn't have done that, would he? Not with Gabriel slurping it down like it was good ale. He had to hide it, in order to ration it carefully."

Gwen canted her head. "Where is it now?"

"In my cell." He acted like they should be thanking him, which maybe they should. Now the commandery really would have enough to be going on with.

"Back to Geoffrey," Gwen said, as if this conversation was going anything like she'd expected. "What did he say to you when he entered the remedy room that last time?"

"They know about me, but I won't say anything about you. Keep your head down, and you'll be fine."

Gwen was impressed that Geoffrey cared enough about Thomas to protect him. "If you had told me he entered the room, collected a remedy, and left, I never would have connected you to any of this."

Thomas's chin came up. He was so used to being the smartest person in the room that he was upended when he wasn't—and was anxious to regain his standing. "When it came to it, Geoffrey had no real idea what really going on at the commandery either. He didn't know about Commander Reginald's need for the elixir. He didn't know Efa was supplying us. If not for me, everything would have fallen apart ages ago. It wasn't Geoffrey who saved us. It was me. I've been the one in charge for a long time."

Yet again, the courtyard was a place of revelation.

Gareth tapped a finger to his lips. "When did Iago come to you with his concerns about the deaths in the infirmary? How long did it take for you to realize he couldn't be allowed to tell anyone else?"

Thomas opened his mouth to speak, and then closed it, looking mutinous—and much more like himself. Maybe he'd finally realized he'd said too much.

In response, Gareth whipped out the foxglove bloom, much the worse for wear for having been carried around in his purse for days.

At the sight of it, Thomas took a step back, his eyes flicking around to each of the people around him, but with Dai's hand on his upper arm, he had nowhere to run. "He was going to ruin everything."

"In what way?" Gareth said.

"He had discovered how many of our brothers were taking the elixir, and that this number included the commander himself. By that time, I'd already taken care of several who'd become too needy. Iago came to me, afraid for the commandery's reputation, with no idea that I was in any way involved."

"Taken care of?" Gareth's tone was dangerously quiet.

Thomas's eyes were on the foxglove flower. "Just a measure of dried leaves with their wine. That was all it took." He shook his head. "They even thanked me because I was giving them their elixir. Their lives would have been a misery without it anyway. In the end, it was for their own good."

48

Day Eight

Gwen

Gwen and Saran had been taking it in turns watching over Commander Reginald over the course of the day and night since Geoffrey's death and Thomas's confession. Thomas himself was confined to a cell, awaiting punishment for his crimes. It could have been Prince Hywel, as the lord of Ceredigion, who sat judgment on him, but the Hospitallers were a military order, with a distinct chain of command. While the Grand Master of the Order was all the way in Jerusalem, Prior Walter, the authority for Britain, was in London.

He was still far away, but not inaccessibly so. With Gareth's permission and oversight as Hywel's steward, Bardolf drafted a letter describing Thomas's crimes and asking for guidance, as well as, finally, a delegation. Bardolf seemed resigned to the possibility that the whole of the commandery would face general punishment, maybe even disbandment. Ironically, it was the very thing Everard had been trying to avert when he put off Brigid at the inn. In part, Geoffrey and

Thomas had become murderers because they were worried about it too. And it was the reason Reginald had hidden his dependency on the elixir. In the end, fear had been at the heart of everything.

But Bardolf felt, in his heart, they had fallen far from grace and deserved whatever punishment was meted out.

By chance, Gwen was sitting at Commander Reginald's bedside when he woke in the early hours of the morning. Commander Reginald had already told them, in a brief moment of lucidness, that he'd had *just a sip* of the concoction Geoffrey had left on his bedside table. He'd been thinking (naturally) that it was the elixir. That the poison (foxglove or otherwise) had been diluted with wine was the only reason Reginald was still alive.

"Who are you? Where am I?" Reginald reared upwards in agitation, trying to push himself out of bed.

"It's Gwen, Commander. You are in your infirmary." Gwen was truly afraid for a moment that the poison had caused Reginald to lose his memory entirely.

But he subsided as he focused on her face. "Of course. Of course. Don't mind an old man." Frowning, he settled back in the bed, looking around the room as he did so. "Why are you here? Why am I here?"

"You were made ill because you had run out of Everard's elixir." Gwen held her breath, wondering how much she'd have to explain, and how remembering would affect him. They didn't need a relapse on top of everything else wrong with him.

He blinked. "You know about that?"

"We all do."

His stopped meeting her eyes, instead looking down and plucking at his blanket. "Do you know who murdered Everard?"

She kept her voice even. "It was Geoffrey."

His head came up at that, and his blue eyes were watery as he gazed at her. "Why?"

She told him.

"This is all my fault."

"You didn't murder Everard, and you didn't make Geoffrey murder him either."

"My dependency prevented me from carrying out my duties. I brought shame upon the Order, upon myself, and upon my brothers."

"We are more concerned in this moment if you knew that Thomas killed some of his brothers to cover up that shame."

"Th-Th-Thomas did what?" His face showed real surprise.

She nodded to see it. "You really didn't know, did you?"

He shook his head, his eyes wide and staring.

And then the intelligence that had won him the commander's post in the first place asserted itself. "You are speaking of Iago, aren't you? He was on the mend, and then he was dead. That was Thomas?"

"He told us so himself."

"I should resign." Reginald struggled to throw off the blanket that covered him, as if he intended to do so right there and then.

Gwen pressed down on his shoulder, stopping him. "I think you will find, when you are well again, that your people need you now more than ever."

And then Efa bustled in, all smiles, to take Gwen's place. Now that her relationship with Lucan was public, and she was no longer responsible for dosing members of the commandery with Lucan's elixir, it was as if the natural sunlight within her had come out from behind a cloud. If Everard genuinely had been worried about her impact on the men in her care (instead of speaking to her about her role in the poppy trade at the commandery, which had turned out to be the truth), he would truly have been concerned now.

But oddly, the completeness of her joy made her seem less like she was flirting. Even Saran had admitted that her contrition and apology appeared genuine.

It was Saran whom Gwen sought out after leaving the infirmary. Iago had been her brother, and Thomas had murdered him. She had been as impacted by the crimes in the commandery as any of them. So it was no surprise to find her stepmother in the churchyard, standing over Iago's grave. Tangwen and Taran, who for that hour had been in her charge, were somersaulting down the gentle slope a few yards away.

Once Gwen told her what Reginald had said, Saran sighed and rested her hand on the top of her brother's gravestone. "Maybe, with this truth, Iago can rest in peace. Maybe now I can close the book—or ledger, or journal—" she looked over at Gwen with a wry smile, "—on this quest."

"I can't help but wonder how much of what we discovered this week Iago had known but couldn't tell us," Gwen said. "How extraordinary that Thomas was murdering patients with foxglove at the same time that Earl Richard's spies were using the flower to identify each other."

Saran lifted one shoulder in a half-shrug. "Then again, maybe not so extraordinary. Foxglove is one of the more powerful poisons. Thomas could have thought to use it precisely because he worked so closely with Everard, and Everard's attachment to it had been planted, so to speak, in his own mind."

"Like when Tad sings a song which I then can't get out of my head?" Gwen looked ruefully at her stepmother. "Maybe it's the same for physicians, except with herbs."

"I'll have to ask your father." Saran laid the flowers she'd brought, none of which were poisonous, in the grass newly growing over Iago's grave. "In the end, we must be grateful. We might never have solved this mystery if Iago hadn't sent us that single bloom of foxglove."

49

Dai

A fortnight later ...

"Loose!"

Dai obeyed the command, watching his burning arrow arc through air. He couldn't see the thatched roofs of the buildings in the outer bailey of Llanrhystud Castle, but since he had been the one to tell Prince Hywel how they were situated, he could picture them in his mind's eye. One moment they were there, and the next they were burning brightly against the darkness of the night sky.

A few moments ago, the wind had started to pick up, giving greater life to the flames. Rain would come soon, but by then it would be too late for Cadfan and the defenders of the castle. Dai had overheard Prince Hywel say that he hoped Cadell's forces were already inside, since that would mean they were engaging a worthy enemy. Cadwaladr, they presumed, was not here or he would have made his presence known by now.

With the resolution of the mystery at Ysbyty Cynfyn, Dai, Llelo, and Gareth had followed Hywel's trail, riding into his encampment late on the third day of riding. The news of Cadwaladr's betrayal could not wait, and they had to be the ones to bring it—along with Brigid's offer to ally with Earl Richard.

Hywel had listened to all they had to say with hardly any reaction, only a slight narrowing of the eyes.

He could have been overjoyed that at long last they had real proof of Cadwaladr's duplicity. Instead, the weight of this new-found knowledge seemed to bow his shoulders. Even the prospect of an alliance with the Earl of Pembroke didn't lift it. Negotiating any agreement would take weeks, which they didn't have.

"What do you want to do?" Gareth had asked him.

"Since you sent warning of an assassin to my father already, we'll take Cadwaladr's castle next. And then we'll see."

Thousands of arrows flew across the ramparts, some flaming, some not, all deadly. The wooden gate into the outer bailey burned fiercely. They had attacked after midnight, on a clear night, since darkness provided the only means to approach the castle unseen. They'd targeted the outer defenses first, along with the guards on the battlement, every one eliminated in the first wave of arrows by Hywel's expert marksmen.

A shout finally came from the top of the gatehouse. Cadwaladr's flag came down, to be replaced by the red and yellow banner of Gwynedd, waved back and forth with intent by one of the defenders.

Gruffydd, the captain of the Dragons, approached Dai. "You met Cadfan, Dai. Can we turn him?"

The Dragons, those that could shoot anyway, had been put to use along with the rest of the army. The hand-to-hand fighting would have come only once the gate had been pulled down. Now, it might not be necessary.

"I wouldn't have said so. He appeared absolutely loyal to his father, in the sense that his father's aims were his own." Dai looked intently at Gruffydd. "Primarily, his desire would be power for himself, the more the better. He reveled in the fact that he was ruling the castle on his own, even for only a few days."

"Is it possible he could be angry at his father for not returning? Or afraid of what Hywel will do to him?"

"If he's afraid of anything, it would be of letting down his father. Part of me thinks he is too stupid to be afraid, but sometimes that level of stupidity looks a lot like bravado. I am surprised he is surrendering so soon, which makes me think it isn't his choice. Either he is incapacitated or his own men have turned on him to make this happen."

"I will tell the prince." Gruffydd turned to go.

"Don't let my father talk to him."

Gruffydd turned back. "Llelo is with your father right now and told us the same thing. Why are you?"

Dai couldn't decide if he should be honored that Gruffydd had been sent to listen to what he had to say or offended for Llelo that the prince felt the need to confirm his assessment with Dai. Better to be honored—and to say what he really thought. "Cadwaladr detests Hywel, that's clear, but his hatred for my father is outsized. If you want these negotiations to go smoothly at all, he should stay behind."

"Won't Cadfan view his absence as a sign of weakness?"

"If he knew he was here, he might. When Hywel took Cadwaladr's castle at Aberystwyth seven years ago, Gareth was the one to care for Cadfan. He put him on his own horse. If you thought Cadfan would remember that moment fondly and view my father as a knight who treated him well, you would be wrong."

In the end, and maybe even because of these warnings, Hywel decided not to attend the negotiations for surrender either, sending Gruffydd and his foster father, Cadifor, instead. They were both men of standing, among the highest ranked in Hywel's court.

When Dai finally entered what remained of the castle, he found Cadfan in the great hall, lying among those wounded in the bombardment.

He was on a pallet, white and sweating from an arrow wound to the thigh. He didn't seem to recognize Dai and simply said, "It hurts."

He was like any other twelve-year-old in that.

Hywel had come up behind Dai and now crouched at Cadfan's side. "I brought wine for you, son. The healers say you should be fine, in time." Dai noted he didn't suggest *dwale*, though this was an instance it might be called for.

Cadfan clutched Hywel's hand as he helped him to raise his head, in order to take a sip from the cup Hywel held. For a moment, they were just cousins, one older and wiser and the other young and afraid.

Then, as Cadfan lay back down on his pallet, he seemed to remember where he was and, more importantly, how he should behave in Hywel's presence. His face screwed up into the same visage of hatred Dai had seen when he and Llelo had met him in his receiving room. "Stay away from me! Ceredigion doesn't belong to you. My father left it to *me*." He thumped his chest with his fist. "It belongs to *me*."

"Not anymore, cousin." As he pushed to his feet, Hywel's voice held nothing but pity. He had come far in the seven years since he'd last taken a castle from Cadwaladr. "And never again."

HISTORICAL NOTE

As always, the events related in the *Gareth & Gwen Medieval Mysteries* are as accurate as I can make them, given the available evidence. In the case of *The Admirable Physician,* the Welsh chronicles tell of an event in 1150 where Hywel, son of Owain Gwynedd, captured his cousin, Cadfan, son of Cadwaladr, and seized his land and castle at Llanrhystud. It also tells of the sons of Gruffydd—Cadell, Maredudd, and Rhys—who came with an army into Ceredigion to attempt to take the region for Deheubarth.

Furthermore, Ysbyty Cynfyn is a real place, located along the pilgrim road that led to a native Welsh abbey, referred to in *The Admirable Physician* as Mynachlog Fawr, that later became the Cistercian Abbey of Strata Florida. Although my husband had marked this particular church, dedicated to St. John, on a map, I hadn't realized its significance as a Hospitaller commandery until we visited it one day, stopping on a whim during a drive down the length of Wales.

Hospitaller commanderies in Wales were initially clustered in Norman-held territory and founded by Normans (as with Ysbyty Cynfyn). We find their commanderies in places where the word *ys-*

byty, which means *hospital* in Welsh, is attached to a church, particularly one dedicated to St. John (since the Hospitaller's complete designation is *The Order of the Knights of the Hospital of St. John of Jerusalem).* There are indications that the Hospitallers took responsibility for their first churches in Wales as early as 1115, shortly after the founding of the Order.

Other known Hospitaller commanderies in Wales include *Ysbyty Ystwyth* (where years ago in an early book in my *After Cilmeri* series I sited the *Healing Waters* spa), Ysbyty Ifan in Gwynedd, and Slebech, which by the dissolution of the monasteries in the sixteenth century was the third wealthiest monastic site in Wales.

No trace of its commandery and infirmary remain today, but the church of Ysbyty Cynfyn, still dedicated to St. John, is situated as I describe in *The Admirable Physician.* As in the book, it lies within a wall that incorporates ancient standing stones. The churchyard is also circular, an indication that worship has been taking place here for millennia. Also as described, on the other side of the Rheidol gorge are the remains of a bronze age burial mound that has eroded away to reveal the stone circle that formed its base. It isn't any wonder that the local people believed it home to the *Tylwyth Teg,* or fairy folk.

Llys Arthur, located to the northeast of the commandery, is also a real place, as is the mine associated with the estate.

All in all, it seemed the perfect setting for a book in the *Gareth & Gwen Medieval Mysteries!*

About the Author

With over a million books sold to date, Sarah Woodbury is the author of more than forty novels, all set in medieval Wales. Although an anthropologist by training, and then a full-time homeschooling mom for twenty years, she began writing fiction when the stories in her head overflowed and demanded that she let them out. While her ancestry is Welsh, she only visited Wales for the first time at university. She has been in love with the country, language, and people ever since. She even convinced her husband to give all four of their children Welsh names.
She makes her home in Oregon.

Thank you for continuing this journey into the Middle Ages with me! Please don't worry that this is the last *Gareth & Gwen Medieval Mystery*. There will be more! If you'd like to know as soon as the preorder for the next book is available, feel free to subscribe to my newsletter at
www.sarahwoodbury.com